SF Books by Vaughn ...

Visit www.Vaughnheppner.com for more information.

Star Soldier

(Doom Star 1)

by
Vaughn Heppner

ISBN-13: 978-1496145697
ISBN-10: 1496145690
BISAC: Fiction / Science Fiction / Military

7 AUGUST 2346 A.D.

Father and son floated swiftly, silently, with purpose, through a seldom-used maintenance shaft. They refused to sell their souls to Social Unity. Three years of hiding like rats proved that and culminated tonight. They had just placed thirty-six bombs onto the space habitat's outer skin and had eleven minutes to go.

Father and son looked nothing alike. Marten Kluge was nineteen, lean and blond-haired, handsome of face like his mother. He cradled a stubby tangler against his vacc-suit and had a high-tech kit on his belt. The old man, Ben Kluge, was massive and hard-eyed, with a needler attached to his silver suit. In the last half hour he'd killed four men, two with his hands. No one had heard or missed the men so far. The Sun-Works Factory circling Mercury was vast beyond any space habitat in the Solar System. The corpses were left to float in dark shafts. Father and son now donned helmets, activated oxygen tanks and opened a hatch for the next phase of the operation.

Mercury spread below, a dead planet buzzing with activity. In appearance, it looked remarkably similar to the Earth's Moon, pockmarked with craters and having almost no atmosphere. On the dayside, a sodium potassium vapor existed, but it was negligible. Only forty percent larger than the Moon, Mercury had a very much higher percentage of metals. Those ores, unbelievable lodes of fissionables such as uranium, thorium and more basic metals like iron and copper, were catapulted off-world, caught by space tugs and fed into the Sun Work's reactors and smelting furnaces. Like Saturn's rings, the tubular-shaped, world-spanning Sun-Works Factory circled the entire planet of Mercury.

Mere specks against the gargantuan space station, father and son pushed off the inner ring. Because Old Sol blazed nearby they were forced to remain in the station's shadows—it was either that or commit quick suicide by sunshine. Mercury was at aphelion, its farthest orbital position from the Sun: seventy million kilometers. At perihelion, a mere forty-six million kilometers, the Sun's radiation would have been more than double the intensity. Space walking, even in the station's shadows, would be impossible then.

As they floated high above Mercury, Marten clicked his com-unit. It emitted a powerful, code-scrambled pulse—the Sun's harsh electromagnetic waves demanded such strength. The pulse sped through the exosphere before it was caught and de-coded by his mother's bio-computer. The biocomp immediately released a virus into the Sun Work's tracking systems. Nineteen seconds later a beep sounded in Marten's ear. He gave a thumbs-up signal to his father. They ignited thruster-packs.

Three years ago, station security—Political Harmony Corps—had brutally suppressed the unionization attempt of the engineers. Social Unity, it was said, provided for all, was all. The State and its people were one, thus unionization was an absurdity, a non-sequitur. So the strike had been *dispersed*: a word that failed to convey the savage fighting, the interrogations and the police murders of the ringleaders and their lieutenants. A few Unionists had slipped into hiding among the millions of kilometers of passageways and maintenance corridors. Most of those

2

had been caught, tortured and killed. Marten, his father and mother, and a handful of determined survivors, had kept one step ahead of the hunters and built an ultra-stealth pod in an abandoned, high-radiation area. The long-range goal was to slip away from the Inner Planets to the Jupiter Confederation or anywhere beyond the reach of the Social Unity fanatics.

Father and son shut off their thruster-packs, rotated ninety degrees and let the packs glow once more. Gently, they landed on the inner ring, on the Mercury-facing-side of the space habitat, kilometers from where they'd jumped. Unlatching the packs, they attached them with magnetic clamps to the nearby hatch.

Ben Kluge faced his son. Hard, dark eyes peered through his plexiglas helmet. He put a hand on his son's shoulder, and squeezed.

Marten nodded. His mouth was so dry that he didn't dare try talking. He turned to the hatch and punched in the entry sequence—between them, he had the better memory. A puff of air escaped the opening hatch. Seconds later, they floated into the compression chamber. Marten's heart hammered. He readied his tangler, licked his lips and checked his chronometer: two minutes to detonation.

CLANG. As the hatch swung closed, Marten twitched, and he berated himself for his fear.

His father flipped off his helmet, letting it hang against his broad back as he scratched his crewcut silver hair. He drew his needler, a wicked little gun of black plastic that seemed to disappear in his hand. He opened the inner hatch and floated into a utility corridor. Following, Marten kept on his helmet. The corridor was uniformly gray, with float rails on the walls. They pulled themselves along, traveling fast to a bank of elevators, choosing the third from the left.

"Which floor?" asked his father.

Marten checked his HUD (head up display) that played on his inner visor. "Fifteenth," he whispered.

His father punched that in, the door closed and they rode the elevator in silence, the orange numbers on the function box changing rapidly. It was "night" shift in this part of the Sun Works, the reason so few people were about. Soon number 15 glowed brightly and the elevator halted. The door swished open and they entered a light-gravity area. Loping along the passageway, they turned into a larger corridor. Green and yellow arrows on the walls showed the directions to various terminals. They followed the yellow arrows and soon came to a door labeled: FUELING STATION 943.

With his heart hammering, Marten re-gripped his tangler. This was it. His father's lips peeled back like a wolf's as he reached for the door.

They entered a circular room lined with consoles and screens. Soft classical music played over the PA. A dark-bearded technician in a blue and gold jumpsuit sat with his back to them at a fueling board. He listened to a tall, red-suited PHC officer, a harsh-faced youth who spoke with the customary arrogance of his kind.

"Then double-check it! Triple-check it if you have to! We can't have any more reactor leaks in the transports."

The technician stared up at a screen showing fueling bots at work on a utilitarian space vessel. Perhaps he saw their reflection in the screen. He turned and his eyes widened. The PHC officer also turned, and after a second's hesitation, he clawed at his holstered sidearm.

Marten was faster than his father was. He brought up the tangler as he pressed the firing stud. A black, egg-shaped capsule exploded against the technician. Strong, sticky strands wrapped around him, entangling the man as his dark face flushed with fear. His father's needler shot slivers of ice. Noiselessly, they punctured the PHC officer's chest. A look of shocked surprise tore the

4

arrogance from his face. The officer gurgled as his knees buckled.

Ben Kluge leaped to the dying PHC officer, touching the needler over the heart as he pumped in extra shots.

The technician's features twisted in terror. "L-look..."

"Shut up," said Ben, pressing the needler against the technician's forehead.

The man worked his mouth silently. Ben dragged him upright and propelled him toward a second exit.

Marten avoided looking at the dead officer as he edged into the technician's seat. Sweat prickled under his neck-seal and his stomach lurched. He fumbled a plastic credcard cracker out of his tech-kit. He checked his chronometer, waited twelve seconds and then slid the card into the function box. His mother's bio-computer had worked six long months on the credcard cracker, perfecting it to fool the system's checks. He waited what seemed forever and then the fuel board's green light blinked.

Marten heaved an explosive sigh. Kilometers from here in a secret docking bay, liquid hydrogen filled their stealth pod's fuel tanks. He turned to tell his father.

Ben Kluge stumbled backward from the exit. Blood squirted from his neck—so bright and red. His needler fired ice slivers. Then the gun went *click, click, click.*

Marten was too shocked to speak.

With blood running down his vacc-suit, Ben Kluge turned toward his boy. Then his head blossomed, blood and bone showering everywhere.

Time slowed as Marten screamed, "NO!" He swiveled toward that exit. Combat-suited PHC personnel—police in bulky, red-colored armor—poked their carbines through the door. Slugs whined around Marten, shattered screens and *pinged* off the consoles.

Marten's tangler made exploding popcorn sounds as he fired back. Then he ran and slipped a bomb out of his pouch, flicking the activation switch. The bomb hit the floor with a thud, rolled. Marten's chest felt hollow as his receivers picked up curses from the entangled PHC officers. He dove through a different door. It swished shut and an explosion shook the room. Hot shrapnel tore through the door. A moment later Marten leaped up and raced down the corridor. Tears burned in his eyes.

"Hey, you!" shouted a technician. Marten tangled the man.

Soon he was back at the compression chamber. Klaxons wailed and emergency codes locked all hatches. Marten overrode his and floated outside where a million stars and a dead planet provided him background. A glance showed him that the planted bombs hadn't blown.

"Marten?" he heard over his com-line.

"Mom!"

"What happened, Marten?" She waited back in their cubbyhole HQ, an abandoned shaft near the station's outer Sun-shield.

"They got father, and the bombs didn't work. What are we going to do?" As Marten talked he wrestled with the thruster-pack.

For a time she didn't speak. It was long enough for him to don the thruster-pack and jump off the habitat wall.

"I want you to listen carefully. You can't come back here. Not…"

"Mom! What's happening?"

"Shhh. You must keep calm, Marten. The outer locks just blew, which indicates they're coming for me. Simon gives it a ninety-four percent chance it's over." Simon was her name for the bio-computer.

Marten swallowed hard as his thruster burned, and he sped like a speck across the face of Mercury below and between the inner surfaces of the Sun-Works Ring.

6

"We always knew this might happen," his mother was saying. "I want you to listen closely, Marten. I love you. Your father loved you."

Why was she talking like this?

"Check your last card, the black one."

Marten fumbled with his tech-kit, almost spilling it and sending the contents tumbling into orbit. Then he saw it, a black credcard.

"Go to A-Twenty-three. Do you understand?"

He was being monitored, that's what she was telling him.

"But—"

"Good luck, Marten. Go with God." He heard an explosion in her background—the inner locks being blown—he heard shouting, gunfire and a scream.

He almost howled like a beaten dog. Instead, a hard knot formed in his gut. Much of their iron, their fire and resolve lived in him. So he slipped the black card into his hand computer. What he read on the tiny screen astonished him. His mother's brilliance had almost insured them a new future in the Jupiter Confederation.

Marten readjusted his flight path and zoomed toward the inner curve of the habitat. Soon numbers and markings flashed underneath him.

The fifth Doom Star battleship had just been completed. Now more space-welders were needed around Earth to make another farming gigahab. Since the sixth Doom Star was still in the planning modification stage, welding wouldn't begin here for another year. That freed enough space-welders so five transports would leave the Sun Works Ring and head for the Earth System. Marten wondered if one of those transports was the vessel with the reactor leak.

Alarm codes rang in Marten's helmet. That meant the alert had gone station wide. PHC officers hunted for him. To listen to the alarms was more than he could handle. So he shut off the com-unit. Despite his best efforts, he could no longer control his emotions. On his arm-pad, he punched in a command to his vacc-suit's medical unit. A hiss sounded in his ears, the suit's hypo-spray. A cooling numbness spread over him and the awful agony in his chest faded. The double dose of tranks allowed him to breathe normally and relax clenched muscles as he rode the thruster-pack a bare few feet above the habitat.

In the distance floated bulky transports, boarding tubes snaking out of the Sun-Works Factory to them. Farther a-field winked the blue and red work-lights of space tugs and their accompanying bots.

Marten concentrated as he slowed his momentum. Then he unhooked himself and set the thruster-pack on auto. He pushed himself down, sending the pack one way and he in the opposite direction. A moment later, the empty thruster-pack burned for the last time, shooting off at a tangent. Marten watched it go   as he readied himself. He bent his knees and turned on the magnetic clamps at minimum power. As he drifted fast onto the station's plates, he ran lightly, using his boots' weak magnetic force to slow his speed. Finally, he increased magnetic power and brought himself to a halt. He was sweating from the exertion and his conditioners hummed at overdrive.

He studied the nearest markings, turned forty degrees and walked, making the customary clank, clank, clank of a magnetic stroll. Sixteen minutes later, he came to an emergency hatch. He entered a small utility tube and shed his vacc-suit. From there he traveled through narrow maintenance shafts. He floated faster than a man could run in normal gravity. In time, he found Junction Z-321-B and felt under a girder for his stash pod. He extracted a welder's gray jumpsuit, boots and traveling kit, along with a wallet that contained a single ID card. It was one Simon had carefully created. Marten stuffed his old clothes into the pod and carefully weighed the tangler.

For three years he'd carried it, kept it under his pillow at night.

He broke it in half, slipped it into the stash pod and attached the pod back under the girder.

He swallowed. Without the tangler, he felt naked. Fortunately, the double dose of tranks kept him easy. He began to float-travel.

After several kilometers, he slipped into a main corridor with light-gravity. Brown Earth tones, soft music and the occasional shrub changed the feel of this corridor. The usual arrows pointed out the nearby destinations.

He waited, sitting on the lip of the pot that contained a shrub. Finally, a group of welders marched past. They were hard-faced men with thick necks and gnarled hands. They wore regulation gray jumpsuits; a few of them had synthetic-leather jackets, most had hats. Each welder carried his kit and had his ID ready. Marten rose with a grunt and jointed the back of the group. A welder glanced at him, taking in his clothes and kit, maybe wondering about his youth.

Marten nodded, keeping his features even. "Got lost in this maze," he said. "Been waiting for you guys to show up."

The welder shrugged noncommittally. It wasn't wise to ask too many questions. He ignored Marten.

The noise level grew and the group marched into Docking Bay Thirteen Terminal It was circular-shaped and, spacious, with tall palms, several modern sculptures and a fountain in the center. Along the sides stood lockers, restrooms and waiting cubicles. It seemed packed with welders, technicians, bureaucrats, military personnel and bulky-armored, red uniformed PHC officers on the prowl. Overhead, plexiglas windows five stories up allowed

9

everyone a view of the nearest shuttles and the twinkling stars behind.

Marten slipped from his group and sat hunched on a stool at a refreshment booth. He ordered a beer and sipped, waiting for announcements. His dark thoughts threatened to overwhelm him. Deciding he'd better stay clear-headed, he ordered a cup of coffee.

"A-Nineteen," called a bored docking clerk over the PA. "Report to Area Eight."

Marten drained his coffee. His stomach tightened as he saw the long line of welders. They snaked toward a small booth and the entrance to the boarding tube. Two PHC officers at the booth checked IDs. Marten stepped into line and advanced slowly. Would PHC simply kill him? His tension increased. Simon had picked up rumors of a new experimental station for political undesirables. Would they send him there?

Marten deliberately recalled why he was in line, why he'd been forced into this long shot. "Bastards," he muttered.

A tall welder with dark eyebrows glanced at him.

Marten bared his teeth in a savage smile, a parody of his father's combat grimace. As the tall man jerked forward, Marten pictured his mother, and he balled his fists. He couldn't do anything about her death now. But the anger was useful.

Soon, a PHC officer growled, "Next."

The tall welder in front of Marten held out his ID.

A PHC woman snatched it from the man and fed it into her computer. After two seconds, the unit beeped. The woman jerked out the ID and shoved it at the welder, waving him through.

Marten gritted his teeth, and stepped forward.

"What's wrong with you?" the woman asked, eyeing him. Her hair had been shaved down to her scalp and her black-tattooed lips were twisted into a sneer.

Confusion froze Marten's tongue.

The woman leaned near, sniffed his breath. "You've been drinking. That's against regs for an out-system traveler."

Speechless, Marten could only stare into her pitiless eyes.

"Step out of line you," ordered the PHC officer beside the woman, using his carbine to poke Marten in the chest.

Marten recovered his wits. "I heard our transport has a reactor leak. I needed something to calm my nerves is all."

The woman narrowed her already hostile gaze.

"Who told you that?" she asked.

"What?"

"About the reactor leak!"

"Two maintenance men," Marten said. "I overheard them talking."

"An eavesdropper, eh?" growled the man.

"Forgot about that," the woman said. "Maintenance was warned to keep quiet."

"They'll have to be told again," the man said, "after they exit the agonizer."

The woman grinned as she lifted her com-unit to report this delicious news.

As he waited, Marten fought off a deepening sense of exhaustion.

Finished reporting, the woman snatched his ID, eyed him closely, licked her lips in an evil manner and then waved him through with an arrogant flick of her wrist.

The released tension almost made Marten buckle. But he didn't. Instead, he moved through the exit portal, floated down a tube and entered the transport. Like most transports, the interior was plain, with endless brown cushioned seats set in tightly spaced rows. Welders buckled themselves in. A few chatted, some napped. Others put on vid-goggles and watched porn.

Marten settled down and waited. His tranks wore off and his stomach twisted. He envisioned a hundred different problems. Finally, however, he was pressed without warning into his cushioned seat. That's what he hated most about Social Unity. They treated you like cattle. As the growing acceleration shoved him deeper, he said a silent prayer for his parents. Then he wondered about his forged passes to Australian Sector. Would they work? He had no idea. But even if they did work—Earth was the birthplace of Social Unity, the epicenter of the most suffocating political creed ever invented. If the Sun-Works Factory had been hell, what would it be like on Earth?

Part I: Civilian

1.

Concrete, glass and plasteel buildings sprawled for kilometers in all directions, but especially down. Greater Sydney, Australian Sector wasn't as congested as Hong Kong or New York, but its fifty-one million inhabitants seldom felt the sun's warmth. There wasn't anything wrong with the sun or its ability to shine upon the populace. Ozone depletion, long a concern of earlier generations, had been taken care of a century ago. Nor was smog any worse than it had been at the beginning of the Twenty-first Century. The problem for sun-lovers had taken a different turn.

To feed Earth's hordes took more land than the world had and more than all the resources of the sea-farms. Thus, a hundred agricultural gigahabs orbited the planet. And even in the middle of the greatest civil war the Solar System had ever known, laser-launched transports went up and came back down every hour of the day. To save land the cities burrowed into the Earth rather than sprawl outward in ever widening circumferences. If humanity hadn't taken this radical turn, concrete, glass and plasteel would have covered the entire planet by 2349.

Greater Sydney boasted fifty-nine levels, neither the greatest nor the least among the planet's megalopolises. Mole-like machinery eternally chewed into the stygian depths, expanding and mining, growing the city at a pre-determined rate.

Most of the fifty-one million inhabitants carried their Social Unity cards with pride. They had been taught that the Inner Planets needed people who could work together for the good of the whole. Loners, hermits and individualists who were found out—and eventually they all were—underwent strenuous re-education or a stint of labor-learning in the algae tanks.

Sometimes, however, even in this age of social paradise and raging civil war, certain officials took advantage of their rank or failed to perform zealously all their duties.

2.

Marten Kluge claimed he wasn't angry, upset or even nervous. So he didn't understand why Molly kept telling him to relax. As they stood alone in the narrow corridor outside the hall leader's office, she tweaked his collar, fidgeting nervously with it.

"Didn't I tell you not to miss any more of the hum-a-longs," she whispered, her pretty face creased with worry. She picked a speck of lint off his collar. "Maybe you could say you had a cold. That your throat hurt."

"The hum-a-longs don't have anything to do with this," said Marten. It was almost three years since he'd escaped out of the Mercury System. He'd turned into a lean, ropy-muscled young man with a handsome, expressive face and bristly blond hair.

He wore black shoes, tan pants and a modest tan jacket with a black choker, suitable attire for such an important meeting, or so Molly kept telling him.

Earth was amazingly different from the Sun-Works Factory. Marten had thought it would be worse, and in a way, it was. The cage was gilded, cleaner than the Sun-Works Ring that built the Doom Star ships. Because of that, the people of Earth had lost... something essential. They couldn't even see the cage anymore. The enormous changes to his life, the sheer impossibility of affecting

15

anything, had depressed Marten and worn down his resolve. He missed his parents, missed talking to people who thought for themselves. All he wanted now was to throw off his Social Unity pretense and be who he really was, if only for a few hours.

"It must be the missed hum-a-longs," Molly whispered, brushing his collar and bringing him back to the moment.

"Tell me," said Marten, "has the hall leader made another advance on you?"

"...What difference would that make?"

Silence was his only answer.

Molly lifted worried green eyes. And with a gesture he'd come to adore, she brushed her stylish bangs. "Promise him you won't miss any more hum-a-longs. Maybe offer to watch your neighbors more diligently."

Before Marten could reply, the door opened and a thin woman in a mufti robe stepped out. "Marten Kluge?"

Unconsciously, his face tightened and his shoulders tensed.

"Be careful, Marten," Molly whispered. "And don't say anything rash."

As Marten followed the mufti-robed woman, his throat constricted. So even though it was ill-advised, he tore off the choker and slipped it into his jacket pocket. The chokers were the latest craze, the latest symbol of social unity. Molly had bought him one expressly for the meeting.

The outer office—the woman's—was as coffin-small as his rental. Her desk and computer terminal filled it. So when she turned to open the hall leader's door, she brushed his shoulder.

"Excuse me," he said.

She frowned, staring at his now bare throat. Then she turned, and said, "Hall Leader Quirn. Marten Kluge seeks your guidance."

16

The hall leader glanced up from behind his computer desk. He was small with narrow shoulders and wore a crisp brown uniform and military style cap—that to hide his thinning hair. He had ever-vigilant eyes and a mouth habitually turned down with disapproval. His eyes narrowed as he viewed Marten, and he touched the choker around his own throat.

Marten's bare throat felt exposed, naked, and it made him fidgety. Without thinking about it and before being bidden, he squeezed past the woman and stepped into the hall leader's office.

"Lout," the woman said under her breath.

The hall leader's mouth twitched with annoyance as he studied Marten.

"You sent for me," said Marten.

"I requested your presence," said Quirn. To his secretary, "Hold any inquiries until we're done."

"Yes, Hall Leader." She closed the door.

Marten marveled at the office's spaciousness. It held the desk, *two* low-built chairs and a stand to the left with a potted plant. A holoscreen "window" showed crashing ocean waves.

"I appreciate your promptness," said Hall Leader Quirn, although he didn't rise or offer his hand.

Marten ignored the slight as he forced himself to act pleasantly.

"Please," said Quirn, "take a seat."

"Thank you," Marten said, sitting in one of the low-slung chairs. He noticed that the higher-seated hall leader now looked down at him.

Quirn gave him a superior smile as he picked up a plastic chart and tapped it against the desk.

"Marten, I'm afraid we have some unfortunate business to discuss. Yes, troubling business."

Marten lurched to his feet.

"What's wrong?"

Marten grimaced and touched his forehead. Then he looked up. "The pain comes and goes. But I feel better now."

"Splendid. If you'll retake your seat."

"I'll stand if it's okay with you? Sitting too much...." Marten shrugged. "You know how it is."

"What I have to say is better discussed if you sit."

Marten could picture Molly advising, "Sit down, Marten. Don't be rash." Despite this common sense and the feeling of weakness in his knees, Marten resisted.

"No. I'll stand."

Quirn leaned back in his chair, eyeing him.

Marten smiled, trying to placate the hall leader with a social gesture.

"Hmm." Quirn sat forward and placed the plastic chart on the desk, smoothing it with his fingers. "Very well, we shall proceed."

"Good."

"No, Marten, I'm afraid that it's not good. And that pains me. Of all the tasks a hall leader performs, this is personally the most difficult. Yet none of us is allowed to shirk his responsibilities. There would be chaos otherwise. Now then, your profile... Marten, it's taken a decided turn for the worse. It's come to my attention that you've actually missed three hum-a-longs in a row."

"I-I had a cold," Marten said, the excuse sounding lame even to his ears. "My throat hurt."

Quirn's voice became an octave more menacing.

"During that time you've also missed two discussions and quite incredibly failed to fill out any community charts. Now," he cleared his throat, reaching for one of the drawers. "I will allow you to fill out several charts here this very moment. Particularly, I would like to know how Mr. Beerbower spends his quiet time from four in the afternoon to—"

"Uh," Marten said, "I'd rather not."

18

Quirn looked astonished. "Everybody fills out community charts. We watch out for one another."

"Yes, but—"

"Now see here, Marten, the entire thrust of Social Unity demands that we *care* about our community. In a time of grave crisis such as this we must be certain that the group functions as smoothly as ever, as one." Quirn opened the drawer and took out a plex-sheet, holding it across the desk.

Marten hesitated. He could take the plex-sheet and fill in nonsense as he'd done in the past. But that didn't really matter today, did it? It was a known fact that the hall leader switched partners with amazing regularity, and his partners were always attractive and energetic. Whispers abounded that Quirn saw such couplings as conquests. Few dared refuse his advances. Molly had dodged him the most persistently, and Marten was certain the hall leader now took it as a personal challenge. Quirn was clever, too. He must realize that if he sent Marten to the slime pits, without real justifiable cause, that might embitter Molly. Therefore, the two of them today were going to have to go through a charade.

"This is quite unprecedented, Marten. Failing to fill out the charts shows a decided lack in political duty. Perhaps...." Quirn's eyes narrowed. "Perhaps you hold heretical views."

Marten still couldn't reach out and take the plex-sheet. He knew he couldn't tell Quirn that he was tired of pretending, especially now that the Highborn attacked Earth. The genetic super-soldiers had rebelled against Social Unity, just as he wanted to rebel. The Highborn had started the civil war, it was said, through an act of rage. Marten squinted. The truth was that he was soul sick, cramped, feeling as if he should have gone down fighting with his Mom and Dad. He'd watched *Quasar* several weeks ago and had seen a documentary on the cave paintings in Southern France Sector. What had fascinated him was the whole idea of cavemen. Free to roam wherever they willed. Hunting for food, really protecting their mates. It had seemed so... alive. He'd imagined himself bellowing at other cavemen, a club in his hands. A man who fought for the well-being of his woman would cherish her. He would treat her as the greatest thing in his free-living life. Like his Dad had treated his Mom. Definitely heretical views.

"No?" Quirn asked icily. "Very well." He put the plex-sheet back in the drawer, closing it with a thump. Then he folded his hands on his desk, and his mouth quivered with distaste. "I've given this much thought, Marten. I've talked with Reform through Labor and found that openings are available."

"You're sending me to the slime pits?" For a wild instant, Marten envisioned himself leaping over the desk and attacking the hall leader.

Quirn raised a hand. "You know very well that a political crime such as yours—"

"Missing three hum-a-longs is a crime?"

"Please don't interrupt. And the answer is yes, for refusing to join your friends and neighbors in sanctioned political harmony, for willfully staying away, that is a political crime. And that translates into an assault upon humanity. Almost as repugnant are your thought-crimes— surely you have some. Fortunately, for you, Marten, the guidelines unequivocally state that thought-crimes occur to most citizens at one time or another—thus the need for a firm teaching party like Social Unity. Yes, a stint in the 'slime pits ' as you put it might be in order."

Quirn let the threat hang in the silence for a moment while he watched Marten narrowly.

"However, in your case I don't believe that would help. And in these trying times even heretics like you must pull their weight. Marten, you need to understand that the

State wants to correct your bad tendencies so that you can become fully functional again. So, I've thought of the perfect job that I believe will help teach you this."

Marten stared at the hall leader, wondering what the man's devious mind had thought up.

Quirn shoved a small slip of plex-paper across the desk.

Marten picked it up. *Biocomp engineer*, it read. Then he noticed the hours: Early morning shift.

"I'll have to get up when everyone else is asleep."

"Yes," said Quirn.

Marten understood. With these new hours, he wouldn't be able to spend as much time with Molly. In other words, she'd have more time alone. And because he hadn't been sent to the slime pits, Molly would surely be grateful to the hall leader. Very neatly done, Marten thought sourly. He looked at the slip of plex-paper again: Biocomp engineer.

…Interesting.

3.

OFFICE OF THE SUPREME COMMANDER
PLANS AND OPERATIONS DIVISION
BEIJING, EAST ASIA SECTOR
TOP SECRET

14 April 2349

Directive No. 1
For the prosecution of the war

"Ultimate victory demands objectivity. Due to their bioengineering, the Highborn rebels automatically have certain advantages. These can neither be wished away nor ignored. Simply stated, man for man the Highborn are smarter, quicker, stronger and perhaps even wiser. Their intense training also heightens their military advantages. Breakthrough ship design and technology has armed them with craft superior to any in the Solar System. Combined with a surprise assault, the genetic super-soldiers have gained mastery of Earth-Luna space.

"It can be expected that total enemy space-fleet control of Venus and Mercury will occur in short order.

"Recommendation: All fleet units randomly retreat into deep space until our superior production gives us a two to one advantage in ship tonnage.

"Army Units, it should be noted...."
***

The microphone snapped off. Even thought he couldn't see them, Secret Police General James Hawthorne stared steely-eyed where the ancient men and women of the Directorate were sitting. Or he assumed they sat behind the polished surface in front of him. Otherwise, he sat alone at a table, a spotlight shining in his eyes and a mike in front of him.

Whoever sat behind the polished wall had been given the chance of a lifetime. The orbital bombardment that had destroyed Geneva had also slain the entire Social Unity Directorate and the SU General Assembly. These new members were a mystery to him and the world at large. He'd carefully studied the files of two aged women who had made it onto the Directorate. They were products of extreme longevity treatments. The others on the Directorate were still blanks to him, although he assumed most of them to be old. In any case, they had gained supreme rank in a single amazing bound. Which of them would come to dominate the Inner Planets hadn't yet been thrashed out.

General Hawthorne wore the green uniform with red piping along the sleeves of Directorate Staff Planning. He was tall and gaunt with wispy blond hair, and many said he had the emotions of granite.

The wall speakers warbled into life.

"Our military ships are to flee?"

Whether a man or woman had spoken was impossible to tell. The shiny, metallic wall confronting General Hawthorne gave him no clue. Such caution bespoke the Directorate's fear. Not fear of the Highborn, necessarily, but fear of his access to secret police files. The Geneva bombardment had stirred a hornet's nest of intrigue and deadly political jockeying. No one trusted anyone—not that anyone really ever had. It was just many times worse now.

For all that, General Hawthorne had a war to run. He leaned toward the mike. "A strategic retreat, yes."

"Don't be fatuous, General."

"That wasn't my intention."

"Humph! Do you care to explain this, this *treason?*"

"Don't they say he's a military genius?" asked someone else.

General Hawthorne wished he had complete biographical data on these ultra-ambitious men and women. A misstep could land him in the Brutality Room. His eyes tightened, and he dared ask, "Am I on trial?"

"Yes."

"Then—"

"We will set the agenda, General."

His bowels turned hollow. But General James Hawthorne clamped down on his fear.

A stylus moved against a plex-pad somewhere behind those polished surfaces. An audible *click* issued from the wall speakers. They were recording his trial—a bad sign.

***

Transcript of Directorate Interrogation of Secret Police General James Hawthorne #4

10.9.2349

Q. Why do you recommend that our space fleets flee?

A. So they won't be destroyed.

Q. Why do you assume automatic destruction?

A. The Highborn are superior to us, Director. We cannot ignore that basic fact.

Q. Nor am I—not that I accept your assumption. But for the sake of argument let us pretend I accept it. Why did you not suggest suicide tactics?

A. Too inefficient.

24

Q. (sarcastically) Granted I'm not an expert on strategy, General. But ultimate victory sometimes entails an inefficient use of resources. It's better than giving up.

A. Agreed.

Q. Maybe you'd better explain yourself.

A. The Highborn have certain advantages, Director. What I wish to avoid is playing into those advantages.

Q. For instance?

A. For instance, they are superior soldiers in every conceivable way. Their strategies and tactics will probably prove superior throughout the conflict.

Q. Are you saying we can't win?

A. Not at all.

Q. But if their strategies are superior, if they themselves are too... I don't see how we can win.

A. History supplies us with several answers.

Q. By all means, please enlighten us, General.

A. We could liken the Highborn to the Spartiates of the ancient Greek world.

Q. Don't you mean the Spartans?

A. No, Director. Spartiates were the full-fledged Spartans, the only ones with complete political rights and decision-making powers. They formed the core of the dreaded Spartan army, which was primarily composed of allies and *perioeci.*

Q. I'm afraid you've lost us, General.

A. Sir... Director, the Spartiates as a class dwindled over the centuries. As they dwindled, so did the efficiency of the dreaded Spartan army. Like the Spartiates, the Highborn are few in numbers.

Q. You call over two million few?

A. In comparison to us, yes. My point is this, Director: When the Athenian General Cleon took one hundred and twenty Spartiates prisoner on the island of Sphacteria—

Q. (interrupting) While we appreciate your historical acumen, General, please tell us in plain language what you're trying to say.

A. (pause) The historical records tell us how to defeat superior soldiers, soldiers who lack sufficient numbers. The primary method is to trick or force them into attrition warfare. In other words, we must fight battles where the Highborn themselves, personally, take crippling losses. For instance, Roman Dictator Fabian defeated the Carthaginian Hannibal in just such a way as I'm suggesting. To state briefly, Hannibal's superior cavalry obliterated Rome's legions whenever they marched onto the plains. So Fabian kept the legions in the hills. He fought siege battles against cities that had gone over to the Carthaginians, sieges conducted behind carefully built earthen outer walls and trenches to nullify Hannibal's cavalry in case they showed up. In the end, Fabian bled his deadly foe to the point where Rome could deal with him in the open. Hence the term: *Fabian tactics*. Or in modern terms, delaying tactics.

Q. Yes, we see your point.

Q. (different Director) Wait! What bearing does any of this have on the treasonous suggestion that our fleet units scurry into deep space?

A. Space battles are the wrong place for our attrition tactics, Director. This being so, we should save what fleet units we possess until such a time as the odds rework into our favor.

Q. (icily) I see.

Q. (different Director) Where do you suggest we stand and fight, General?

A. Planet-side. On Earth, Venus and Mercury.

Q. But that's nonsense. They'll simply bombard us from orbit.

A. Will they?

Q. We're asking the questions. (pause) Why don't you believe they'll simply bombard us from orbit?

A. They need the Inner Planets. They need our industrial might in order to keep their fleet in being. Thus, ground troops will have to land to secure these things. That's when we fight them.

Q. But orbital bombard—

A. Will give them great advantages for a time, granted. We'll have to develop better beam and missile batteries to drive the Doom Stars away from near-Earth orbit and better point defense systems to destroy any orbital debris they rain upon us. Still, the essential point is attrition. If they want North American Sector, for instance, they will have to land troops and take it. We will of course fight them on the ground, in the cities, under the cities. Then, once they hold North American Sector, we will continue the struggle via guerrilla warfare, political assassination, terrorism—

Q. And once they own all Earth, General?

A. No. I'm not suggesting that.

Q. Perhaps I missed something then. You've implied they will beat us wherever we stand and fight. For how otherwise will they take North American Sector?

A. Initially, they will be victorious, yes. But you said two million soldiers before, Director. Two million soldiers cannot control forty *billion* people. Don't forget that they must man their space fleet at the same time. After the first few victories and once their men are garrisoning what they've won, then we can overwhelm them here and there. We can assassinate a lone Highborn who visits a prostitute, say. Attrition, Directors. Bleeding the enemy to death one attack at a time. That's why our space units must flee. An existing fleet, which we'll have if we keep our ships, means the enemy will still have to *worry* about them.

27

Q. Yes, I'm beginning to see your strategy. But one thing worries me, General. Won't they recruit, well, regular people into their armed forces?

A. Unquestionably.

Q. Then your entire theory is destroyed.

A. I don't believe so. Because now *we* will operate in an area of *our* advantage.

Q. Which in your opinion is?

A. Secret police ruthlessness and superior political theory.

Q. Perhaps you'd better explain that, General.

A. In a word, egalitarianism. Modern Social Unity philosophy teaches us that one man is as good as the next. The Highborn have exactly the opposite view. They are an elite, a master race, if you will. (pause)

Q. Yes?

A. If you will permit one last historical example.

Q. Make your point, General Hawthorne.

A. Nazi Germany preached a racial superiority philosophy in the middle of the Twentieth Century. They invaded Socialist Russia—a precursor to our own political system, I might add—and won titanic battles. Yet the Nazi political philosophy insured the hatred of the people. The people were treated as inferiors even though the Germans were no different in terms of real ability versus the Russians.

In our day the Highborn actually *are* superior. No doubt, this will cause them to act arrogantly, especially as they rub shoulders with the conquered peoples. The masses will learn to hate the Highborn. What men fear they hate, and when a man is looked down upon, he hates that even more. Added to this is our modern thinking. People will become incensed at the idea that someone actually could be better. That, Directors, is one of our key advantages. Secondly, military governments seldom produce as ruthless a secret police as a one party political government. The Prussian General Staff thought they could outfox and be more ruthless than Lenin and his Bolsheviks back in World War One—

Q. We perceive your point, General. And that point really amounts to kill them on the ground.

A. Yes.

Q. But it entails risk.

A. Great risk. For their battle-skills may prove superior to our political skills. War hysteria and extreme paranoia of the supermen must be drummed into everyone until all Inner Planets hate the Highborn. We must ensure that our troops fight with fanatical zeal. In other words, they must fight to the last man and the last bullet in every encounter.

Q. Then we will win?

A. Yes. We will win.

End of transcript #4: Interrogation of Secret Police General James Hawthorne

4.

The weeks sped by with the news of the expanding civil war on everyone's lips. Then a fateful day arrived for Marten Kluge and in a way for all humanity. Thanks to Hall Leader Quirn, Marten woke up in his cubicle at one in the morning, when the rest of his complex slept the sleep of the just.

His cubicle, the standard single rent, seemed barely big enough for Marten's tall frame. So when the alarm buzzed he slid out of his sleep-shelf and in two steps reached the shower. No mementos, paintings or statuettes cluttered the tiny room or gave it a personal flair. It was stark, minimalist, clean, a holdover from his years of hiding in the Sun-Works Factory.

He went through his toiletries, ate breakfast, donned a gray jumpsuit, hardhat, and work boots. As he chewed his last bite of vitamin-reinforced algae bread, Marten squinted at the holoset—he hated its constant noise. By law and technology, the holoset was impossible to turn off. The set showed armored Social Unity infantrymen hiding behind rocks and dunes and lasering Highborn as they bounded toward them in powered battlesuits. The giant invaders crumpled one after the other, dead. Then fighters screamed over the scene, missiles zooming from their underbellies and slamming into huge tanks, which exploded soundlessly behind the commentary.

A talking head droned on the set: "Bitter fighting in the Mullarbor Plain yesterday forced the Highborn Third Army to retreat to their initial drop zone. Reinforcement fighters from Japan Sector helped stem this latest breakout attempt.

"In the east...."

Marten sneered as he picked up his lunch pail. According to the news, this was the third time this week the Highborn had retreated to their initial drop zone. How much farther could they go? He believed that instead of retreating, they advanced. He shrugged. It really didn't matter what he thought.

He stepped out of his cubicle, closing Door No. 209 and strode along Corridor 118 until he reached the nearest conveyer belt. He rode it out of the twenty-story complex and onto the darkened street. Terraced gardens of sleeping tulips and marigolds drooped away from him, while dwarf palms rustled in the breeze. Gigantic fans connected to vents that led all the way to the surface created that breeze. High overhead, the sunlamps of Level Thirty-nine glowed at dim and soft "sleep" music played from hidden speakers. Automated street sweepers swished by Marten as he strode fast along the sidewalk. Passing him zipped a caravan of cyclists training for the upcoming Festival Games.

Others on the early morning shift passed Marten or headed in the same direction. Many shouted hearty greetings to each other and spoke of the latest Highborn defeat. Uniformed peacekeepers on patrol nodded approvingly. Once or twice, the black visor of a peacekeeper turned in Marten's direction. He shouted no greetings to his fellow workers nor made any comments on the news. A tall peacekeeper spoke into a hand

31

recorder. Marten wondered if he'd gained another demerit for unsociable behavior.

He entered the Far-Forty Lift Tube with twenty other people, a mixture of manual laborers and office workers. The door closed with a hiss and down they plunged. Ads played on the lift vid. A shouting emcee told of the prizes to be won on Tell-a-Friend. Then dancing girls in sequins wiggled by, singing of the wonders of algae protein shakes. "Mmmm, great!"

The lift stopped, people struggled out and others shouldered their way in. Hiss, close, down they plunged.

Fifteen minutes later Marten and five other men in gray jumpsuits, hardhats and boots strode out of the elevator. No music played down here; no vids or holos blared. The only sound was that of their boots drumming on the cool earth. They peeled away in different directions, one or two waving, and then Marten strode alone deep underground and in a semi-dark corridor.

His shoulders relaxed and the stiffness in his neck went away. His somber features softened. He walked and walked and walked, turning many times into many different corridors. Finally, in the distance he heard the grind and roar of Tunnel Crawler Six as it chewed into deep sedimentary rock.

This was end of the line for Greater Sydney. This was the bottom of the city, where Level Sixty was under construction.

Marten inserted his earplugs, snapped on his helmet lamp, fixed his oxygen mask and strolled closer to his monster.

The mighty Tunnel Crawler Six was a vast metallic worm. The huge segmented sections slithered after the main mouth that tore at the rock twenty-four hours a day. The chewed up parts went on an internal conveyer belt to the central dump. Some of the rock was mined for useful minerals. Some went topside for construction and the rest went down the deep-core mine, there to be turned into lava and added to the Earth's interior. Pollution as such was nonexistent with the deep-core dump. Nuclear wastes, toxic chemicals, fuel sludge—anything unwanted or non-reusable—was simply dumped deep into the Earth and never worried about again.

Marten's job wasn't repairing Tunnel Crawler Six. His specs called for maintenance of the biocomp that ran the beast.

Fine particles of dust drifted in the corridor. Marten's light beamed through it. It got thicker up ahead as he neared the machine's maw. The clank and roar of the chewing mouth shook the air. No one could talk here. The roar became a blanket covering other noise. It brought... well, after awhile the roar seemed to fade in one's thinking until it became a kind of silence.

"Silence is golden," Marten mouthed under his oxygen mask.

For such an utterance—if he'd been heard—peacekeepers would surely have drawn their shock rods and beaten him down as anti-social.

Marten reached the cab, which was three hundred meters from the mouth, and hoisted himself up the rungs. The long beast shook and vibrated. He opened the cab and slipped in, shutting the heavy door behind him. Much of the roar and clanking faded away, although the vibrations were constant.

He sat at the controls and turned on the Bioram Taw2. The cab was cramped with coils, leads, tools and screens, but the control chair was heaven compared to anything Marten had ever used.

The Bioram Taw2 was a marvel of modern technology. Human brain tissue, from a criminal who'd been liquidated for the good of the state, had been carefully teased from the main brain mass. After a good personality-scrubbing, the brain tissue was embedded in cryo-sheets and surrounded by programming gel. One point five kilos of brain tissue_had replaced tons of specialized control and volitional systems. Unfortunately, the cryocyorgic environment accelerated decay and eventual death. Still, biocomps were the wave of the future.

Here, away from prying eyes and busybodies, Marten had given rein to his impulses. He'd written brand new software for his Data-Five auxiliary computer. The auxiliary computer was only to be used as backup for the biocomp, but Marten had ignored that reg. In fact, he'd erased many of the D5's programs in order to make room for his own. Then, with infinite patience, he'd teased memories out of the biocomp's brain tissue.

The pros upstairs thought they'd scrubbed all personality from the biocomp's gray matter. Marten knew it wasn't as easy as that. His mother had known more about bio-computers than the so-called experts had, and she'd taught him before she'd been killed on the Sun-Works Factory.

Marten took off his work gloves, turned on the D5 and logged onto his Bio-Speak Program. Then he settled the keyboard on his knees, put the mike near his mouth and the audio-plugs in his ears.

It wasn't what he learned from the Bioram Taw2 that made the difference. It was that after three long years he finally had someone to talk to again. No one in the cab marked demerits or awarded him honors for his views. What he said was what he felt, no less and no more.

Blake, the Bioram Taw2's name, remembered little of his former life. He'd been married, had two kids and he'd run a big government agency, but of what exactly he couldn't remember. During their talks, Blake upheld Social Unity, sort of. He mostly wanted to hear all about Marten and Molly Tan. Marten thought it ironic that the disembodied brain was a randy sex-fiend, but he never told Blake that.

Blake and he greeted one another this morning, talked about the news, the work, rambled about nothing for awhile, until finally Blake brought up Molly. He asked, "Why don't you move in with her?"

"Because she's not my wife yet," said Marten for the umpteenth time.

"So?"

"So I think a man should commit first before he has sex with a woman."

"What a perverse notion, Marten. Don't ever tell your block leader that."

"I'll punch him unconscious is what I'll do."

"Why?" That asked eagerly.

"He's making moves on Molly again, hinting that he can pull strings for her and maybe even for me if she's nice. When she tells him no thank you, he hints that events can turn the other way just as easily."

"Tut, tut. Women chase power, Marten. Surely, you know that. She's just playing hard to get."

"You don't know Molly."

Something like laughter came over the audio-feed. Marten wondered how Blake did that, because laughter had never been in the program.

"Marten, you punch your block leader and you'll go to the slime pits. You know that, don't you?"

"Yeah."

"Or maybe they'll tear your brain down and hook you into a beast." More of that mad laughter came over the line.

Then the cab shook as the beast tore into the rock with greater intensity than ever.

To Marten's left, a holoset flickered into life. A small, angry, holo-image shouted silently.

Marten picked up the receiver and put it to his ear.

35

"Slow it down, Marten!"

"Roger," said Marten.

In order to keep Blake's mind off his fate, Marten spent the rest of the morning playing chess. He let Blake win three games in a row. Blake hated losing, but he hated even more someone letting him win. So Marten had to stretch out the games.

After lunch, Marten went on a routine inspection walk. His mind began to wander as he checked well-oiled segments of machinery… neatly maintained like his life. He didn't know any more what he wanted. Not to live in Greater Sydney forever, that's for sure. He wondered sometimes if he had the balls to take an excursion into the slums. Where had his daring gone? Had seeing his Dad's head explode stolen something out of him?

Despite the so-called glories of Social Unity, slums had formed in paradise. Each city seemed to have them. Greater Sydney wasn't an exception. In fact, for reasons unknown to the social engineers, Greater Sydney's slums proved nastier than the common run. Sydney's deep-core mine reached down to Earth's mantle, drawing planetary thermal power. Many of the larger cities did likewise.

None of the levels reached anywhere near the mantle. The deep-core mine was a narrow shaft that went far beyond Sydney's living space. The slums were always near the mine, or the upper part of it, anyway. Sydney's slums were from Level Forty-one to Forty-nine and for a full kilometer outward. Police raids seldom helped keep control there. Social workers rarely ventured into the slums even if guaranteed army patrols. Hall and block leaders kept a low profile there. Ward officers seldom set foot in their own territory. Desperate people lived in the slums, uneducated, violent people with bizarre modes of thought and behavior. Gangs roved at night, youth gangs being particular bloodthirsty. Drug-lords hired people called mules, bodyguards and enforcers.

The honest, card-carrying citizens on the fringes who lived above and below the slums cried out for stronger police patrols. So at elevator openings and stairwells and at strategic tunnel doors thick knots of heavily-armed shock cops formed.

Marten wondered sometimes if the people in the slums had a greater form of freedom than those living in the better levels. Could he find the freedom he desired in the slums? Maybe he could, but maybe at too bitter of a cost.

Marten kicked a rock out of his way. Where had his courage gone?

Later, near quitting time, he turned left at a dark corridor and opened an emergency shed. Inside stood a makeshift kettle, a flame box underneath and strange fumes bubbling out of it. From a nearby bin, he took the last slices of algae bread and fed them into the kettle. He readjusted the still, switched bottles and examined a clear liquid in the light of his helmet lamp.

The liquid was clear, hard liquor: synthahol. He sniffed it and screwed up his nose. It had an awful odor. He put the flask to his lips and threw back his head. He didn't dare taste it, but he relaxed his throat and let the synthahol slide into his belly. Oh, it burned so nicely in his stomach. Then the alcoholic fumes shot up to his brain like fire—Liquid fire!

He checked his chronometer, finished the contents of the flask and put it back under the drip.

Comfortably numb, he strode for the main lift-tube about a kilometer away. He then reversed the process of this morning. The neck and shoulder stiffening wouldn't occur until the synthahol wore off. But the cramped lift, the peacekeepers, the endless corridors of his complex... these things remained dreadfully the same.

Marten doffed his clothes in his cubicle, showered, put on new clothes, ate a bowl of gruel and thought about calling Molly. He decided against it. Then his door chime sounded.

For a moment, he froze as fear crawled up his spine. Then he shrugged. They didn't have anything on him he could think of. But if it was cops, well, then it was the cops. He was more thankful than ever for the synthahol. When they took him, as they surely must in the end, he wanted to play it cool. He slouched against the wall, set his face in a neutral mask and said:

"Enter."

The door opened and beautiful Molly Tan stepped within. She wore shimmering sequins similar to this morning's ad girls, and she wore a silky red skirt and silver slippers. She had short red hair combed to the left, freckles galore and a body to kill for. Her legs—Marten puckered his lips and imagined kissing them.

Molly hopped near and pecked him on the lips. Then she frowned.

"Marten, you've been drinking again."

He shrugged.

"But you can't be drinking this afternoon."

"Why not?"

She pouted as she ran her hands over his chest. "Discussions start in fifteen minutes."

"So?"

"Hurry, Marten, get dressed or we'll be late."

He almost said no, forget it, not today. Then they'd fight, Molly might storm away, and then that bastard, Hall Leader Quirn, would drape his slimy arm over her shoulder and console her at the discussions.

He threw on a synthetic leather jacket and boots.

"You should wear a shirt under the jacket," she said.

Marten left the jacket open, exposing his lean stomach, and he didn't comb his hair. Maybe it was the synthahol whispering. He dressed slum, the daring new style. It wasn't the right sort of dress for discussions, maybe more an outing to the zoo.

Molly told him all that. He kissed her to silence. She told him to take a mint. She hated synthahol breath.

"And it's illegal, Marten. You know that."

"I know."

"I should report you."

"Then who will you have to move in with?"

"Oh, Marten!" she said, brightening, clapping her hands. "Are you serious? Do you want to move in today?"

He blinked at her in confusion, uncertain what he'd just said.

She pouted. "We can't get married. Marten, that's... that's *reactionary*. Do you know what my friends would say?"

Marten took the mint, ushered her out the cubicle and in silence they rode the conveyer to the discussion room. He tried to take her hand. She jerked it away. He rubbed her shoulder, whispering, "Don't be anti-social."

She glared at him. He gave her a playful pinch. Finally, she relented and gave him a smile. He kissed her. She kissed him back.

They jumped off the conveyer and strolled to the large double doors of the discussion room. Crowds poured in. The women dressed in silky, knee-length skirts and slippers. Some had sequined blouses like Molly, others wore frilly blouses with the top three buttons open. Every female dressed in bright, "happy" colors. The men wore brown shorts and sandals, and typically yellow sleeveless shirts with red cloth-cuffs. Within the building ferns abounded everywhere. They hung from the high ceiling and lined the walls. Couples and triplets mingled freely. Giggling came from the hidden lanes created by the ferns. Pleasant, sing-along-humming issued from wall speakers.

When a chime sounded people moved to the center of the room, sitting on mats. The men sat cross-legged, the ladies tucked their legs under themselves. A few people frowned at Marten's attire. More than one woman shook her head at Molly in sympathy. She shrugged, rubbed Marten's shoulder and finally started scolding him for wearing such improper garments to discussions.

Molly brooded even as the speaker moved toward center stage. The speaker was a terrifying ogre of a woman: large, massively shouldered, with ponderous breasts and a big gut. She wore the tight-fitting red uniform with black epaulets of Political Harmony Corps. She stomped her black boots on the platform as if on parade. She came to a sudden halt and wheeled toward the crowd, glowering at them from beneath the low-slung brim of her black cap. She had heavy jowls that wobbled as she spoke. Her thick right hand rested on the butt of her holstered stunner. Her tiny black eyes, dots within folds of flesh, seemed to glitter as she searched for those who lacked social harmony.

"Depressingly formidable," whispered Molly.

Marten squeezed her hand. Few here would dare joke about a political police officer. That Molly could was one of the reasons Marten liked her.

The PHC officer barked out in a drill parade voice, telling them how evil the Highborn were, how the genetic soldiers hated everything good and proper. Their political philosophy, as low and primitive as could be imagined, was based on the master-slave relationship. The Highborn could never win, everyone knew that… and on and on she roared. Finally, her voice broke as she burst into praise of the Directorate's bold new plans that would throw these space deviants off the good old Earth.

Cued, Hall Leader Quirn stepped onto stage. His community persona was utterly different from his office presentation. Today he wore attire similar to the men but with the added features of a short "block leader" cape and his military style cap. He clapped loudly as he limped toward the major. The crowd leaped to its feet, clapping and shouting approval for the major's speech. As Marten rose, Molly cheered beside him.

Quirn motioned them down as his voice came over the speakers.

"Thank you, Major Orlov, thank you. That was very informative. Yes, I understand now how in the end our military will defeat the Highborn. Their very... *evil* gives them a certain advantage over good folk like us, trusting folk that we are. How vile it was of them to have taken advantage of our good nature. But soon, very soon they will be defeated."

"Correct!" barked Major Orlov.

Quirn and she vigorously shook hands on center stage. She dwarfed him like some medieval monster. Then he faced the crowd again. "Major, I'm sure that many, many of the folk of Hall C-Two hundred and seventeen have questions for you, burning questions that I'm certain only you have the expertise to answer."

From her spot on the floor, Molly hissed at Marten, who swayed on his feet, not having yet sat down again like everyone else.

"Yes, that man over—why, it's Marten Kluge," said Quirn in surprise. "Dearest Marten, do you have a question for the major?"

A thin man in a yellow zipsuit hurried toward Marten. The man excused himself as he stepped over seated people until he shoved a mike under Marten's nose.

"Uh..." said Marten, and it came over the wall speakers.

People laughed.

Quirn held up exquisitely clean hands—they shone as if lacquered. "There are no bad questions. Only questions that haven't yet been asked."

"Quite correct!" barked the major.

"Yes, I do have a question," Marten said.

"Splendid!" cried Quirn. He nodded for Marten to go ahead and ask it.

"Don't you say anything silly, Marten," Molly said from the floor.

The mike picked that up and broadcast it throughout the room. Nervous laughter greeted her words.

"A woman's wisdom," shouted Quirn.

Clapping erupted everywhere from the women.

Marten growled into the mike. "Yeah, I got a question. How many times can the Highborn retreat to their drop zone? The news said three times already. That seems two times too many to me."

Silence greeted his words.

Licking his lips in a nervous gesture, Quirn glanced at the major. She stared at Marten with obvious hostility.

Marten leaned his face toward the mike. "I know there aren't any bad questions."

As if pricked, Major Orlov snarled, "Far better to die fighting for political equality and social equity than to fall into the hated hands of the Supremacists! Humanity stands shoulder to shoulder against these caste masters, against the peerage of supposed genetic superiority. I for one refuse to buckle under these grandees, these supposed lords of creation. United together and no matter the cost, we will hurl these interlopers into the depths of space."

Major Orlov's pin-dot eyes shone. "How many times can the Highborn retreat to their drop zone? That, my arrogant friend, is a matter of state security and only told to those who need to know!"

"Ahhh," went throughout the room.

Marten allowed Molly to drag him down beside her.

"How could you, Marten?" she said, tears brimming.

Marten might have been worried, but good old synthahol came to his rescue. He blanked out and time seemed to leap forward. The next thing he knew they mingled among the crowds, discussing what had been said. No one asked him about his question. Molly fidgeted and she kept touching his jacket until he zipped it.

Hall Leader Quirn limped up, a glass of punch in his hand. His eyes appeared glassy. Rumor said he sniffed dream dust, but surely, he'd not slipped a dose here. Beside him strode Major Orlov.

"Be careful, Marten," Molly hissed into his ear.

"Ah, dear fellow," said Quirn, slapping Marten on the shoulder. "What possessed you to ask such a question?"

"Sorry," Marten mumbled. Beside him, Molly heaved a sigh of relief.

"Ah, well, must have been a hard day at work," said Quirn, his right eye fluttering, a sure sign of dream dust usage.

PHC Major Orlov wasn't so gracious. She planted herself in front of Marten, her burly arms akimbo. "I never believed there were alarmists. Not until I saw you."

"Asking questions is wrong?" Marten meekly asked.

"Certain questions are. Any patriot knows that."

Tears leaked from Molly's eyes as people turned and stared.

"Molly!" cried Quirn. "Please don't cry." He moved forward as if to console her.

But Molly turned away and fled toward the nearest Lady's Room. Marten took a step after her. A hard grip on his arm jerked him to a stop and spun him around.

"I'm speaking to you," said the major.

Marten scowled, and out of the corner of his eye, he saw Quirn limping after Molly.

"Can you comprehend the odds our soldiers face?"

"Huh?" said Marten.

People moved closer, interested in the information and wondering if Mad Marten would give this political policewoman something to think about.

"The odds, the difficulties, the *danger*."

Marten eyed the major, and he wondered how much real information she was privy to. Certain that it would annoy her and maybe loosen her lips, he shrugged.

"Are you dense?" the major asked outraged.

"These are Supremacists we speak of," Marten said, "deviants, I believe you said."

"Yes, yes, of course they are. But surely you would agree that a rabid dog is dangerous."

"Surely."

"Then think of a dog *bred* for battle, and that dog rabid and running loose."

"So the odds are bad?" Marten asked innocently.

The monstrous major decisively chopped the air.

"Orbital Highborn fighters scour the skies until nothing of ours can move. Powered troopers land behind any fixed positions we try to hold and in hours the surrounded units are annihilated." She shook her head so her jowls wobbled. "They have complete fluidity, we die in…"

The faces around her had turned ashen, silent, still.

"Please," said Marten, "continue. Your information is absorbing"

Major Orlov turned crimson and shot him a venomous glance. Then she turned and ponderously marched elsewhere.

Marten glanced around for a sign of Molly. Then his features hardened as he failed to spy Hall Leader Quirn. Marten strode to the nearest Lady's Room as he considered the major's revelations. It was as he'd suspected. The Highborn were winning, at least in Australian Sector. Rumors said they'd already taken Antarctica, New Zealand, Tasmania, New Caledonia, the Solomon Islands and New Guinea. Their strategy didn't seem difficult to decipher. Grab Earth's islands first, because except for submarines the islands would be impossible to re-supply with Social Unity troops. The rumors he'd heard said that Earth's surface vessels had all been destroyed—only the submarines had survived and could survive the Highborn orbital laser platforms that burned anything that moved. Other rumors said the Directorate's high scientists devised new beam and missile batteries to drive the hated enemies away from Near-Earth Orbit. The news shows ominously stated that Political Harmony Corps intended the Highborn to gain no useful victories.

"Marten!" said a woman.

Marten turned. "Oh, hello Beth."

Beth was Molly's best friend. She constantly urged Molly to see someone else. Beth worked in records, wore her dark hair short and never smiled except during hum-a-longs when it was considered bad manners not to.

Beth eyed Marten's leather jacket with distaste, hesitated and then moved closer.

"Really, Marten, don't you ever think of anyone but yourself?"

He didn't want to argue with Beth. So he said, "Sometimes. Have you seen Molly?"

Beth took another step. "Marten… why do you have to make it so hard for Molly?"

"Beth, please, not now."

"No, listen for once. She'd like you to move in with her. But your insistence that you get married first, Marten! That's so…."

"Reactionary?"

"It's worse than that. What if she wants to see other people?"

"What?" he said. "Like who?"

"See. That's what I'm talking about. We all belong to each other. To insist upon marriage—you don't own her, Marten."

"I know that."

"Do you?"

Maybe it was the synthahol, because he wasn't sure why he asked, "Haven't you ever wanted to belong solely to one person? To be a team, you and your partner, against the world?"

Beth drew back in horror. "We're all one, Marten. No one is better than anyone else."

"Yes, but—"

"How dare you want to be..." she sputtered for the right word "...elitist!"

"No, that's not what I mean."

"Do you think you're the only one good enough for Molly?"

"Beth..."

"I think she should see Quirn more."

"More? What do you mean *more*?"

Beth blinked in surprise. "Uh, what I mean is—"

"She's been seeing Quirn?"

"Not seeing, really."

With his heart hammering, Marten turned and glanced for sight of the hall leader.

Beth plucked at his sleeve. "She can't just see one person. People might think her odd. Really, Marten, sometimes I think you're corrupting her."

Marten could hardly think as he stalked away.

"Don't be elitist, Marten! Or—Where's the major?" he heard Beth ask someone.

Quirn! He couldn't believe Molly was actually seeing him, maybe even kissing him. Rage flared within him. He hunted for the hall leader. Then he saw ferns thrash and he heard a muffled, "Stop. Not here."

Hall Leader Quirn struggled to hold onto Molly.

Several quick strides brought Marten near. He yanked back the fern.

"Marten!" said the hall leader, his features a mixture of rage, surprise and drugged lethargy.

Marten lunged at Quirn.

"Marten, no!" Molly cried.

"Take your hands off me," Quirn warned, who finally released Molly to defend himself. "I can—"

He never finished. Marten slugged him in the mouth. Quirn slammed against the wall. Marten grabbed the front of Quirn's shirt and...

"You!"

Marten looked over his shoulder.

With her sidearm stunner, PHC Major Orlov shot Marten in the back.

5.

Each day the forty billion people of Sol III consumed billions of kilograms of food. The government's nightmare—even before the civil war—was where to find all those calories. Earth's environment was strained to the maximum and still there wasn't enough to go around. A hundred of the solar system's biggest gigahabs orbited the planet. On the gigahabs were fish farms, wheat farms, chicken farms and rice farms churning out food around the clock in order to provide the teeming hordes with their daily bread. Still that wasn't enough. Beef had vanished long ago for the average man. Fish, chicken and rabbit returned more meat per bushel of feed than a steer did. Also, cows weighed ten times more than goats and ate ten times as much feed. Unfortunately, a cow only produced four times as much milk as a goat. For the same amount of feed, a goat produced twice what a cow could. For this reason, Earthmen in 2349 drank goat milk and ate goat-derived cheese.

Breakthrough food technologies became stopgap measures. Massive starvation would have occurred but for humanity's creativity. "Necessity is the mother of invention," went the ancient saying. And men invented with a passion in the area of food production.

In the end, one of the oldest foods in the chain came to humanity's rescue. It happened partly for another basic need: oxygen. Near each major city gargantuan algae vats were constructed underground. In order to increase growth, powerful sunlamps burned every minute of the rotation cycle. Many names abounded for these life-saving, sustenance-rich algae a vicious, thick, goopy scum that clogged all known machinery. The nearest to the truth in terms of its rawest form was pond scum. Everything about this high-grade algae production required around the clock maintenance. From the heat flats, to the chutes that drained excess algae to the settling tanks, to the processing bins, the churn cycle and then the constantly cleaned canals that brought the vitamin-rich slop to the enhancing vats. Robotic machinery and androids cared for ninety-seven percent of the process. The last three-percent took flesh and blood workers in slick-suits slaving harder than any Egyptian had raising the pyramids.

The slime pits became one of the supreme teaching tools for Social Unity. Reform through labor, first raised to an art centuries ago by Mao Zedong in the Great Proletarian Cultural Revolution, now once more came into its own in the middle of the Twenty-fourth Century.

For those who found normal social interaction intolerable, for those too thickheaded to understand the beauty of the system, well, a long stint in the slime pits often cured them of their pathological malaise. Perhaps as importantly, for the first time many of them performed a socially useful function. It wasn't nice or easy. Sometimes, regrettably, workers lost lives to drowning, heat exhaustion, algae gorging, excess bleeding from torn limbs in the choppers, red-syrup lung, sludge parasite and a vicious form of black gangrene. Studies showed that unless the trainees bonded quickly with their counselors, their probability for survival was minimal. Upon initiation, each trainee or student was encouraged to develop the proper work ethic and enthusiasm for his instructor.

Marten Kluge found himself placed among the incorrigibles, due in large measure to Major Orlov backing up Hall Leader Quirn's testimonial. No one thought Marten's odds very good for survival, least of all Marten Kluge. But he'd be damned if he were going to just lie down and die.

6.

For four days, Marten Kluge uttered no word to anybody. They cut his rations in half, quartered them, and then they told him he could eat when he decided to cooperate and talk. Stubbornly, day and after day, he kept his lips shut and his eyes peeled. His cellmates stole food from the refectory, he discovered on his fifth day after the judgment. On the eighth day, he successfully performed his first theft from them. The day they caught him started ordinarily enough.

The squad worked in the heat flats for ten hours straight, twice the legal limit. Exhausted, they dragged themselves through decontamination, peeled off their slick-suits and staggered under the showers. Seven men of various shapes, sizes and ages slumped against the tiles as icy water needled their skin. Marten tilted his head back and gulped water. His blue eyes were bloodshot. His skin was blotchy and his stomach seemed glued to his spine.

The water stopped. They shuffled to the vents and like patient animals endured the heated air. When it quit, they donned coarse, itchy tunics and marched barefoot to their cell. Each man crumpled to his mat on the steel floor and fell asleep.

A klaxon woke them. They rose, with black circles around their eyes, and they shuffled out of their cell for dinner. Marten brought up the rear. Just before reaching the door, he knelt, felt the open stitching of the nearest mat and drew a hidden wafer, popping it into his mouth.

"So it's you!"

Startled, Marten looked up.

A short, swarthy, stocky youth glared at him. He was Stick, a knifeboy from a pocket gang in the slums.

Armored guards stood outside, as did over a hundred men and women trooping out of their cells to dinner. Now wasn't the moment to fight. Stick knew it, so did Marten, but Stick didn't seem to care. He launched himself into the cell, aiming a karate kick at Marten's head. Marten dodged, and the foot slammed against his shoulder and spun him to the floor.

Stick snarled, "Where I come from we kill thieves."

Marten staggered to his feet. He felt lightheaded and his vision was blurry. He was taller than Stick, probably weighed more, but the scars on Stick's body had come from a hundred different street fights.

In the corridor, there was shouting and shrill whistle blasts, and then the loud *zaps* of shock rods striking flesh.

Stick roared a battle cry and rained a flurry of blows at Marten. Smack, smack, smack, Marten's cheek stung. He grunted as a fist snapped into his stomach. His ribs ached where Stick connected with his heel. Then red despair boiled into Marten. He gave an inarticulate cry as he charged the knifeboy. Knuckles thudded atop his head. Then Marten lifted Stick off his feet and shoulder-slammed him against the wall. He grappled as Stick gouged with his fingernails.

"Stop!" shouted the guards, blowing whistles as they piled into the room.

Neither man heeded the call. So shock rods fell on them, stunning them into submission. Armored guards separated them and hauled them to their feet and forced-marched them out of the cell and down the corridor filled with open-mouthed trainees. Marten glared wildly at everyone. Stick had eyes only for Marten. The look promised murder.

A guard twisted Marten's arm behind his back. Marten ground his teeth together, refusing to cry out.

"Think you're a tough bastard, huh?"

Marten remained silent.

The guard twisted harder.

Marten yelled. The guard laughed in his ear. Marten struggled to free himself, and to his amazement, the guard let go. Marten turned toward his tormenter. Shock rods hit him in the face. He saw their black visors and the gleaming white teeth of their sadistic smiles. Then he blanked out into unconsciousness.

7.

Marten woke to the sound of a hissing hypo. Groggily, he realized someone had shot him full of stimulants. He was also aware of a body beside him. He checked and saw Stick sneer. They sat on a bench together.

"You're meat," said Stick.

"The prisoners will not speak unless they are spoken to."

It was an effort, but Marten swung his eyes toward the front. Ogre-sized Major Orlov sat there, her black cap snug over her beady eyes. Brutality shone on her face. Behind her stood two, red-uniformed PHC thugs, men with the zealous glare of the hypnotically adjusted. They were in a small room, the lights bright and the walls bare.

"Marten Kluge, the State believes that you are worse than an incorrigible."

Marten said nothing concerning her statement. He was too shocked and dismayed to discover her here.

Major Orlov, her ham-like hands resting on her knees, shifted her attention to Stick. "What could possibly drive a trainee to strike another member of society?"

Stick took a leaf from Marten's book, saying nothing.

Major Orlov nodded curtly, as if confirming a suspicion. "Intransigence is punishable many different ways."

Stick's eyes darted around the cell.

"On the other hand, cooperation shows willingness to reform, which means the incorrigible might possibly be returned to the labor battalion he originally came from."

"Uh..." Stick shifted on the bench. The two thugs behind the major grew tense. Stick's shoulders slumped in a submissive way. The guards relaxed and the major stretched her lips in what she surely assumed was a smile.

"We had an argument," Stick said slowly.

The major's bushy eyebrows rose. "Does Marten Kluge slack off during work hours?"

Stick shrugged.

"No. Mannerisms don't interest me."

Stick stared at her.

"Truth interests me. Factual, precise, measurable truth." She glanced at Marten.

He glowered, but he didn't glower at her. In fact, he didn't really listen to her. He stared straight ahead and let rage consume him. His eyes grew glossy and his breathing deepened. He let rage wash over his thinking as he brooded on how much he hated everyone here. How everyone here was against him and plotted to thwart him. They tried to make him talk. He would never talk. He would rather they slice open his belly than give them the satisfaction of hearing him talk. They tried to subdue his will. They had taken away all his personal freedom. No. He refused. He wouldn't budge a millimeter.

Major Orlov pursed her lips. "The truth is both of you broke regulations. These regulations are not frivolous guides haphazardly written. Indeed not! They are here to reform you. But we can only reform you if you will help, if you will cooperate. Truth…. It is a precious commodity. Those who cooperate will only wish to speak truths. Now, I will give you each a chance to tell me factual, actual truth."

Marten breathed heavily through his nose. For the moment, he subsisted on rage.

Stick, however, thoughtfully rubbed his chin. He eyed Marten and then he judged the major and her two killers.

"You want the truth?" asked Stick.

Major Orlov bared her teeth. "At this moment we attempt to solve deep-seated issues. I admit to a personal interest—I wish to show the sluggards who run Reform how to… how to correct an incorrigible." She glanced at Marten, before she continued with Stick.

"I tell you frankly, the tank awaits both of you if we fail. But you must never think of the tank as punishment. Indeed not! The tank is merely one of society's many tools of reform. Unless each of you is reformed, we have failed in our assigned task. I hate failure. It mocks the State, which is the engine that gives the greatest good to the most people. So yes, truth must now step forth so that the proper correctives can be applied to each of you."

Marten vaguely understood that hoarding food was punishable by death. Not that he planned on turning Stick over to them. To cooperate was the first step toward giving in.

Stick seemed to think about his answer as he gauged the major. "We don't get along."

Major Orlov leaned forward. "Indeed. Why did you choose that moment to publicly reveal your dislike?"

Stick hung his head as if defeated. "He spoke profanities."

Major Orlov sat straighter, her interests obviously engaged. "Marten Kluge spoke to you, verbally?"

Stick nodded miserably. He was a good actor.

Major Orlov scowled and snapped her thick fingers. One of her red-suited killers stepped forward.

"Give me your agonizer."

The man placed a small disc with a dial into her huge hand. She twisted the setting onto high as the two thugs swung behind Stick and held him fast.

"Mannerisms annoy me. They indicate frivolity."

She placed the agonizer to his neck. Stick arched his back and winced horribly, but he made no noise other than a croak. Finally, she removed the agonizer and handed it back to the thug.

She addressed Marten. "What did you say to him?"

Marten glowered at the wall.

"My patience is not unlimited, Mr. Kluge." After a moment, Major Orlov pursed her lips. She asked Stick, "What did he say to you?"

"It don't matter."

Her tone turned glacial. "I will determine that."

"He called me a dirty gook."

"Ah... a racial epithet?"

"Yeah."

She swung back to Marten. "That is a serious crime, Mr. Kluge. You shall spend ten days in the tank unless you admit to your racial bigotry and make a formal apology to everyone in squad eleven."

The glassy look left Marten's eyes. He grew aware of the conversation, playing it back in his mind, as it were. He glanced at Stick, who wouldn't meet his gaze. A small, tight smile played on Marten's lips.

"And what do you find so amusing?" asked the major.

Marten fixed his gaze upon her.

"Here, Mr. Kluge, insolence is a costly attitude to sustain."

Major Orlov could hurt him, hurt him very much. Despite that, Marten let his contempt for her freeze onto his face.

She flushed. She leaned forward and deliberately slapped him across the face. Marten checked his impulse to leap upon her. Instead, he laughed.

57

She bolted upright, seemed on the verge of falling upon him and then whispered, "Into the tank with him this very instant."

8.

Nine-foot tall glass cylinders lined the sides of a sterile auditorium. In the middle stood what seemed to be an emergency medical operating theater, complete with green-clad doctors and nurses. Several interns strolled around a working cylinder.

As he was marched past them, Marten saw green-colored water pouring into the cylinder from the top, splashing upon a naked woman inside. The water swirled up to her thighs. Drenched and wretched she worked the lever of a hand-pump built into the cylinder. At every stroke, water exited via a tube and drained out through the auditorium floor.

Marten's scrotum tightened and he stumbled.

From behind, Major Orlov steadied him with a hand on his shoulder. He felt her breath on his neck.

"Ten days in there, Mr. Kluge. Either that or speak to me now."

Marten calculated the fall of the water. It wasn't gushing, but it was constant. He felt dizzy, lightheaded. He considered the medical unit. They wouldn't let him die, it seemed. So he steeled himself for the worst and kept repeating in his mind how he'd never give in.

"Foolish," said Major Orlov, perhaps noting the set of his jaw. "There are constant miscalculations. Often the trainee dies of heart failure. Sometimes the pumping malfunctions and more water pours into the tank than was required. Before anyone can draw the trainee to safety, he or she drowns."

A small, balding doctor with a clipboard stepped up. He kept blinking his eyes rapidly. He said hello and explained the pump to them, the water temperature—icy—and that at times "elements" were added to the tank to increase the discomfort and thereby help prod the recalcitrant to speedier reform.

"Any questions then?" asked the doctor when he had finished.

Marten stared rigidly ahead.

"He refuses to communicate," Major Orlov explained.

"Indeed? Interesting."

"Incorrect, Doctor. It is social maladjustment."

"True, true." The doctor, with his right cheek twitching, indicated that Marten should enter the tank. Two beefy interns rolled a platform beside the cylinder. They ripped off Marten's tunic, attached a harness, lifted him with a winch and released him into the nine-foot tube.

An intense feeling of shame filled Marten. Distorted through the glass he saw Major Orlov and the doctor inspecting him, Orlov pointing at his privates. Marten turned his back on them and studied his surroundings. The glass was cold and the floor was wet and slimy under his bare feet. Above, the interns slotted a stopper over the top.

"Are you ready, Mr. Kluge," the doctor asked over an intercom.

Marten refused to acknowledge him.

"Hmm, I see. Well, in your case, Mr. Kluge, the simple expedient of verbal communication will end your stay. Otherwise—" the doctor glanced at his clipboard. "Ten days?" he asked Major Orlov. "Is that warranted?"

"You exceed your authority, Doctor."

"No one has survived ten days in the tank. It's physically impossible."

Marten glanced over his shoulder at them.

Major Orlov smiled as her eyes lingered on his buttocks. "Yes, that gained your attention. You are a madman, Mr. Kluge. This time you will have to talk."

"I must protest," said the doctor, his cheek twitching.

Major Orlov raised her eyebrows.

After a moment, the doctor backed away, his tic worsening. He turned and strode to his place at the medical center.

Major Orlov regarded Marten once more. "Ten days, Mr. Kluge. My estimation is that you'll break in three." She waited a moment longer, glanced at the muscles of his back, then turned and made a gesture to someone.

Water gurgled overhead. Marten glanced up as green-colored water splashed him in the face. He groaned. His facial bones ached as if someone had slammed a board against his face. The water swirled at his feet, crept up his ankles and lapped at his calves faster than he'd expected. He grasped the lever. It was a little higher than waist level. The pump resisted movement. He strained, and he found the angle awkward. Then water sluiced out of the tube at the bottom. He worked faster. More water drained away. He pumped as fast as he could. It was hard, and soon he was gasping. By then, the water was no longer icy.

The intercom came on and Orlov's voice was insidious. "How long do you think you can keep that up, Mr. Kluge?"

Startled, Marten saw that the major still watched him.

"I must admit that you have an excellent physique. Perhaps there are other ways for you to exit the tube."

Marten ignored her. The idea of sexually wrestling with the major, a brutal woman lacking all femininity, nauseated him.

So he pumped, and time soon lost all meaning. His muscles ached and after each stroke, he yearned to quit. The hours grew second by agonizing second. Sweat poured. His shoulders, arms and torso felt as if they were afire. His eyes burned from lack of sleep. His stomach growled and gurgled by the minute—he was ravenous. When he wanted water, he tilted his head and drank. When he needed to relieve himself, he did so. A hundred different times he almost turned and shouted that okay, yes, he'd talk. Each time something hard and unyielding inside him refused. From time to time, an intern or doctor passed by, stopped, watched a moment or two, sometimes nodded, sometimes shook their head, often marking a slate and finally strolling on. Twice the major returned. She spoke to him over the intercom. He ignored her until she went away. Minute after minute he levered the handle up and down in stupefying monotony. After twenty-eight hours, sharp pains knifed into his back. He groaned, came close to collapsing, but then he gritted his teeth and pumped on.

Finally, he stopped and let the water cascade upon him. It rose to his thighs, his stomach, up to his chest.

"I suggest you pump quickly, Mr. Kluge," the doctor said over the intercom. "The water acts as a drag and will make pumping later many times more difficult."

The work stoppage felt so glorious that Marten almost let the water reach his neck. He didn't really believe they'd let him drown. Then a sudden and elemental wish to live bid him grasp the pump and move it! Pain exploded in his back and shoulders. His forearms knotted and the lever slipped out of his grasp. A desperate cry tore from the depths of his being. He concentrated on grasping the handle and pumped with a will. Water touched his chin. He pumped as air wheezed down his throat. He pumped as the horrible pain in his forearms receded. He pumped as ever so slowly the water inched down to his chest, his stomach and finally to his mid-thighs. Then he could no longer keep up the ferocious pace. He leveled off and tried to think. It was impossible. Life was one long agonized blur of pain and pumping.

Later, through the distortion of his glass and that of the cylinder beside him, he saw a woman drowning. Her hair floated freely as she banged her fists against the stopper. Marten released his pump and banged on his glass. A nearby intern faced him. Marten pointed at the woman. The intern followed the finger, and his mouth opened in shock. The intern shouted. Marten couldn't hear the words. Men rushed the platform to the tank.

As Marten pumped, he watched them take her out, carry her to the medical center and work on her. After a short time, the doctor shook his head and covered her face with a blanket. Terror filled Marten. The woman had drowned, died, ceased living! They hadn't paid enough attention. He became depressed and paranoid. He might die in here. Perhaps he *should* talk. The very idea stole his strength. He felt his pains more than before. His will grew weak.

"What's the use?" he whispered.

He turned his head to call, but then a burst of pride made him clamp his mouth shut. He pumped the lever. His hands were like lumps and his arm muscles quivered. Air burned down his nostrils. The endless rhythm was agony, and the agony stole pieces of his pride minute after minute. The woman had died. He would die soon. Up and down, up and down. The sheer exhaustion was too much. He couldn't do this anymore. It was time to give up.

At that precise moment, Major Orlov marched into the room and halted at his cylinder. Perhaps she saw his despair. She grinned, and her eyes roved over his nakedness. Marten closed his eyes, refusing to look at her. But... yes, if that's what it took. A great and mighty weariness stole over him. He opened his mouth and croaked, "You win."

In the silence, the water rose around him. Marten opened his eyes. Major Orlov had left. He wildly looked around. She wasn't in the room.

Marten pumped, and through the fog of exhaustion, he considered what that meant. Slowly, a new form of pride renewed his will and gave him more energy. He checked the wall clock. Thirty hours he'd been here. Could he go ten days?

"Pump," he whispered.

He did.

At thirty-one hours, a final numbing fog came over Marten. *Just a little longer*, he told himself.

Then a thud, a shiver, shook the room and shook the cylinder. Marten blinked, wondering what had happened. The doctors, nurses and interns looked alarmed and pointed at the ceiling. Marten glanced up. He didn't understand what caused their concern. Miraculously, the water falling onto his head slowed. It slowed and became a trickle. The trickle stopped. Marten didn't understand. He didn't need too. He simply collapsed and fell asleep.

He woke to the sound of interns removing the stopper. Groggily he looked up. They lowered hooks. He grabbed hold and they lifted him.

Major Orlov brooded at the bottom of the platform. Red-uniformed PHC thugs stood beside her.

"This is highly unusual," the doctor told her.

Major Orlov glared at him. The doctor fidgeted with his clipboard

An intern draped a tunic over Marten. The thugs each grabbed an arm and marched him out of the auditorium and down a hall. Marten could barely walk. The muscles in his back, shoulders and arms had frozen. The thugs deposited him in the interrogation room with the bench.

This time, however, Stick wasn't there. The two held him up. Otherwise, he'd simply have fallen over.

"Your time runs short, Mr. Kluge."

Marten wasn't sure, but Major Orlov sounded desperate. A spark of something bade him keep his mouth shut.

"Give me your agonizer."

Incredibly, the thug seemed reluctant. But at this point, Marten couldn't be sure about anything.

Major Orlov twisted the setting and touched the agonizer to his chest. Marten bellowed and fell backward.

"I have decided to accelerate the process," said the major.

The two thugs picked Marten off the floor and set him back on the bench. Smiles twitched across their lips.

Major Orlov lowered the agonizer for another touch. Marten squirmed as they held him tight.

"Well, Mr. Kluge?"

Marten stared at the agonizer. It moved closer, closer—

The door opened, and a guard said, "You're needed, Major."

Major Orlov hesitated. Then she tossed the agonizer to a thug. She glared at Marten and hurried out of the room.

After several moments, the red-uniformed PHC men moved to the door. They whispered urgently together. Somewhere outside a klaxon blared. Marten lay down on the bench. They didn't say anything about it. So he closed his eyes and fell asleep.

9.

Months away from Earth in terms of space travel time—Tanaka Station orbited blue Neptune. Vast cargo ships circled this commercial clearinghouse. In the distance, a fat ice-skimmer worked its way up from the blue mass of the gas giant.

The Ice Hauler Cartel, which owned much of the Neptune System, also owed Tanaka Station. The habitat was run on strict capitalist lines. The general principle of the Solar System seemed to be that the farther one left the Inner Planets behind the purer became the capitalism. Unfortunately, for a first class-rated space pilot from Jupiter, this "pureness" came as a shock.

Osadar Di huddled miserably in a bar close to the docking bay where she'd berthed her ship. The owner of the vessel had just departed, leaving her in a dim cubicle. She held onto a beer, but she hadn't sipped it. Around her in the packed bar mingled pilots, dockworkers, sex objects and gamblers. It was different from the Jupiter Confederation where she'd been born and raised, and only recently fled. The bar was like a caricature of an Old Asteroid Mining vid she'd watched as a child. The pilots and gamblers played cards, cheating, drinking and getting into fistfights. In other cubicles, shady deals were being hatched and nefarious plots conceived.

Osadar Di had short dark hair, dark worried eyes and an unremarkable nose. On the tallish side, she had long shapely legs in a tan jumpsuit. Along with her excellent piloting skills, she'd developed a deep-seated paranoia. Beginning at the orphanage, life had been out to get her. Now she was certain her bad luck had run out—from now on she'd have miserable luck.

Her friends had died in the Second Battle of Deep Mars Orbit. She remembered that time. The Jupiter Confederation had recognized Martian independence, and the rulers had sent a massive expeditionary fleet to the Red Planet. Social Unity had outfitted a reinforcing fleet, and the First Battle of Deep Mars Orbit had surprised everyone. The allied vessels of Mars and Jupiter won an annihilating victory. Back then, Osadar had wondered if she'd made a mistake, as she'd already fled the Jupiter system to escape service. Social Unity had outfitted a huge retaliatory fleet and sent it to Mars. The next battle with its grisly results had proven her wisdom. Ever since then, the Jupiter Confederation had scrambled to rebuild its fleet and had scoured everywhere for pilots.

Two months ago on a seedy hab in the Saturn system—still much too near Jupiter and its extradition treaties—Osadar Di had hired out to a disreputable ship owner who wished to travel to Neptune. Presently, Neptune orbited farther away from the Sun than even icy-dark Pluto with its eccentric orbital path. Now she waited for the ship owner to return from selling his cargo so he could come and pay her.

Osadar stared at the beer. What was the point of being alive anyway? She'd just suffer more. Maybe she'd be better off dead with her friends than sitting in this dump waiting for some sleaze ball who would probably run off with her wages anyway."

"Osadar Di?"

Startled, she looked up. A beefy man wearing an armored vest and a visored helmet stared down at her. He held a computer slate and seemed to be studying it. A massive stunner rode on his hip.

"W-Who are you?" she stammered.

"Tanaka Station Security. Are you Osadar Di?"

"Yes. But how do you know me?"

He hooked the computer slate to his belt and drew the stunner. "Come with me, please."

"What did I do?"

"Do you refuse to comply?"

"No, I—"

He waved the stunner. "Stand up and come with me."

A dejected relief filled her. Here it was—the worst she'd been expecting. All her friends were long dead: space debris still floating around Mars. Why should it be any different for her? Only... she set her face into a grim mask as she marched out of the bar and into a tiny bubble-built vehicle on the street. She had to place her hands into the dash restraints and then they were off. Despite her paranoia, there was a spark within her, a willingness to resist. She was going to go down to some dark fate—she knew that with certainty—but that didn't mean she had to like or accept it.

"Can you at least tell me what I've done?" she asked.

Upon entering the vehicle, he'd punched in the destination code and now watched the various pedestrians, centering upon the slinky women in outrageously revealing costumes. He glanced at her with his dark visor long enough to ask, "You were the pilot, right?"

"What do you mean?"

He snorted and went back to examining the skimpily-clad women who accosted the various dock and office workers along the street.

"Did... Did someone turn me in? Is that it?"

"Save it for the judge," he said.

Thankfully, the ride was short. By the time they jerked to a halt in front of a squat gray building, Osadar was certain the ship owner had done something illegal, been caught and then spilled his guts in an effort to wriggle out of whatever he was in. In other words, he'd probably sold her out.

The security man released her from the dash restraints and marched her inside. A knot of security people stood to the side by a water dispenser. Other people in outlandishly long suits with enormous collars held onto computer folios and bantered together. Two men wore long red robes that reached the tiled floor. They wore large hats with three sprouting prongs and seemed older and graver than anyone else. Several burly-shouldered, combat-armored protectors hovered at their elbows. Everyone showed deference to the two robed men.

"In here," said her security man, pointing to a door that had just swished up.

Osadar followed him into a tiny room—it seemed more like a closet—and sat down beside a bored old woman at a computer terminal. She wore a loose orange dress and wore silver bangles on her wrists that clashed as she typed on the keyboard.

"Name?"

"Osadar Di."

The old woman typed that in and studied the screen. "From the Jupiter system, Taiping Hab?"

"Yes, but—"

"Pilot rated first class?"

"That's right."

"You piloted the *Manitoba* from the Saturn system, Winnipeg Hab?"

"Yes," Osadar said with a sinking feeling.

"Do you freely admit to smuggling—"

"The owner lied to me about his cargo."

The old woman glanced at Osadar. Then jangle, jangle, jangle went the bangles as she typed some more. "Your credcard number, please."

"I don't see what bearing that has on this."

The old woman wouldn't look up, but she said, "Dear, don't be a trouble-maker. Just give me your card number."

"MC: 3223-233-6776."

The old woman typed that in, jangle, jangle, jangle, and she blinked at the screen. Her face tightened.

The security man noticed. He'd been leaning against the wall, watching. He groaned as he stepped near. "No credit?" he asked.

"None," said the old woman.

"What!" said Osadar Di. "That's impossible. I have over three thousand credits."

"Deserters don't carry credits out of the Jupiter Confederacy," the old woman said sourly.

"That's just great," complained the security man.

"Why are you upset?" Osadar asked him.

"Come on," he said, grabbing her by the arm and dragging her out of the room. The hall was empty now. She squinted. Far down the corridor, she saw the ship owner, a fat man with baby soft skin. He spoke urgently to one of those people with huge collars.

"Hey!" Osadar yelled.

The ship owner looked up and had the decency to blush. Then he turned his back on her and gently led the huge-collared man with the computer folio farther down the corridor.

Osadar tried to follow. The security man tightened his grip. "Forget it," he said.

"He sold me out."

"What did you expect?"

"Huh?" Osadar asked, looking into the security man's dark visor.

"His fine was stiff. So he must have sold information to the court."

"You mean about me?" Osadar asked angrily.

"You piloted the ship, didn't you?"

"He hired me."

"So you admit your guilt. I fail to understand your anger."

Osadar shook her head. She knew this would happen. It was fated.

He marched her down a different hall. By a side door, they entered a larger room. In the front, a short man in a black robe and with thick gray hair sat behind a computer terminal. The rest of the room contained tables and benches. The two long-robed men with their three pronged hats sat apart in throne-like chairs. Their protectors stood behind them. The others sat at the tables, with computer styluses poised.

The black-robed man, the judge surely, studied his screen as Osadar entered.

"Osadar Di, a deserter from the Jupiter Confederacy Military Branch," the security man said.

"That's not right," Osadar said.

"The smuggler?" asked the judge in a surprisingly high-pitched voice.

"Yes, your Honor," said the security man. "She piloted the *Manitoba* from the Winnipeg Habitat, Saturn system."

"Look," Osadar said, trying to use a reasonable tone, "I think there's been a mistake."

"Silence," said her security man, shaking her. "Stand over there." He pointed to a red square near the judge.

Osadar debated refusing. She shrugged and stepped deliberately into the red square.

The small judge read from his screen. "Pilot rated first class. Induced into the Jupiter Confederacy Military Force for orbital fighter duty, Two-Five-Twenty-three Thirty-nine, went AWOL the same year. Pilot of the *Manitoba*,

Winnipeg Habitat. Charge: smuggling dream-dust onto Tanaka Station. Status: Vagrant."

"No credits?" asked a huge-collared woman.

"None," said the judge.

Another of the huge-collared people, a man, raised his hand.

"Yes?" asked the judge.

"I'd like her to disrobe."

The judge nodded to Osadar.

She frowned in disbelief, certain that she hadn't heard correctly.

"Disrobe," the judge told her.

"What do you mean?" Osadar asked.

"Mean?" asked the judge. "I mean take off your clothes. All of them."

"B-But why?"

"So the gentleman over there can assess your worth."

Osadar stared at the man. Between his purple suit and orange hair, his face looked pasty. His small eyes burned hotly as he licked his lips at her.

"No," Osadar said, disgusted.

The judge raised his bushy eyebrows.

"Contempt of court?" he asked. "That's a stiff fine. I'm afraid your former employer sold us all the information we need. If you can't pay, and I don't see how a creditless person can, that means immediate spacing."

Outrage filled Osadar. "For not taking off my clothes?"

"Of course not," said the judge, "for your contempt of court."

Blank incomprehension filled Osadar.

"Come now," said the judge in a reasonable tone. "Why the surprise? You have no funds for accommodation. As a deserter, no one will hire you as a pilot. Who would dare with your history? You might

72

simply mutiny and sell the ship cargo elsewhere? Your only hope is indenture status with one of the services."

"I'm to become a slave?"

"No, of course not," said the judge. "Indenture status. We in the Neptune System allow anyone to advance if he or she is willing to work. I imagine the gentleman from Sex Objects Incorporated merely wants to see if you have the, er…" the judge coughed into his fist. "If you qualify as a possible… employee."

"You mean as a prostitute?"

"A crude reference," said the judge, "but close enough to the mark."

Osadar Di glanced in horror at the huge-collared man with the hot eyes. She began shaking her head.

"Very well," said the judge. "Contempt of court. Because of your vagrant status that means immediate spacing."

"Wait," said one of the long-robed men from his throne.

"Yes, Dominie Banbury?" the judge asked in a reverent tone.

"You said the rulers of the Jupiter Confederation had inducted her for orbital fighter duty?"

The judge checked his screen. "Yes, Dominie."

"Yet she piloted a Class II space vessel?"

"That is correct, Dominie."

The long-robed man pursed his lips. He was a large man with a high forehead and shrewd eyes. "Young lady," he said, "why did you desert?"

Osadar shrugged. "I didn't want to die."

She scanned the seated throng, noticing that some of them looked at her with contempt and haughtiness. "All my friends died in the Second Battle of Deep Mars Orbit. Social Unity killed them, but at least I'm still alive."

"Just so," said Dominie Banbury. "Tell me. Would you like the chance of piloting an experimental space craft for the Ice Hauling Cartel?"

That sounded better than being spaced. "I would."

"What is the bid?" Dominie Banbury asked the judge.

"Five hundred credits, Dominie."

"So much?" he asked.

The judge swallowed hard and spread his hands.

Dominie Banbury whispered with a huge-collared woman at a nearby table. A moment later, he looked up. "Yes, done."

The judge typed that onto his keyboard. In a moment, he said, "Next case."

"You're lucky," said the security man, who grabbed Osadar by the elbow. "And so am I," he said with a laugh. "I get my finders-fee after all."

Osadar Di wondered what 'experimental space craft' really meant. Maybe it was merely a paranoid premonition, but working for Sex Objects Incorporated would probably have been a better option than the one she'd just chosen.

10.

Marten opened his eyes in terror. Then he squinted against the bright light…. This wasn't the cylinder. Ah, he'd been having a nightmare.

He tried to sit up, and winced painfully. Back, shoulders and sides, every muscle protested the slightest twitch. If he lay perfectly still and didn't breathe too deeply he'd be okay.

Then he wondered where everyone was. He'd have to sit up to find out. He wasn't sure he wanted to know that badly.

Finally, with a moan, he lifted his torso and swung his feet off the bench. He sat there panting, and groaning. A muscle in his side quivered and cramped. He shot to his feet, yelling, and clutched his side, all his muscles complaining at the movement. He paced until the cramp eased away.

Where was everybody? He might have shrugged, but that would have hurt.

Oh, to finally be out of the dreadful cylinder. A ripple of fear, like electricity, shivered through him. He didn't *ever* want to go back. They'd have to kill him first.

Frowning, Marten faced the door. The last thing he remembered was someone calling the major. Was this some sort of test, a means to make him talk? He decided no, that was too sophisticated for these brutes. He shuffled to the door, waited and dared touch it. It didn't shock him, which he'd half suspected it might.

"Did they steal your balls, Marten?" he whispered.

A hideous smile stretched his lips in lieu of an answer. He twisted the doorknob, his heart pounding. He stared into an empty corridor. Lines of puzzlement creased his forehead. He opened the door wider. The corridor went about twenty paces before coming to a T-junction. He listened, but heard no one.

Okay. He had nothing to lose and everything to gain. So he moved down the corridor. The lights glowed overhead, and somewhere a generator hummed. He came to the junction, and he knew that to the right was the auditorium. Left were the cells. The only way he wanted to go back to the auditorium was with a machine gun in his hands. So he went left. Where was everybody?

This didn't make sense.

He laughed bitterly.

Why did it have to make sense? An opportunity should be taken, not analyzed to death.

He crossed a line painted in the middle of the corridor. On one side, the corridor was white. The other side was green. Cells doors lined the green walls. He peered through a tiny glass window in the first door. Empty. He moved to the next. That cell was also empty. He tried the knob. Locked. So he kept moving, increasing his pace. The truth came to him that it frightened him to be alone. He shook his head. It had never frightened him down in Level Sixty.

Marten passed another painted line as he headed for the guard areas. The corridor color changed from green to blue. At the next door he came to, he opened it and went through. The air was damp and hotter than in the hall. He paused. To his left were the showers, the slick-suit dressing room and a hatch to the heat flats. To his right…

he didn't know what lay behind the door he'd always seen the guards enter.

So he tried it, and to his surprise, the door opened. Marten stared into a room with a wall of TV screens and a control panel. His heart thudded as he entered. Then he stopped, unbelieving. A grin transformed him as he picked a shock rod off a chair. He clicked it to its highest setting, feeling it hum in his hands. He barged through the next door. In the room was a lunch box. He tore it open and crammed a sandwich into his mouth. It tasted like egg and hurt his throat because he swallowed such big chunks. He didn't care. He guzzled orange juice and gnawed on a chocolate bar. For a moment his gut hurt, then strength seemed to ooze into him.

Back in the control room, Marten tested switches. The TV screens flickered into life showing the heat flats. He peered more closely. People in slick-suits floated face down in the scum, with glaring sunlamps hanging three feet above them in the ceiling. Workers usually crawled through the algae, using a bar to break apart clumps and scrape hardened slime from the bottom. Five-hour stints were all a person could take before heat exhaustion set in. Marten cursed under his breath. None of those bodies so much as twitched. He saw that slime had crusted on some of them. That took at least three hours to form.

Marten pressed more switches, jumping views. There were more dead floaters. A lump stuck in his throat. Then he saw movement. He counted them, seven people at a lock—wait. It was this hatch and it looked like his old squad. One man slowly banged against the iron door.

Marten moved out of the room, down the corridor, through the showers and decontamination center. He hurried to the hatch, cranked the lever and spun the wheel. The hatch opened with a *whomp*.

A vile, swampy stench blew into the room and a blistering humidity caused him to sweat. He staggered from the entrance. Picking up an emergency hose, he waited. His old comrades dragged themselves into the room, flopping onto the plasteel floor. Scum clung tenaciously to them, making them look like swamp monsters.

Marten twisted the nozzle, hosing them with detergent. One of them closed the hatch with a clang. When they were clean, he helped them peel off their slick-suits and masks. They looked worse than he did, with hot, feverish skin, some with tiny blisters on their face, neck and torso. As they crawled to the showers, he sprinted to the control room, experimented until he found the right switch and turned on the water. He hurried back. They lay on their sides or stomachs, slurping water off the floor. Then they lay still, blissful in the drizzle.

Later, they crawled to the drying area. Stick was one of them. He struggled to his feet and tried to face Marten down.

"You want some?" wheezed the street fighter.

Marten wasn't sure what he felt, whether the man's bravado was admirable or laughable. The truth was it would be simplicity itself to beat Stick to death. Then the scarred street fighter, the former knifeboy, flexed his hands in classic karate style. Well, maybe it wouldn't be so easy.

"You lied about me," said Marten

"Yeah?" said Stick, hunching his shoulders.

"They almost killed me for it."

Stick glanced at the others.

One of them, Marten saw, tried to sit up. Then he noticed another working his way to his feet, a mean-faced, muscle-bound Asian. Marten stepped back so he could keep all three in view.

Stick frowned. "Wait," he told them. "How come..." He tilted his head in puzzlement.

"How long were you in the heat flats?" Marten asked, giving the knifeboy time to orient himself.

Stick examined the tiny blisters on his arms. He seemed bemused. "Where'd they go?"

Marten shrugged.

"Ain't anyone here?" asked a tall, stork-like man called Turbo, who leaned heavily against the wall.

"You're incorrigibles, right?" Marten asked.

That deepened their scowls.

"You're from the slums, right?"

"So?" said Turbo.

"You feel like eating more crap?" Marten asked, "Or maybe dealing it out for a change?"

Stick cracked his knuckles as he glanced at the other two, the only ones who showed interest in Marten's words.

"What do you have in mind?" asked the muscle-bound Asian, a Korean.

Marten lowered the baton to a water slick. A spark jumped from the instrument, the electrical current making momentary tracings in the water.

"What about between you and me?" asked Stick.

Marten shrugged. "There is bigger game afoot."

Stick grinned.

"Yeah?" said Turbo. "Count me in."

11.

In dull horror, Marten crept into the auditorium. He had to walk carefully because water made the floor slippery. Six of the twenty cylinders contained occupants. They floated rigidly; their hands like claws and pressed against the stoppers.

"What...?" Stick couldn't finish the question. He was pale.

Turbo made retching noises, but there was nothing in his stomach to vomit. The bullet-headed Asian, a gunman by the name of Omi, stared steely-eyed at the scene.

Marten moved to his old cylinder, noting that it was filled with water. He gazed about the auditorium. For some reason everyone had left. His chest hurt as he visualized what had happened. The water had started again, gushing too fast to pump. Rage gripped him. He stalked to the medical center where Stick yanked open drawers and examined equipment.

"Anything?"

Stick shook his head.

Marten rummaged around and picked up a little black disc. He pressed it against his arm. It beeped as it diagnosed him, a red light winking. It was a medkit, a biomedical-monitoring device and drug dispenser, usually giving Quickheal, Superstim or Hypercoagulin. A pneumospray hypo hissed, using compressed air to inject him with drugs. Marten licked his lips and tossed the kit to greedy-eyed Turbo.

"Oh yeah," whispered Turbo. He punched in override codes and pressed the disc to his lean chest. Then he moaned pleasurably and shivered.

"Sweet." Stick drew a long knife out of a drawer and by clicking a switch made it hum. It was a vibroblade, a hideous close-combat weapon. The blade vibrated thousands of times per second, so fast the motion was invisible. The knifeboy's delight was obvious.

Then they froze. From the nearest corridor, there sounded the pounding footsteps of someone in a hurry.

Marten and Stick exchanged glances hardly daring to breathe. Marten flanked the door, his two-handed grip tight upon the baton. Stick waited on the other side. The sounds came closer and closer. Plastic body armor rattled. Then a guard exploded through the door, a short-barreled gun in his hand. Stick chopped and his knife sang. The guard's knee disintegrated in a spray of blood and bone. With a scream, he went down. Marten roared and swung. *ZAP!* The guard's head flipped back and his helmet went spinning. *ZAP!* The guard's chin snapped against the floor as his entire body flopped downward. Rage, fear and hatred drove Marten's muscles. *Zap, zap, zap!* He hammered the guard's head until Turbo and Stick dragged him off.

Marten nodded after a moment. They let go.

Without a word, Omi picked up the dead guard's short barreled .44 off the floor. He checked the slide and tested its heft. Then he rummaged the dead man for extra bullets.

Stick knelt beside the corpse and began unbuckling the body armor.

"What about me?" complained Turbo.

"The helmet is still good," Stick said.

Turbo scooped it off the floor, inspected it, put it on and snapped the chinstrap. "What do you think?"

"Beautiful," said Stick.

Marten trembled and forced himself to move. He wiped the gory shock rod on the dead man's clothes. He felt surreal. Hollow. Used up.

Stick said, "Bet I know what happened."

"Huh?"

"Where everyone went, bet I know."

Marten focused on him. "Yeah?"

"Highborn! They must've finally got here and gone underground. The army needed the cops to help fight."

Marten nodded. Could be.

"So what now?" asked Turbo, his face twitching in the manner of the over-stimulated.

Marten glanced at the cylinders, at the floaters, at their dull stares. Something in him hardened. He said, "We kill more of them."

12.

Endless corridors and empty rooms, wherever they trudged the vast algae production center had become a desert. They found regular clothes in a storage bin and donned splay jackets, dungarees and boots. Marten found an extra energy cell for his baton. In a guardroom, Turbo shattered a candy bar machine. Several floors down, they opened a hatch into a settling tank. Turbo peered at the thick soup below. He blanched, drew back and shook his head.

Marten looked in. About a hundred workers floated dead in the brine. They'd been shot in the back or in the back of the head. Their blood slicked the goop like oil.

Marten clenched his teeth until they ached.

"Mass murder," slurred Turbo.

"Like they're covering their tracks," said Stick.

"Who is?" snapped Marten.

"PHC." Stick must have noticed Marten's incomprehension. "Things got really rough in the pits several months ago."

"Yeah," said Turbo. "When the war started."

Stick nodded in agreement. "When Major Orlov arrived."

"No way are they gonna lose to the Supremacists," Turbo said.

"But why are they gunning down all the prisoners?" growled Marten.

Omi smiled sourly.

"Did I ask something stupid?"

"Naw," said Stick. "It's just that Omi does the same thing, only in the slums. He takes out the troublemakers, makes sure those he's hurt can never come around to hurt him back."

"It's insurance," Omi said flatly.

"It is cold-blooded murder," slurred Turbo. "It's because they're bastards."

Omi shrugged.

They moved on warily, to scenes of greater mass death. Gleaming corridors often ended in piles of gory butchery. Many of the dead had been dumped unceremoniously into the various stages of algae production.

They rode an elevator down to an office section and prowled the next corridor. The halls were shorter and narrower, constantly twisting and turning.

Marten felt overwhelmed. The mass death appalled him. What kind of choice was there for anyone? Earth was trapped between implacable enemies, with PHC killers on one hand and Highborn on the other. There was no hope for a better future.

Turbo stopped short, his long face twitching. "No, no, no!"

The others watched him.

Turbo tore off his helmet and threw it at the floor. "Why'd they kill everybody?" he yelled. "It don't make sense."

"Easy," said Stick.

"Easy?" shouted Turbo. He laughed wildly.

Marten jerked around. He thought he heard a click from ahead.

"You're just feeling the stims wearing off," Stick told his friend.

Turbo laughed even more wildly, a bit hysterically.

"Look—"

"Duck!" shouted Marten. He hurled his body against Omi, throwing him to the floor. He saw a blur fly past, strike the wall, bounce and ricochet around the corner. It exploded with a roar, hot metal pinging off the walls.

With eyes blazing and mouth open, Turbo zigzagged in a crazy-man's rush around the corner. They heard him roar an insane oath, and then a thud and a rattle sounded. A second later, Turbo yelled, "It's safe!"

Gingerly, they turned the corner and found Turbo with a short, stubby, shotgun-like weapon, the Electromag Grenade Launcher. It was a small mass-driver that used a magnetic impulse to propel grenades. The guard who'd shot it lay on the floor, gasping. There was a trail of blood leading up to him. It was like a smeared barcode, thicker in the places where he'd stopped to rest. The man had been crawling a ways to get this far.

"Someone must've gut-shot him," said Turbo, his voice ominously flat.

The man's face was pinched and his eyes were glassy. He had thinning white hair plastered to a sweaty skull and a colonel's emblem on his shoulders.

Omi crouched before him. "Why'd you shoot at us?"

The colonel lay panting, his life ebbing away.

Marten marveled at the trail of blood: so thick and wet.

"What made him to crawl so far?" asked Stick.

"Wonder who shot him?" said Turbo.

"And why?" Stick added.

Marten crouched beside Omi as he dug the medkit out of his jacket. He pressed it to the colonel's neck. For a moment, it did nothing. Then it beeped shrilly, as if it couldn't figure out what to do.

"Override it," suggested Stick.

Marten waited.

Turbo swore and bent down to do it. Omi grabbed his arm.

Marten thought about it. "No. Let him."

Omi's stiff face stiffened a little, but he let go of the lanky junkie. Turbo tapped in override and shot a batch of stims into the dying man. The colonel's eyes flickered. He shuddered and drew an agonizing gasp.

Deep in thought concerning the colonel, Marten reclaimed the medkit.

The colonel groaned as he dragged his hand from his wound and examined his own blood.

"Can you tell us what happened?" asked Marten.

"Help me sit up," whispered the colonel.

Marten found him surprisingly light as he propped the colonel against the wall. Blood soaked the colonel's pants and half his shirt. Marten never knew so much blood could be in a man. A gaping wound in the colonel's gut kept pumping out more.

"Bastards couldn't even shoot me face to face," the colonel wheezed. "Had to do it to me in the back."

"Exploding bullet," said Omi with professional detachment. "You should be dead."

"I am," the colonel said wearily.

"Who did it?" asked Marten.

"PHC."

"Why?"

A great and final weariness seemed to settle on the colonel. Before their eyes, he aged into a brittle old man. The drugs gave him a final burst, but at a terrible cost.

"I thought you were them," he said, "coming back."

"Where'd they go?" Marten asked.

"Down."

Marten frowned at the others. Then he told the colonel, "They've shot everyone."

"Wretched villains, murderers, scum. They don't want to leave anybody for the Highborn."

"What do you mean?"

The colonel made a supreme effort to focus. With his bloody hand, he clutched Marten's wrist. "Sydney's lost, son. All Australian Sector is lost."

"That's no reason to go on a murder spree."

"Don't tell PHC that." The dying colonel coughed blood. His pale skin turned sickly yellow.

"You said they headed down," Marten prodded.

"To the deep-core station, the bottom one."

"And?"

"And they're gonna blow it."

Marten was puzzled. "They're going to destroy the mine?"

"No!" The old, old man wheezed air. He had maybe ten seconds left. "They're gonna let it spew, geyser. They're gonna use lava to destroy Sydney." His eyelids fluttered and his head almost drooped for the last time. He kept it up with an iron will. "Use the heat flats to the flow canal. Elevator there goes to level forty. There's an emergency drop to the deep-core station. Stop them. Stop them or everyone in Sydney's dead."

They glanced at each other for about three seconds, long enough for the colonel to die.

"We gotta get out of Sydney," whispered Turbo.

"How are you gonna do that?" asked Stick.

Fear washed over Turbo. He began to tremble.

Omi rose, his face hardening.

Marten considered the colonel's information, turned it over and thought about the implications. "We can't go up, right?"

"Not with the Highborn coming down," said Stick.

"We don't know that," said Turbo.

"If you don't then you're an idiot," Stick told him.

"Or a junkie," Omi added.

"Yeah, that too," agreed Stick.

"Okay," said Marten. "Then we have to down."

"Meaning what?" asked Stick.

"I mean to stop them like the colonel said," Marten told them.

Surprise and then comprehension filled the knifeboy. He seemed bemused rather than fearful. Turbo kept shaking his head.

"If we don't stop them nobody will," Marten said.

"You can't know that," Omi said.

"That's right," Marten said. "So we hide and cross our fingers and hope somebody else stops them. Is that it?"

"What else can we do?" Turbo whined.

"We can stop them," said Marten.

"You're crazy," said Turbo.

"Crazy is better than waiting to die," Marten countered.

"I don't know," Stick said. "It sounds like quick suicide to me."

"It's like this," Marten said. "Either we do it ourselves or it's not going to get done. Now we can sit tight and hope the State sends someone else to do the job. Only right now the State is dying and turning on itself and wants to die in a pyre of immolation."

"What?" Turbo asked.

Marten stood, glancing at each of them. "You coming?"

The three slum dwellers wouldn't meet his eyes. But as the moment stretched into silent discomfort, Omi finally shrugged.

"Yeah, why not, it's as good a way as any to die."

13.

Transcript of Directorate Interrogation of Secret Police
General James Hawthorne #7
10.13.2349
Page 11

Q. General Hawthorne, I'm concerned about the
wording of one of your statements yesterday. Hmm, let's
see.... 'Civilian sacrifices cannot be too great for
Highborn unit destruction of company or higher.' Please
elaborate on that statement.

A. Director?

Q. Please don't be evasive, General.

A. I believe the wording is as accurate as I could state
it.

Q. Do you? Do you indeed? Then let us see if we can
narrow the definition. By 'cannot be too great,' does that
mean up to and including a million people?

A. Most definitely.

Q. (pause) For a company of Highborn?

A. Yes.

Q. And a company is how large?

A. A Highborn drop troop company's estimated
strength would be approximately two hundred and fifty
soldiers.

Q. You would willingly trade a million of our people for two hundred and fifty enemies?

A. A million civilians, Director.

Q. Civilians or soldiers, either way the comparison is incredible.

A. I disagree, Director. A million civilians are largely useless. Two hundred and fifty Highborn are deadly in the extreme.

Q. (coldly) I see. Then you would trade a city perhaps for a battalion of these heroes?

A. It would depend on the size of the city.

Q. Let us say a major city. One hundred million civilians?

A. I would hope for a division of the enemy in such an exchange.

Q. (pause) I find your sanity questionable, General.

A. Sacrifices are never easy, Director. Two million super-soldiers are, however, not an endless supply. Nor do we even need to exchange on the levels you're suggesting for all two million warriors. Once their casualties rise to a certain level, their defeat becomes inevitable. The trick is to make them take staggering losses as quickly as possible. Hence, what seems at first glance to be irrational exchanges quickly transfers into a logical strategy.

Q. I'm uncertain my colleagues or I agree with you, General.

A. The Dutch of the Sixteenth and Twentieth Centuries likewise faced such decisions. Much of their land had been reclaimed from the sea. When first the Spaniards and later the Germans tramped across the land in conquest, the Dutch broke their dykes and allowed the sea to swamp their hard-won farms. In each incidence, the flooding proved invaluable in military terms.

Q. We're speaking of people, General, not land.

A. In a war, people and land are similar in this regard: they are ciphers that lead to victory or defeat. Not enough land often spells defeat. Too few people likewise can be devastating. To defeat the Highborn we must decrease their numbers to manageable levels. Out of a population well over forty billion, we can easily afford to lose three quarters of our people and come out ahead. Many cities will be destroyed in the coming conflict. Why not make their losses constructive to our eventual victory?

Q. (different Director) You have a particular strategy in mind?

A. Indeed.

Q. Elaborate.

A. I'm thinking of cities that use thermal power, the deep-core mines in particular. Studies have shown how to breach the safety features.

Q. (long pause) No one would survive a lava flow, General.

A. Correct.

Q. But…

Q. (different Director) The entire populace of Earth might well rise up in rebellion if it found out we that engineered core bursts.

A. Agreed. Thus, the Highborn will be blamed for such 'savage' attacks. It will help whip up war frenzy.

Q. Quite ingenious, General. But I must point out that the safety features of each deep-core mine are embedded in the deepest levels.

A. True.

Q. In other words, General, only someone willing to die could bypass the safety features. For each deep-core has such codes and preventive devices built into it. I believe these security measures are to prevent terrorist core bursts by remote control.

A. Your information is quite accurate, Director.

Q. Then I am at a loss. Who would do such a deed? Only madmen would, and you couldn't trust a madman.

A. A madman, maybe, but I was thinking of PHC officers.

Q. They are the last people one thinks of as suicidal.

A. Correct. Hypnotic commands would have to be embedded deep within the chosen officer's psyche.

Q. PHC Command is willing to do this to its operatives?

A. Directors, PHC is your tool. Willing or not, the deed must be done if you command it.

Q. You recommend this action?

A. Yes.

Q. When and how?

A. My recommendation is the soonest opportunity possible. After such a deed, and with blame laid on the Highborn, Earth will fight every battle with back-to-the-wall ferocity.

End of transcript Interrogation of Secret Police General James Hawthorne #7

14.

The exhausted quartet halted behind a flipped-over, bullet-riddled police cruiser. Several SU infantrymen lay dead within it. Squat, gray cylinders hummed all around them—Sydney's power generators. The lift they'd tried to take to Level Forty had pinged an emergency warning and they'd been forced to exit at Level Thirty-eight. They were looking for a stairwell down. Up the street they heard the crump of mortars, the rat-tat-tat of machine-guns, explosions and screaming.

"I don't wanna be no hero," whined Turbo.

"What'cha you gonna do then?" asked Stick.

"Pop topside and run."

"How many times I gotta tell you that you'd never get to the surface. The Highborn would blast you."

"Right," Turbo said. "I've been thinking about that. We could tell them about the deep-core as our ticket out."

Stick jeered. "Sure! They're gonna believe a junkie."

"Why not? I ain't no liar."

"Yes you are," Stick said. "And look where we're at: in the middle of a battle. Soldiers shoot first and ask later."

Turbo blew snot out his long icicle of a nose as he grumbled. His drugs had worn off a half-hour ago and Marten had refused to hand him the medkit for more.

Their eyes were hollow, and like Marten sweat shone on their faces and their chests heaved. Marten's legs quivered as he leaned against a twisted piece of car framing.

"Look," Omi said, pointing into the crumpled police cruiser. "There are guns in there."

"Where?" asked Stick.

"In there with the soldiers."

Stick looked into the wrecked vehicle, but made no move for the guns.

With a grunt, Marten rolled onto his belly and crawled into the pile of dead men. They stank of blood and guts and he avoided looking into their staring eyes. With their dead fingers, some of them held on to their weapons tightly, forcing him to pry and jerk to free them. He rummaged through torn armor, body parts and slags of metal. Soon he handed back short assault carbines and extra ammo clips. He even found a few grenades for Turbo's Electro-launcher. He crawled out and wiped gore from his hands and checks. A small part warned him that it wasn't good he was becoming used to such carnage.

"Hey, you're not saying we join them up there?" Turbo said as he slapped the grenade clip into his launcher.

Marten peered over the wreckage. Omi rose and peered with him. He saw explosive flashes among the smoking rubble and half walls of former generators. Most of the sunlamps over there were broken shards in the ceiling, so it was eerily dark amid the red glares. Marten jerked his head, and in a crouch, he sprinted for a gray building closer to the firefight, one that still seemed intact. Omi sprinted after him. They threw their backs to the wall and slid toward a corner, peering around it.

Tracer rounds, plasma and lasers crisscrossed the darkened street in either direction. Orange plasma gobs gouged sections of wall, causing them to slide molten to the ground. Bullets chipped concrete. The bright lasers hurt their eyes.

Marten and Omi ducked back around the corner.

"That route's blocked," said the tough Korean.

"Perceptive. But did you notice the dead?"

Omi shook his head.

Marten found that he was shaking. Watching war videos was one thing, being near the real thing was infinitely more straining.

"Several of the dead were PHC," Marten said.

"Red suits?"

Marten gave him a wan smile. Then he sprinted back for the overturned police cruiser. He soon lay panting behind it. Turbo and Stick chewed on protein bars, a pile of them at their feet. Marten noticed that some of the wrappers were bloody.

"You didn't get them from in there?" Marten asked in outrage, jerking his thumb at the dead infantrymen.

Turbo shrugged.

Marten blanched. "That's… that's ghoulish."

"You grabbed the guns," Turbo said, his mouth full of chewed bar.

"I'm not eating my gun!"

"Relax," said Stick. "It's not like we're cannibals."

Marten dropped it. He inspected his assault carbine, figuring out how it worked.

Omi shook his shoulder. "The red-suits must have gotten caught before they made it to the emergency elevator. My guess is they've having a tough time ordering people out of their way."

"You think the red-suits are in charge of Sydney?" asked Stick.

Omi jerked his thumb at the firefight. "The Highborn are deep in the city. Bet they know, or guess at least, what the PHC are capable of."

"So what?" said Stick. "What I wanna know is how to get around this battle and to deep-core."

Marten cudgeled his mind, thinking back to his planning meetings in Construction of Level Sixty. There were three different types of levels, each conforming to a preplanned pattern. The ones with power generators like here on Level Thirty-eight were business levels, so…. He snapped his fingers. "There should be a maintenance shaft…." He glanced at the ceiling to get his bearings. "South," he said, pointing away from the firefight.

"Down to Level Forty?" asked Omi.

Marten nodded.

Omi took off running the direction Marten had pointed. Stick and Turbo followed, getting away from the firefight as fast as possible.

Marten glanced at the leftover pile of bloody protein bars. He wrinkled his nose, shrugged and grabbed a fistful, shoving them into his pockets. Then he took off after the others.

15.

Conflicting emotions, fear predominating, warred within Major Orlov as she bulled through a terrified sea of civilians—they choked the streets with their masses and kept pouring out of the complexes. As loud and elemental as thunder, their combined shouts echoed off the ceiling and rolled from one building to the next. It created an emotional, supercharged atmosphere that drained everyone of reason. Individuals weren't strong enough to resist such power, and a new entity had been born: the mob. Primeval, powerful, pregnant with horror, the mob paralyzed the lower sections of Sydney. The hordes within it surged like waves first one way and then another. Eddies, currents and treacherous riptides developed without apparent reason, which was deceptive. A rational mind couldn't comprehend, but the grim thing that yet reeked of the primordial slime—the mob—understood perfectly.

The beings who had once been human—and who would be again if they survived this night—bore tightly strapped packs or clutched onto prized heirlooms. Their hysterical faces spoke more eloquently than words. Children were often torn from their parents' grasp and became flotsam in the fleshy ocean. The major, as best she could, used her bulk and bearish strength to shove toward the Deep-Core Station. Behind her followed the picked men of her flying squad. The screaming crowds flinched from her killers. The crowds retained enough sense for that. Women and children cringed. Some men, however, dared to scowl behind their backs. Terrified, the major knew that one thrown bottle, or any hard object in fact, could send the mob howling upon them. She shoved more brutally. Mercy would only be seen as weakness, or even worse, as fear.

Each of her men wore the red uniform of Political Harmony Corps. Beneath it they wore body armor. Silver packs attached by wires joined the slim pistols in their fists. Behind their clear visors, glazed eyes showed their post-hypnotic conditioning, and so perhaps did the set of their lips. They marched to death, to supreme suicide, and it had turned them into something akin to zombies. That in turn gave them an aura even the mob dreaded.

Wherever the squad went, they had left a litter of the dead and dying. The major had ordered scattered army formations directly into the fray against the Highborn with orders that no one retreat in face of the enemy. A few times the lasers flared and stubborn police units fell dead at their posts. The truth was that nobody had expected the Highborn to fight with such grim élan underground. In Greater Sydney, everybody had agreed, the traitors from space would learn what real fighting was all about. Once the Highborn crawled in the Earth like moles, their vaunted superiority would prove false. That thought had been the illusion.

Major Orlov staggered through the last of the shoulder-to-shoulder masses, which now surged toward Stairwell One hundred and six to Level Forty-one. Groups of people huddled together on the street in shock or dashed off to points unknown as fast as they could. Slowly the size of the mobs thinned. Still, wherever Major Orlov marched, people ran by screaming or grimly silent or stood numb as they gazed intently at the ceiling, as if expecting it to collapse at any moment.

The major squared her massive shoulders and tugged her uniform straight. The berserk hordes frightened her. Some people had actually dared to hiss as they'd passed. Terror, as she well knew from those she'd tortured, often destroyed a lifetime of social conditioning. She shook her head, silently berating herself. She had played too long with Marten Kluge, had wished too fervently to see him broken. That was why Highborn had gotten so far into Sydney before she'd moved, why they had been able to block the normal route to her destination. It amazed her how efficient the enemy was. How extraordinary their martial accomplishments. She'd wasted time with Marten Kluge. And there had been something else, something she wouldn't allow herself to admit. It's why she hadn't killed him in the interrogation room. She glanced at her men. No matter. Marten Kluge along with everyone else in Sydney would serve the greater good by their sacrifice.

Yet…

Major Orlov ran a dry tongue over equally dry lips. She didn't want to perish, to become nonbeing. The idea made her guts churn. After this life, nothing, blank, deleted. But… sweat prickled her collar. What if the old legends—the nonsense from the ancient world—really were true? That was foolish. There was no Hell, no Judge in the afterlife. There was this one life, then nonexistence. She'd lived well. But she wanted to live still! And maybe Hell was real. Maybe for all the wretched evil she'd done—

"I did it for the good of the State," she told herself.

Major Orlov removed her cap and wiped sweat from her forehead. The she placed the cap firmly on her head. A sick feeling thumped in her chest. What if the Great Judge didn't view it that way? What if He consigned her to Hell for her errors of judgment?

She left the blocks of barracks-like living complexes and entered a financial zone. In the distance roared the mobs. It made her shiver and hope with everything she had that they didn't turn this way. The buildings changed from long edifices to smaller cubes of credit unions, banks, repo-houses and travel agencies. Plants and trees abounded in greater profusion. The streets and sidewalks switched from plain ferroconcrete to colorful bricks. They made eye-pleasing plazas with umbrellas, and table and chairs outside small eateries.

The major stopped and tried to get her bearings. Being out of the mob was like leaving a high-pressure cage. She could breathe again, normally, but she felt funny just the same. Every so often, a group of people raced by, running to join the mob or to get far away from it. They avoided her, but they no longer seemed in awe. She didn't like that. They thought perhaps that they had a new master to fear. Well they were wrong! She snarled at her zombies. They stiffened to attention, alert, eager to kill again before their finality.

A sergeant hurried beside her and brought an electronic map. She traced her blunt finger over it, tapping the red dot.

"Here."

He gazed at the buildings around them. Then he grunted, "Seven blocks over. That way."

"Yes."

"Major?"

She squinted at him, a little man with a deadly laser. Not that he was so small really, just that all her life she'd been bigger, larger than practically everyone. Sometimes she found it annoying; mostly it proved useful for intimidation purposes.

"They will be wary," the sergeant said. "They might shoot first."

Major Orlov bit back the retort that maybe it would be just as well if they did shoot. *That* thought she mustn't allow herself, not after such an illustrious career. So she lifted a haughty chin and rapped an order. The squad, their trigger fingers overly sensitive, jogged behind at the double as she marched to face down the Deep-Core Personnel.

Deep-Core took orders straight from the SU Directorate and no other. Neither the Army nor the PHC nor the Political Action Committee had any authority over them. To ensure Deep-Core's independence and protection from terrorists they had their own police units and security directives. Some called them a state within a state. The practically limitless energy that came from this advanced technology and the awful risks it entailed demanded such a condition. Deep-Core Security guarded the emergency elevator on Level Forty that sank far into the Earth. The Regular Army had demanded reinforcements from them. The answer, as always, had been, "Don't be absurd."

After a brisk walk, Major Orlov rounded the last corner and marched toward the entrance of a low-built building that looked just like the others in this district. A spacious plaza fronted the glass entrance, not for gracious living, but to provide a wide field of fire. The building looked like a bank, but that was illusion. It would be a vault over a vault, in other words, a well-constructed fortress. Apple trees rustled along the brick-laid plaza, while soft music played overhead. The war hadn't yet reached here, although a bloodstain here and there showed where Security had slain refugees foolish enough to head here for safety. And of course, Security had quickly removed the bodies, undoubtedly dropping the corpses down the chute to the core waste dump.

Major Orlov knew weapons tracked her. Security operatives watched their every move. It made her back itch, and she wondered if they would simply cut her down without a warning. The farther she walked, the more certain she became they waited until none of them could get away before they opened fire. Her belly muscles clenched and her mouth grew drier. It became agony to take another step.

"Halt!" rumbled a command, as if out of the very air.

Major Orlov almost collapsed right there. She froze in the middle of the plaza and waited. The short hairs on the back of her neck prickled. Her red-suited zombies halted behind her, their programmed eyes absorbing every detail. She vaguely wondered if being so near to death heightened one's senses. Did knowing that she would soon not-be make her want to live these last few hours with all the zest she could muster? The seconds dragged, and she wondered if security personnel debated about talking first or just going ahead and killing them. She wanted to scream, 'Wait, we're PHC!' Yet maybe that fact was going against them in the debate.

Her thoughts stopped as the glass door opened. Her knees felt weak, and she felt absurdly happy that she could live a few more hours.

Out marched a slender man in a brown uniform. He smoked a stimstick, the tip glowing red, and he wore his cap at a rakish angle. He smiled at them, but his mean little eyes took in their lasers, their red uniforms.

He smiled to show her she didn't frighten him. Major Orlov was certain of it, the arrogant prick! He probably relished his position. He no doubt delighted in cowing people when he knew snipers would back his every word. So she took a wide stance and put her hands on her heavy hips. She glowered at him with the PHC look.

It didn't impress. He saluted, allowed himself another drag on his stub of a stimstick, then took it with his slim fingers and flicked it far. In fright, Major Orlov and her men watched the smoldering stub. It seemed too much like a signal. When the stub hit the bricks and broke into sparks they all winced. But nothing bad happened.

"It's major, I believe," he said, with a cursory glance at her epaulets.

Major Orlov maintained her glower, and she hated him more by the nanosecond. She wasn't used to such disrespect and she silently damned him for scaring her.

He darted a glance at her killers, and the down turn at the corner of his lips said he saw something nasty about them that one shouldn't really talk about. So he regarded her again. "This is a restricted area, as I'm sure you know."

Major Orlov drew a plastic computer card from her side. It was her directive. She thrust it at him.

He made no move to take it. "You must move along now, Major, and, uh, take your *men* with you."

"This is direct from Beijing." The first hint of uncertainty entered his eyes, and oh, that thrilled her.

"This is Deep-Core." He spoke reverently.

"The SU Directorate supersedes Deep-Core."

Momentary awe flickered across his face—that she could bear orders stamped by a Director. He suppressed the awe, and then he snatched the card and dropped it into a scanner slung on his belt. He stared at the scanner longer than necessary. Finally, he glanced at her, murmuring, "This is highly unusual."

"Notice the seal." She couldn't keep the glee out of her voice. "SU Directorate."

"Hmm." He spoke into his cuff. Then he drew a second stimstick from his uniform.

Her men stiffened, as if this slender officer would actually do the killing. He need merely twitch his finger and lasers would cut them down. He had no need to draw a gun, not out here.

The Deep-Core officer inhaled, and the end of his stimstick glowed into life. He blew narcotic smoke into the air. Suddenly he cocked his head as if he heard an inner voice. No doubt, an implant communicator had been embedded in his skull. He lifted his eyebrows, glanced at Orlov. It took him a moment to formulate the words. "This way then," he said, "but your goons stay behind."

"I beg to differ. My orders clearly state I'm to help defend your station."

"You can't mean inside?" he asked in outrage, finally shedding his calm.

"My orders are explicit."

"But…. That just isn't done."

"If you need to, reread the directive," she said.

He spoke into his cuff again, sharply. The answer returned faster. He blinked and took the longest drag of his stimstick yet, holding the smoke in his lungs. He exhaled as if sighing. Finally, he composed himself and muttered, "Very well then, follow me."

Major Orlov marched across the plaza toward the Deep-Core Station, her squad behind her. Inside would be armored security. They would be just as suspicious as this man was. This was a delicate operation. The elevator down would be Security's inner sanctum, the holy of holies for these officers. Deep-Core's orders, training and special conditioning were to destroy the elevator rather than to lose control of it. Oh yes, this would be a very delicate operation, perhaps the greatest of her career.

A pain flared in her ponderous left breast. Major Orlov feared the end, yet…. The good of the many outweighed that of the few. She knew that. It beat in her brain until she wanted to retch. So she set her teeth and marched after the slender Deep-Core officer. At least she'd take all the bastards of Greater Sydney with her, there was that much to console her. And she'd take out the hated Highborn who had brought this awful fate to pass.

Hot molten metal would spew into Greater Sydney, slaying, searing and destroying all. No one could escape. It brought an odd smile to Orlov's lips. Then the brown-uniformed officer opened the glass door into the Deep-Core building. She followed. Behind came her killers. The extra special operation was about to begin.

16.

The frenzied hordes appalled Marten. Faintly, from down the stairwells came the sounds of gunfire and plasma cannons. The sounds lashed the crowds, the masses, and they trampled weaker people, clawed and fought to get away. Illegal weapons appeared. Shots rang out. The moans of the dying mingled with groans of terror. Hundred-man fights raged. Big men with crank bats, wearing the uniform of a local sports team, waded through the mob. Their heavy bats rose and fell. People collapsed, their skulls crushed and their faces bleeding. Kitchen knives appeared in fists, were plunged into tightly packed bodies. An overturned car plugged one lane. People scrambled to get over it, trampling a knot of school kids underneath. The old hobbled, infirm and begging for help, to be thrown aside by stronger, younger people again and again. Some of the frail gave up. Others held up their arms, pleading. Outside a theater, chorus girls screamed offers to whoever would save them.

Where any of these people thought they could hide was a mystery to Marten. But that didn't matter. Panic overrode logic.

The lights flickered as a dreadful quake caused masonry to rain upon the mob. Shrieks and bellows rose to a crescendo as trapped people turned, clawing those nearest them in the need to get away. The crank-bat wielders were attacked from all sides and the big men went down under an avalanche of screaming people. Waves of human flesh turned in any open direction and bolted for safety. Twenty office managers in tweed suits sprinted into a building, to come tumbling back out as a drunken mob bashed them with bowling balls. Crammed bodies jammed the nearest stairwell; several young men climbed atop that packed crowd and slithered over the heaving mass. One was pulled headfirst back into the throng, his screams lost in the noise as boots and shoes crushed the life out of him. A boy, his face pale with terror, refused to move as he stood there, ashen and silent.

To Marten's horror, a mob charged them, led by a tall man with long hair. Inhuman fear stamped their features. Demented, they could not grasp that there was no way out in this direction. Marten and the Incorrigibles were sheltered in a small cul-de-sac. Once the mob reached them, they'd be trampled, perhaps to death.

Omi raised his assault carbine to his shoulder. Flames leapt from the short snout and he trembled from the vibration. Marten couldn't hear the shots over the wild sounds around them. The lead man blew apart in a spray of blood and bone. Behind him, others plunged to the ground, gut and chest-shot. The survivors turned as they bellowed like maddened bulls.

Trembling, Stick led them to a nearby hole in the wall. An artillery shell must have created it earlier. They ducked into what looked like a hotel lobby. There they waited as if sheltering from a storm. The mob had become like a force of nature, this one particularly unpredictable.

"Why'd you do that?" Turbo roared into Omi's ear. It was the only way to make himself heard.

Omi didn't say why. Like Marten and Stick, he crouched with his back against a wall. He closed his eyes and pressed the hot barrel of his gun against his forehead.

Perhaps he felt bad for what he'd done. Perhaps he merely rested.

"We gotta keep moving," Marten said.

"Why'd he kill them?" shouted Turbo.

"I don't know."

"We ain't murders!" the junkie bellowed.

Omi moved like a spark, jumping into Turbo's face. "They would've trampled us! That's why!"

"You murdered them!" shouted Turbo, saliva spraying out of his mouth.

Omi swung the butt of the carbine into Turbo's gut. The tall junkie bent at the waist, falling backward. The gunman fed a bullet into the chamber and raised his weapon.

"No!" shouted Marten. He leaped beside Omi and yanked down the barrel.

For a moment, it seemed Omi would use the same trick on him. Then the Korean's shoulders sagged and he threw himself against the wall, his eyes closed as he rested his forehead against the hot barrel of his gun.

Marten helped Turbo.

"He's crazy."

"Maybe we all are," Marten said.

Turbo laughed harshly. "Not like him, baby. He's Class-A crazy."

Stick moved beside them. "Listen."

They did.

"The crowd's thinning out," Stick said.

"Yeah," Marten said. "I'm not shouting anymore."

Omi opened his eyes. He wouldn't look at Turbo. "I have one question."

"Name it," said Marten.

"What's our plan?"

"I plan on living, you murdering bastard," Turbo said.

Omi acted as if he didn't hear. He asked Marten, "You tell me our plan."

"We have to stop PHC," Marten said.

"From doing what?"

"What do you think?" Marten exploded. "From blowing the deep-core mine."

Omi rose, and now he stared at Turbo. "Exactly."

"So you can gun down anybody now?" shouted Turbo. "Is that your excuse?"

"So we can save Sydney. Yes."

"Just like the cops say," Turbo sneered. "You're doing this for everyone else, huh?"

"That's right," the gunman said.

"Yeah?" said Turbo. "Well—"

Marten grabbed Turbo's skinny arm, shaking him. "Save it. Let's go."

They followed him out of the hotel and back onto the street. A group of teenagers armed with bricks sprinted past. They hurled the bricks at windows, cars, stores or dwelling places, their laughter hysterical. Two old men helped up an old woman with a bleeding gash on her forehead. Crushed bodies lay everywhere. The relative quiet after the mob had passed an eerie feeling to it, making the world strange.

"Come on," said Marten.

Exhaustion dragged at their muscles. They'd been tortured for many months, Marten not as long but to the point of death. So he allowed each of them another shot of Superstim. Turbo begged for more, until he noticed Omi's haughty eyes. After that, the tall junkie slouched down the street without complaining.

Luckily, they made a straight run to the Deep-Core Station. Most of the crowds streamed to a lower level, starting stampedes there. Marten wondered what would happen when they reached end of the line Sydney, Level Sixty.

"There it is," whispered Omi, who held up his hand to stop them.

They peered around a corner at the bank-like building. The large plaza was empty, rather silent compared to the noises of only shortly ago.

"If we charge across they'll just shoot us down," Omi said.

Marten shook his head. "We have to bank this on PHC already being successful."

"Meaning?"

"Meaning PHC will have taken this place out, killed everyone so there aren't any witnesses."

"You can't know that," Omi said. "Maybe Deep-Core is in with PHC."

"I doubt it," said Stick. "Remember how the Reform people hated PHC sticking their nose into their racket?"

"Yeah," Omi said.

"What's wrong," Turbo jeered, "don't have anybody to point a gun at?"

Omi narrowed his eyes.

"Oh, real tough," said Turbo. "How about you watch this. Marten!"

"What?"

Turbo pointed at his pocket, the one holding the medkit.

Marten thought he understood. Dubiously, he drew out the medkit, weighed it a moment and then handed it to Turbo.

Turbo's fingers flicked over the buttons as he pressed it to his arm. The medkit hissed, shooting him with more stims. "Ahhhh," whispered Turbo, his face one of ecstasy. He pitched the medkit back and strode onto the plaza, his carbine ready. Then he broke into a sprint for the glass door.

"Fool," Omi hissed. "They'll kill him."

They didn't. Turbo made it to the door and bounded within.

"He guessed right," said Marten, who now broke into a sprint after Turbo.

Inside they found more carnage. DCM personnel lay sprawled everywhere with laser holes neatly drilled into them. A few times, they found a red-suit with an ugly bullet hole in his skull or torso.

Stick savagely kicked one. Turbo spat on them all indiscriminately.

The door into the elevator room stood ajar. Blood and gore lay splashed on the controls, but the bodies had been cleared.

"PHC beat us here," said Omi.

"So it would appear," Marten said.

"You doubt?" Omi asked.

"No...." Marten said.

"What then?"

Marten looked up, swallowed. "We have to go down after them."

"What?" Turbo asked. "Down? How about up?"

"Highborn say no," Omi said.

"Yeah? And how do you know that?" Turbo asked.

"By thinking."

Marten thought Turbo would jeer. Instead, the lanky man shuffled off to sulk. Marten studied the controls. They seemed basic enough. He pressed a red button. *Ping*! The nearest elevator opened, and before them stood the plush box that could take them farther down into the planet than anything else possibly could. None of them, however, made a move.

"I once heard an old, old saying," Marten finally said.

Turbo refused to be drawn. Omi grunted, but seemed lost in thought. Stick, who stropped his vibroblade on his pant leg, looked up. "Yeah?"

"Those who would lose their life will gain it. Those who would gain their life will lose it."

"That don't make sense," the knifeboy said.

111

"Here it does."

Stick thought about, shrugged. "Maybe."

"No maybe about it," Omi said. "He's right. So let's go."

17.

They plunged toward the center of the Earth, picking up speed until the elevator whined and vibrated so it shook their teeth. Speech was impossible. Turbo thumped against the nearest wall, cradling the grenade launcher between his bony knees as he stuck his fingers in his ears. He closed his eyes and it almost seemed as if he fell asleep. Stick sat beside him and stared fixedly at his vibroblade, switching it on and off with his thumb. Of course, it was impossible to hear its hum. Marten wasn't sure the knifeboy could even feel its vibration. Omi stood and watched the depth gauge and heat-meter. His features showed an increasing dread and desperation.

Marten clamped his teeth together on the nervous urge to laugh. He'd seen far too many people in the last while high on violence. He didn't want to become as uncontrolled as they had been.

Down, down, down they plunged, toward the molten core of the planet. Heavy oppression squeezed these lifelong underground dwellers. A sense, an aura, a *feeling* of extreme pressure bore upon each of them. No python ever tightened its coils like this. Breathing became difficult. Strange sounds, groans, hisses and screeches abraded their hearing, their very awareness.

On the outside of the shaft, the temperature of the Earth increased thirty degrees Celsius for every kilometer they dropped. At one hundred kilometers it would became white hot. Then the rate of temperature increase would slow. No metal or ceramic substance man had ever used in construction could have survived the blasting heat of the deeper reaches of the Earth. Yet incredible heat was the lesser of the two problems. The greater technical difficulty lay in pressure, awful, mind-numbing pressure. Just as a swimmer in a pool experienced pressure as he dove as little as six feet down, so the Earth increased in pressure the farther down one went. At three hundred and twenty kilometers, it reached one hundred thousand atmospheres, twelve hundred times the pressure of the deepest point in the ocean.

Omi threw an agonizing glance at Marten. Marten grunted and moved beside the gunman, watching the deep gauge and heat-meter. Deep-Core personnel were intensely trained for five years before they dared go down. Psychological tests weeded out over three-quarters of the personnel. Many often cracked after a little more than a week in the deep station. Not that any human could withstand one hundred thousand atmospheres. That was impossible.

Omi tapped the depth gauge.

Marten nodded.

They left the Earth's crust and entered the mantle.

A solid layer of rock circled the outer Earth, its crust. On the ocean floor, the crust could be as little as sixteen kilometers thick. On the continents, the crust reached a thickness of forty kilometers. Basalt composed the ocean floor, a combination of oxygen, silicon, aluminum, magnesium and iron. The continental mass was mostly granite. Granite was of lower density than basalt. Thus, the continental granite plates floated on the basalt. The entire crust floated on the mantle.

Twenty-nine hundred kilometers thick, the mantle was composed of molten olivine rock: iron and magnesium combined with silicon and oxygen. Overall, the mantle was solid, but under these terrific pressures, it behaved like a plastic. Under the slow, steady pressure the material flowed like extra-thick molasses, but sudden changes in pressure would cause it to snap and fragment like glass.

Beneath the mantle pulsed the outer core. The Earth's inner core was solid. Both halves were constituted mainly of iron in an alloy form with a small amount of sulfur or oxygen. Because of the heat and pressure, the outer core was molten iron, hot to a degree almost unimaginable.

Heat and pressure of such extremes prevented the use of any known material in shaft construction.. Magnetic force alone formed the walls of the long narrow mine sunk deep into the Earth. Incredibly powerful magnetic shields shoved against the unrelenting pressure of crust, mantle and outer core. The terrible heat from the Earth itself powered these shields, and everything livable had to stay within them. Generators of brutal efficiency and power cooled the temperature inside the shaft. A breech anywhere along the line would destroy the entire deep-core mine. This core heat provided Greater Sydney and much of Australian Sector with its energy needs.

Therefore, the main safety feature was already built into the deep-core. The only way lava could possibly geyser up the mine and onto the surface was to send a tiny plug of it, like a man spitting—a little spurt of molten metal would destroy the magnetic tube behind it as it went. But such was the Earth's ability to spit that Sydney and everything around it for fifty kilometers would be annihilated. The design and safety features of the mine ensured that process could only be triggered at the deepest section of human habitation, the bottom core station, which hung just above the Earth's outer core.

The bottom core station was the elevator's destination.

For a time, Omi and Marten watched the gauges. Suddenly Marten trembled. The psychological weight around him became more than he could bear. He staggered to a cot conveniently provided and slumped upon it. He shut his eyes and his breathing grew even. Exhaustion claimed him. He dreamed of being crushed to death, of Major Orlov sitting on his chest and smothering his mouth with a rag. He clawed against her brawny forearms to no avail. Then, sluggishly, with infinite slowness, he grew aware that he dreamed and fought to wake up. His eyelids unglued and his vision swam in blurry confusion. He groaned, but couldn't hear himself. Nausea burned the back of his throat with threatened vomit. He concentrated, swung his legs off the cot and rubbed his eyes. A horrible headache pounded. He squinted. The blurs wouldn't go away. A bolt of fear stabbed him. He bent his head between his knees and told himself to relax, to breathe deeply. He did, and he found that if he pressed his hands on either side of his head that he could focus.

Turbo lay sprawled on the floor, drool spilling from his open mouth. He stared glazed-eyed at the wall. Stick squeezed his eyes closed with ferocious intensity and breathed in and out as if he were a bellows. Omi kept jerking the slide to his assault carbine open and shut, open and shut. Fifty cartridges lay at his feet, but he seemed oblivious to them.

Marten willed himself to his feet, but found that he couldn't move. Weird gusts of air puffed his cheeks. He frowned. Then he realized that he brayed moronic laughter minus the sound, or the elevator was too noisy to let him hear his own laughter. He slapped a hand over his mouth. Then, after he'd settled himself, he put his hands to his knees and slowly rose to his feet. Systematically he lurched to the depth gauge. The others ignored him. He positioned himself before it and concentrated with everything he had. It swam into view: 2850 kilometers. Just as slowly, he realized they were almost there. It seemed impossible that the pressure could affect them, no matter how terrific, when kept at bay by technology. Maybe man wasn't conditioned to take it, or maybe some sixth sense felt the world's weight. Millions of pounds of pressure per square inch... or maybe the awareness of being buried alive more horribly than any dream was too much for the human psyche. Only a superior will could stand it, only a stubborn mule of a man.

There was something just on the edge of Marten's awareness. It could help him, he knew, but he couldn't think of it. Oh! Yes, of course. He dug the medkit out of his jacket and pressed it against his arm. The red light flashed and stopped. He hadn't felt anything. Was it broken? Then a wave of cool relief flooded through him.

He laughed, normally, although still without sound. He stepped beside Omi and put his hand over the gunman's, the one working the slide. Omi squinted at him, but it didn't seem that he saw Marten. So Marten pressed the medkit to Omi's arm. No red light winked. Nothing. Marten checked the medkit and found that it was empty, or empty of whatever drug could help the gunman.

Marten shook Omi.

Omi scowled, but there still wasn't any focus in his eyes.

Marten went to each of them in turn. It was as if they were in cocoons, in their own worlds. He didn't know the deep-core term for their condition, although he was sure there was one. One thing seemed to make sense, if they had gone schizoid then surely some of the red-suits had too—he hoped.

Marten also hoped the drug in his bloodstream would last long enough so he could do the job. He readied his assault carbine. And on impulse, he went and pried the

117

vibroblade out of Stick's grip, sliding it in his boot. Then he went back to the depth gauge and watched.

In time, the noise level lowered. He shouted, and was rewarded with a new sound: his voice. That made his heart pound. Here it was—savior of Sydney or just another loser to Social Unity. Marten didn't know it, but a vicious snarl twisted his lips.

The elevator pinged.

Marten staggered to the door. It was like wading through gel, slow, difficult work. He had to concentrate to move.

A hand on his shoulder caused him to whip his head around. Omi glared at him, a death's head grin exposing his teeth.

"Do it," hissed Omi.

The box shuddered to a halt, the doors slid open and Marten Kluge waded alone into the deep-core station.

18.

The floor of the deep-core station thrummed. A prickly sensation scratched at Marten's nerves. He'd heard before from a news show or a spy video, he couldn't remember which, that the discharges of magnetic force off the molten metal created strange electrical currents within the station. It felt as if spiders with sandpaper feet scurried across him. He kept rubbing his arms and rolling his shoulders. And he kept a sharp lookout for red-suits.

The station was grimly utilitarian. Thick ablative foam walls, dull gray in color, sectioned the place into what seemed like hundreds of tiny rooms. The hall ceilings hung uncomfortably low. The light-globes embedded in them radiated almost no heat. Every time he entered a new room through a hatch, he had to duck his head.

His mother had once taken him to a museum. He remembered seeing submarines from the Twentieth Century. It had been in a conflict called World War Two. The rooms and the narrow hatchways of the deep-core station seemed similar to those WWII subs. Gauges, dials, control boards and computer screens abounded everywhere. Emergency breathing masks hung on all the walls, along with fire extinguishers and heavy-duty tanks filled with construction foam. When sprayed and exposed to air, the foam quickhardened into a lightweight, durable wall. Riot police and soldiers used construction foam, as did firefighters creating a fast firebreak. Marten realized that fires must be a constant hazard on the station.

He touched the ablative foam wall. Hot. He looked around warily. The foam walls seemed to mute sound. He barely heard his footsteps. They were muffled, almost noiseless.

He crept down a small, steep set of stairs and peered onto the next floor. It was just like the previous floor. Then an odd *clang* sounded. It seemed to come from all around. An eerie c-r-e-a-k of ghostly quality followed. The entire station shuddered. In his fright and surprise, Marten almost lost his balance and tumbled down the stairs.

His heart thudded as he hurried up them instead. Those noises didn't sound good. He wondered if it was stage one of Major Orlov's objective. Or was it merely regular deep station occurrences? He had no way to judge, but he felt that time was running out. Assault carbine at the ready, he hunted from room to room, straining to hear anything that would lead him to the enemy. The thick foam walls absorbed sound, so that the station seemed empty, lifeless, dead. It gave Marten an evil, creepy feeling. Was he too late to change anything?

Then he stumbled onto PHC-created carnage. It looked like a kitchen, a food center with a microwave and a refrigerator. Pockmarked ablative foam lined the wall, where laser beams had hit. Gray smoke curled from each pockmark and gave off a horrible stink. Draped over several small tables were six bodies, each in the brown coveralls of Deep-Core. The laser burns that had killed them still smoldered.

Rage filled Marten, at such wanton murder, senseless slaughter. He had to stop Major Orlov and her killers.

He increased his pace, but it was impossible to run. The psychological pressure wouldn't allow it. It felt as if he *dragged* his legs against a horizontal gravity. Then he heard a sound, a voice. He slowed to a creep, peering ahead so hard it seemed as if his eyeballs would spill out. He mouth went dry. His fingers stiffened.

Two men spoke in monotone voices, and they were just around the hatch. They said that maybe they should rape the system specialist after the major was finished with her.

Marten's rage burned in him and loosened his stiff fingers. He rounded the hatchway and stepped through.

Two red-suits sat at a small table. Their lasers lay in their laps as they stared at their drinks. They looked up as Marten stepped through the hatch. They had hard, tanned faces, like bloodthirsty weasels given human form. For a nanosecond, Marten and they stared at each other.

"You," one of them said in a dull monotone.

Marten vaguely recognized the pointed chin. Yeah, that man had given the major the agonizer. That seemed like an age ago.

The nanosecond ended, and the red-suits lunged out of their chairs, spilling their drinks. They were deadly as serpents, almost as fast. Their lasers lifted into firing position as red beams hosed the floor. Marten's assault carbine spoke—a quiet *cha-cha-cha*. The two red-suits hit the floor dead, riddled and twisted into grotesque positions.

Marten stepped over them, moving faster now. He was certain that because of the walls the sound of his gunfire wouldn't carry far.

The next moment a red-suit walking like a deprogrammed android almost bumped into him. Marten blew him aside, the red-suit only beginning to realize what had happened as his eyes fluttered for the last time. Marten moved like a killer robot now, a machine. Down a steep set of stairs, turn left, right, right. A red-suit tried to poke a stimstick between his own compressed lips. His

121

face was filled with intense concentration, but he kept hitting his cheek or nose with the end of the stimstick. Marten gunned him down, thankful that the deep-core pressure was making them stupid.

Marten kept striding, but it felt as if he moved through water. His head started hurting and it was hard to concentrate. So he watched his feet, willing them forward one step at a time. When had control of them again, he looked up, hunting, searching. He hurried through a hatchway—and he tripped over a foot. Marten threw out his arms to catch himself. His weapon went spinning, but he landed without knocking out his teeth. When nothing more happened, he looked back.

A red-suit pointed a laser at him. The man had razor-thin eyebrows and the deadly intent eyes of a pit bull. On his suit was the name: Ngo Drang. He was the second guard that had helped the major torture him in the interrogation room.

Drang frowned. "I… I should shoot you."

Marten sagged in defeat. He didn't know why Ngo Drang hadn't already done it. Then he looked at the tight face, at the empty, odd stare in the killer's eyes.

"Hissss—splat," said Drang. "A neat laser hole in your forehead."

"You should take me to the major," Marten said.

Drang shook his head. "No. I… I should kill you. I don't know why I haven't done it already. It's…" He shook his head, frowning.

"The major wants you to take me to her," Marten said.

"Yeah?"

Marten rose slowly, noting how the laser tracked his forehead. Deep-core pressure was all he had between him and death. "We'd better go."

The intense frown left Ngo Drang's face. "That way," he said, gesturing with the laser.

19.

When Marten had first stepped off the elevator into the deep-core station, Major Orlov had been twining her thick fingers into the long dark hair of System Specialist Ah Chen. The Chinese technician was exactly the type the major passionately hated: Petite, pretty, with luxurious dark hair and eyes like a vid star. Ah Chen made her baggy brown overalls seem sexy and provocative. Major Orlov hated her on sight. So she gripped the system specialist's thick hair and yanked her head.

"You're going to help us obliterate Sydney, my smooth-skinned harlot."

Ah Chen remained speechless. Tears welled in her fawn eyes and streaked her oval face. She'd squealed in terror until Orlov had forced her to watch the quick and efficient slaughter of her deep station colleagues. The major had grinned and made a running commentary as her killers had hosed the room with beams. Sobs still racked the tiny thing.

"No crying!" Orlov shouted, jerking the small head from side to side.

The little beauty sniffled and sobbed. So the major slammed her face against the wall, listening to the little button nose crunch and break.

"Did you hear me!" roared Orlov, enjoying herself hugely.

Ah Chen bowed her head. Her blood dripped to the floor.

Major Orlov shoved the tiny system specialist ahead of her into the hall, and did so all the way to the main reactor room. It contained a bewildering array of computer screens and keyboards. Openmouthed, terrified technicians stared at them.

Major Orlov shook Ah Chen's head. Then she leaned low and whispered into her ear, telling her what was expected of her.

The tiny Chinese technician turned in amazement. "No. I-I-I cannot do as you ask."

"Pity." Major Orlov gestured to her killers.

The little technician cringed as lasers beamed. More of her colleagues collapsed amid bloody butchery.

She whispered, "You might as well kill me too. I'm no good to you."

Major Orlov barked harsh laughter. "Kill you? I wouldn't dream of such a thing." She indicated the room. "I know several of the steps for prepping the station for a geyser, but not all of them. No. You will help me destroy Sydney."

The small technician's dread was palpable as color drained from her face. So very slowly, she shook her head.

"Are you brave, my dear?"

"No. But I cannot do as you ask."

"Conditioning?"

"You are correct."

"Don't you know that Political Harmony Corps can break conditioning?"

"I must inform you that you cannot break Deep-Core's."

"Oh yes, most certainly we can break Deep-Core's." Major Orlov snapped her fingers.

A pot-bellied PHC officer, with thinning hair and droopy eyes, opened a black case. He had pudgy little hands with dirt under the fingernails. No laser pack was slung on his back. No pistol was cradled at his side. He was known simply as 'the Doctor.' He now took out a pneumospray hypo.

Ah Chen's fawn eyes grew wide with fright.

The Doctor explained. "Oh, it isn't painful, I assure you. This is simply a hyperaesthesic."

The small technician appeared bewildered.

"It heightens your senses," he said, as he pressed the hypo to her arm, letting it hiss.

She jerked her arm back, rubbing it.

"No, I advise against that," said the Doctor.

Her hand shot off her arm as pain creased her features.

"As I said, a fast-acting hyperaesthesic. Your heart rate and breathing will increase, and your senses will become many times more sensitive. For instance, the light in this room will soon hurt your eyes. The clothes you wear will begin to chafe unbearably. Certain odors you've never noticed will now become most pronounced. It's possible that what you now consider an awful stench will make you vomit. In the quantity you've been given—a large dosage, believe me—these new sensations will become...." He exposed small teeth in a rather nasty smile, "...decidedly uncomfortable."

Major Orlov laughed. "You'll never have felt pain like this."

Already the tiny technician twitched this way and that. But that only increased the obvious discomfort she felt from her clothes.

"Let me help you," said Major Orlov. She took hold of Ah Chen's garment and ripped off the top half, exposing the petite Chinese technician from the waist up. "Not too well endowed, are you?"

The little technician covered herself with her hands.

125

The major took each tiny wrist and swung the arms behind Ah Chen's back, snapping handcuffs onto her. The system specialist painfully sucked in her breath.

"It hurts?" asked the Doctor.

"Why are you doing this?" asked Ah Chen.

The Doctor reached into his black bang, pulling out a wand. "The nerve lash," he said professionally. "Notice, I position the switch at one, the lowest setting." The wand purred evilly. "I then apply the tip to your belly."

Ah Chen screamed, her face twisting hideously.

The Doctor popped a rubber ball into her mouth. The technician's eyes widened in shock. "You'll become quite a bit louder," the Doctor told her. "We don't care to wear ear plugs, so you must accommodate us."

Major Orlov giggled wickedly.

"Examine your belly," the Doctor said, taking away the nerve lash.

Ah Chen did. There was no mark.

"This is a marvelous instrument," the Doctor said. "Now notice, I set it to level two. The pain will now increase." He touched it to her left breast.

Ah Chen collapsed into a thrashing heap onto the floor.

Major Orlov cracked her knuckles in anticipation.

20.

Marten stumbled into the reactor room. A small, nude Chinese woman lay in a sweaty heap on the floor. A pot-bellied red-suit straightened, clutching a nerve lash in his dirty hands. Major Orlov sat back in a chair. Her big boots were propped up on a com-board. With obvious relish, she watched the Chinese woman.

Marten took in the scene at a glance. More torture, more PHC brutality. Something snapped in him. This was his last chance anyway. He kept stumbling and allowed himself to trip over his own feet. He fell to the floor, and while lying on his stomach, he reached to his boot and drew the vibroknife. His thumb settled onto the on/off switch.

"Marten Kluge?" the major asked, as if heaven had sent her the gift of a lifetime.

"Can you believe it?" asked Drang.

"Where did you find him?"

"In the halls."

"Amazing. No, shocking." Major Orlov chuckled. "This... This is simply wonderful. Marten! Marten, dear, did you miss mommy?"

"I thought you'd want to see him again," said Drang.

"Doctor," said Orlov, "do you have any more hyperaesthesic left?"

"Certainly."

"Doesn't the system specialist need a rest?" suggested the major.

"Your sense of timing is impeccable, as always," the Doctor said. "I was just about to suggest a cooling off period. She's reached the tertiary point, in any case."

"Gentlemen," said Major Orlov, "I pronounce our deeds approved. For if there is any Higher Form after death—"

"You can't really believe that?" Drang asked.

"Don't interrupt me." Major Orlov cleared her throat. "As I was saying, if there is any Higher Form after death, He can only be showing us His approval by gifting me with these two. Oh yes, Marten and a young pretty. This is splendid!"

"If I'm to inject him I want him standing," said the Doctor.

"Marten. Oh, Marten," called Major Orlov.

Marten lay on his belly, waiting, willing them closer.

"What's wrong with him?" asked the major.

"Perhaps he's finally succumbed to deep pressure," the Doctor said.

"Well, get him up!" snapped Major Orlov.

Drang approached Marten.

"Be careful," said the major.

Drang grabbed Marten by the shoulder, the pistol digging into his back. "On your feet, slum-dog."

Marten groaned, but he allowed himself to be pulled up. Then he twisted around, flicked the knife on and drove the vibroblade into Drang's belly. The blade dug in with ease, singing all the way. Marten sidestepped and jerked the blade out sideways, slicing the laser coil just as Drang clicked the trigger. Substance spilled from the coil, burning Drang, who howled. Marten chopped at the man's head. He had no idea of the blade's power. It sawed through part of the skull, spraying brain and gore. The corpse pitched forward.

Ah Chen screamed.

Marten turned. The Doctor thrust at him with the nerve lash. Marten parried, cutting the lash in two. With a croak of dismay, the Doctor drew back his ruined torture device. Marten snarled, hewing at the Doctor's chest. The knife whined in high glee, punching into the chest. Blood sprayed and drenched Marten. The vibroblade was a messy weapon.

Major Orlov had leaped to her feet and clawed at her holster.

The small Chinese technician, still lying on the floor, used her tiny foot to kick the major's boot at the ankle. The major cried out and momentarily lost her balance. She both drew her pistol and let go at the same moment. The pistol clattered to the floor. Marten whooped savagely, attacked and thrust. Major Orlov, for all her bulk and unbalance, twisted and dodged the singing, bloody blade. She then pivoted on her heel and swung a ham-like fist. Marten heard a rib crack as the air whooshed out of him. The major's touch hurt horribly. She followed with another smashing blow. It rocked him backward and stole his breath. She was incredibly strong, with more than twice his mass.

"Little man!" she snarled.

Marten backpedaled to give himself time, and almost slipped on all the blood and gore.

Orlov checked herself, then turned and lunged for her gun.

Wildly, Marten threw the vibroblade. Orlov dodged. It hit a panel, singing loudly as it buried itself into it. Marten followed. Major Orlov laughed and crashed upon him like an auto-sweeper. They wrestled on the floor. The slick of blood made it hard for either of them to get a good hold. Orlov had size, strength and weight. Marten was faster.

She tried to twist his head around, but her hands keep slipping off. He dug his fingers into her nose. She moaned, and bit his wrist. He jabbed with his other hand, using his thumb like a pick. Bone, bone, he jabbed deeply into an eye, digging until Major Orlov shrieked, using her hands and feet to hurl him away. He landed heavily and rose off the floor. So did she, with ichor dripping from her ruined left eye.

"Hey!" cried Ah Chen. Marten glanced at her. The small Chinese woman handed him the vibroblade. It was turned off.

"No!" howled Major Orlov, charging.

Marten sidestepped to her blind side, flicked on the blade and chopped. Like a thing alive, the blade hummed. It seemed satisfied beyond measure. Major Orlov's head separated from her body and thumped onto the floor. The huge torso jetted blood everywhere. Then it crashed onto the deck, spent, finished, ended forever.

Ah Chen clutched Marten, burying her face in his chest and crying.

He couldn't believe it. He stood there dazed, looking at the carnage. Finally, it came to him that he held a naked woman in his arms and that they were both covered with other people's blood. He flicked off the knife and pitched it aside.

Sydney had been saved from annihilation. Marten wondered if he'd be able to do the same for himself.

21.

Transcript #30,499 Highborn Archives of an exchange of notes between: Paenus, Inspector General, Earth, and Cassius, Grand Admiral of Highborn. Dates: December 15 to December 20, 2349.

December 15
To Paenus:
The training schedule must be accelerated. Hawk Assault Teams and panzer crews are especially needed for the pending Australian Sector Campaign.

To Cassius:
Your Excellency is surely aware of the lack of qualified recruits. Combined with enemy sleeper agents, worldwide anti-Highborn propaganda and terrorist assassinations makes the accelerated training program, especially for these elite units, a daunting, perhaps a hopeless task.

December 17
To Paenus:
Surely not hopeless my dear Inspector General.

To Cassius:

Your Excellency must know that most of my recruits are herded to me at gunpoint. As fodder for bombs and lasers, they excel. As warriors, they are sadly lacking. Hawk Assault Teams and panzer crews require a certain *élan* for maximum effectiveness. Still, I shall comply with your wishes to the best of my ability.

December 18
To Paenus:
I thank the Inspector General for informing me of the need for *élan* in certain shock and exploitation troops. Such graciousness should be returned. Thus, I have decided to solve your training problems as way of reward.

The easiest expedient to help instill fervor in recruits is to show them the folly of lacking it. For instance, a bullet in the back of the head, preferably where many recruits can witness the event, will help energize the others. Every recruit must learn that orders are to be obeyed. Sleeper agents abound, you say. I recommend strenuous mind-probing. When an offender is found, brain-wipe him and send him to a penal battalion. These battalions should be highly visible as deterrents to the others. Therefore, all penal battalions must be designated as suicide troops. All suicide troops must have a mini-explosive implanted in their cortex. Detonation devices will be in the control of the battalion's colonel, captains and lieutenants. I believe that all our Earth draftees should have a cortex bomb, but at some point, the enemy will learn the code and frequency of various sets and they will explode them before it is desirable.

Let me point out to the Inspector General the very urgent need of these soldiers for the coming Australian campaign. Actual Highborn deaths took an alarming turn in the New Zealand and Java Island Campaigns. Yet we cannot afford to slacken the speed of our advance, thus the need for your Earth levies at the earliest possible date.

I surely do not need to point out to the Inspector General that victory in the field automatically diminishes the effectiveness of enemy propaganda. We must strike hard and fast NOW, but we must keep Highborn losses to a minimum. I cannot overstate this need for trained Earth soldiers who can *fight*. Brutality, my dear Paenus, done in calculated doses, will save lives and ensure us a golden future sooner rather than later.

December 19
To Cassius:
I hear and obey you, Grand Admiral.

To Paenus:
I know you too well, my dear Paenus. You held back. I know, because your curt reply plays repeatedly in my mind. Please, share with a fellow warrior what ails you.

December 20
To Cassius:
I am indeed troubled, Grand Admiral. I feel that we are somehow going about this the wrong way. I realize that brutality and hard training can make soldiers of civilians in short order. And yes, our technology allows us a certain leeway that warriors in the past never had. I refer to brain scans, wipes and cortex bombs. I ask myself, however, will we have to garrison our conquests forever? Our enemy blares on the vids and holos against us, and on the airwaves and in the streets.

Grand Admiral, to a space battle we bring Doom Stars, tac-craft and long-range lasers. To a land assault, we brings orbital fighters, heavy panzers and drop troops. My question, Grand Admiral, is what does one bring to a propaganda war?

To Paenus:

My brilliant friend. You are quite right. You fight an idea with a better idea.

22.

The elevator sped toward the surface, bearing its cargo of five survivors. As the horrible pressure of the great deep lessened, Omi repackaged the cartridges littered around him, until his carbine clips brimmed with shells. Turbo wiped spittle from his chin and tried to make conversation with Ah Chen. She huddled beside Marten, who rested his head against the vibrating wall. Stick reclaimed his knife and wanted to hear again how Major Orlov had lost her head.

A tired smile touched Marten's lips.

"That's right," Stick said. "A knife's better than anything else. You feel them die. You don't stand back and let technology do your dirty work. Not like gunmen do it."

"Meaning what?" asked Omi from his side of the elevator.

"Meaning shooting out kneecaps," said Stick.

"And your knife isn't technological?" the muscled Korean asked.

"You know what I mean," said Stick. "You gotta drive the blade into them. It's your own strength that does it, not just pulling a trigger."

"In case you're interested," said Omi, "I've never shot out anyone's kneecap."

135

"That's right," Turbo sneered. "He once had his buddies hold a guy down while he slipped on a leather glove. Then he beat the poor sap to death."

"Well, at least that's better than using bullets," said Stick. "He's doing it himself. That's what counts."

"I don't see how that's any better to the man getting beat," said Turbo.

"Of course it is," argued Stick. "It's more personal. It's between men."

"Between a sadist and his victim, more like."

"Maybe that too, but it's personal."

"So is rape," said Ah Chen. "But I would rather be shot or run over by a car."

Stick scowled until he brightened. "I'm only talking man to man. When you bring women in it's an entirely different thing."

Turbo threw up his hands and started pacing.

"You gotta admit it takes more balls to knife someone than shoot him," Stick said.

"You've been in the slime pits too long," Turbo muttered.

"That doesn't have anything to do with it." Stick turned to Omi. "Am I right?"

Omi shrugged.

"Come on," Stick said. "You gotta admit beating a man with your fists is more manly than using a bat. I mean, you can break your hand doing it."

"Then I'd rather use a bat," Omi said dryly.

"Not me!" said Stick. He slapped his chest. "I'll do it the old-fashioned way every time."

"What are we going to do next?" Marten asked, trying to change the topic.

"Sneak out of Sydney," Turbo said. "That's my plan."

"And how are you going to manage this feat?" Omi asked.

"Maybe she knows of some secret elevator to the surface," Turbo said.

All four men glanced at Ah Chen. She shook her head and snuggled closer to Marten.

"You must know of a way out," Turbo pleaded.

"Leave her alone," Marten said. "She's been through enough you don't have to hound her."

"Sorry," muttered Turbo. He went back to pacing.

Omi glanced at the gauge. "Almost there," he said.

Marten struggled to his feet and then he helped Ah Chen. She wore an oversized coat and still trembled from the abuse and the drugs they'd given her. Marten checked his carbine, then stood before the door, waiting.

Omi stepped near. "We can't head to the lower levels with the mobs. Not if we plan to survive."

"Maybe we can hide out the war in the slums," said Marten.

Turbo snorted.

Marten glanced at him.

"You ain't ever lived in the slums," said Turbo.

"What are we going to do then?"

No one answered Marten.

"You're a hero for saving the deep-core mine," Ah Chen timidly said. "If we could reach Deep-Core Central, they would take care of you."

Omi shook his head. "Forget about that. Marten broke a Directorate plan. There's no hope for him with Social Unity."

"I know one thing," said Stick. "I'm sure not turning traitor." The others gave him their attention. "You're thinking about joining the Highborn," he told Omi.

"Whichever gang is strongest," said Omi.

"Don't you have *any* loyalty?" asked Stick.

"Yes," said Omi, "to my continued existence."

The elevator slowed.

"Get ready," said Marten, interrupting whatever Stick had planned to retort.

The others crowded around him, their weapons ready.

"We should have an emergency plan," said Turbo. "Just stepping into danger every time and hoping for the best is…. It isn't smart."

The elevator pinged. The door swished open and a huge, nine-foot soldier in powered black armor turned to face them. Servos whined as the giant soldier aimed an auto-cannon that had an extremely pitted nozzle—his oversized weapon had obviously seen plenty of use. The combination plasteel/ceramic armor gave him a robotic, knightly look. Humming power packs supplied the energy and an exo-skeleton multiplied his strength so that if there had been enough room he could have leaped a hundred meters in a single bound. Shock absorbers and a Highborn physique allowed him to withstand the landing. A missile launcher was fixed to his slab of a back and the auto-cannon he aimed at their faces fired twenty-millimeter-sized shells.

"Drop your weapons!" boomed his helmet, the faceplate darkened so they couldn't see his face.

Marten dropped his carbine, then so did the others. It was questionable whether their slugs would have even been able to penetrate the armor. Maybe they could have shot out his faceplate if they had hit several times in quick succession. But by then they'd have been obliterated. They raised their hands.

A second Highborn stepped into view. His servos were geared to their lowest setting. He too towered nine feet tall. This one didn't aim an auto-cannon at them. Instead, with his powered gloves, he reached up, twisted the helmet to the left and lifted it off his head. He had china-plate-colored white skin, with harsh features angled in a most inhuman manner. His lips were razor thin and his hair was cut down almost to his scalp. It was more like a synthetic rug than anything else. He had fierce black eyes, and there was an intense, almost pathological energy to him, a hysteria to slay, rend and destroy that was only kept in check by an inhumanly vital will.

"You are not PHC," he said in a deep voice.

"We killed them," Marten said matter-of-factly.

The fierce eyes tightened, as if the Highborn could judge the truth of Marten's statement by an act of will. Perhaps he could.

Marten said, "They were going to blow the deep-core mine and destroy everyone in Sydney."

The Highborn raised his brows. His eyes were sunken deeper into his face than a normal man's. It gave him a skull-like appearance. "It is a worthy way to die, taking down your enemies."

Marten wondered if the man was crazy.

The nine-foot tall Highborn took a deep draught of air, and he lifted his auto-cannon. "By decree of the Imperial High Command—since you showed resistance to your unlawful government—I am forced to offer you the chance to volunteer for the Free Earth Corps."

"And if we don't volunteer?" asked Turbo.

A wicked grin exposed perfect teeth, and a loud clack from within the auto-cannon told of its readiness. The first Highborn, the one who hadn't removed his helmet, lifted a humming sword three times the length of Stick's vibroblade.

"Hey!" Turbo told Stick. "That should you make you happy: a personal sort of death."

For a moment, no one said anything. Then Marten took a step toward the pitted nozzle of the auto-cannon. "I wish to volunteer," he said.

Part II
Recruit

1.

The tall, gaunt general in the green uniform and red piping of Directorate Staff Planning strode back and forth across the rug. His desk was huge. Behind it was an old-style bookshelf with books. He claimed turning pages helped him concentrate. But then most people thought of him as eccentric—and that was a bad thing this near the ruling power. The nine directors of the Social Unity Directorate appreciated men and women they understood. Eccentrics, which in their mind meant "unpredictables," were distrusted. Even worse, they were hated.

Secret Police General James Hawthorne ran a bony hand through his blond, wispy hair. He pivoted and paced back over the worn trail he'd made in his carpet. He had a sure stride, and he clasped his hands behind his back. Pacing helped him think. The pacing didn't indicate nervousness. That was another of his eccentricities. He was trying to decide between two momentous avenues for the further prosecution of the war.

Most people thought he had the emotions of a large slab of rock. The belief occurred primarily because of his patrician mannerisms. The directors disliked such mannerisms. Social Unity preached egalitarianism, not the ways of aristocracy. So Hawthorne strove to keep his true nature hidden.

He read voraciously, military history being his special love. Among the great captains of history, he believed he most resembled Douglas MacArthur of the Twentieth Century, a brilliant man.

Before Hawthorne could pivot and retrace his steps, a chime sounded from his desk. He frowned. Then he forced his features into the blank look that he wore around people in power.

The door swished open and unannounced an old man hobbled into the office. That spoke of the man's power. He had breached Hawthorne's security net without any alarms going off.

The old man seemed more caricature than real. He had uncombed white hair and a leathery face with a thousand wrinkles. He used a cane, and he shivered as he shuffled a few steps at a time.

Behind the old man followed a strange creature. Not quite an android, it was difficult to call him a man. The common phrase was semi-prosthetic or bionic. Specialists had torn down the bodyguard and rebuilt him with artificial muscles, steel-reinforced bones and nerves protected by sheathing. The bionic guard wore a black slick-suit and a senso mask to hide his face.

A barely audible whine emanated from the bodyguard as he took one step at a time behind his master. At a word from the bent-over director, the bodyguard could tear the office apart with his bare hands. Although the bodyguard wore no outer weapons, at least one of his fingers likely contained an embedded mini-laser. Wonder glands could squirt drugs into his bloodstream, dulling pain and adding speed and strength.

"Director Enkov," Hawthorne said, "this is a surprise."

The ancient man with a thousand wrinkles struggled to lift his head. He had pale blue eyes. They were the keen eyes of a killer more murderous than any blood-maddened shark. They stared into General James Hawthorne's eyes. After fifty days of infighting, and two sudden deaths, this wicked butcher had proved himself the strongest force on the Directorate governing Inner Planets.

Director Enkov dropped his gaze and struggled to the nearest chair. General Hawthorne would have sprung to the chair and slid it closer. But a single look into the director's eyes had rooted Hawthorne's feet and caused his tongue to freeze.

Despite his best efforts over the past few months, General Hawthorne had only gained driblets of information concerning Enkov. This much he knew. Unless he pleased this withered old man, the bionic monstrosity behind him.... General Hawthorne regained use of his tongue. He moved it in his cotton dry mouth. One misstep today and the bodyguard would destroy him in an undignified manner.

Director Enkov laboriously maneuvered himself into the chair. He grunted painfully as he sank his crooked back against the rest. He set the cane on his knees. And with a trembling, wrinkled hand, he reached into his coat and drew out a stimstick. He stuck it between his dry lips and inhaled sharply. Stimsticks automatically lit with the first puff. He worked the stimstick to the left side of his mouth and let it dangle.

The bionic bodyguard flanked the right side of the chair. There, he froze into immobility.

"General Hawthorne," wheezed the director. The old man's voice was raspy, pained and still filled with deadly menace.

"Sir!" said Hawthorne, snapping to attention.

Red smoke drifted out of the old man's nostrils. "Shall we spout pleasantries, you and I, or shall we hew to the meat of the matter?"

"I am at the Director's pleasure, sir."

"What is the term...? Ah, yes. At ease, General, at ease."

General Hawthorn's stance grew minutely wider and he snapped his hands behind his back. His features remained blank.

More red smoke trickled out of the director's nostrils. "I deplore subterfuge, General."

"Yes, sir."

"So you may forgo the military routine."

"Sir?"

"You're a pacer, I hear. That's what my profile team told me. When you talk you walk, at least if left to your own devices. So by all means walk."

"I, ah...."

"Walk," growled Enkov, indicating the worn carpet.

General Hawthorne did as ordered, although his stride was no longer as sure as before.

"Comfortable?"

"Yes, sir," said Hawthorne.

"I deplore lying."

General Hawthorne's stride suddenly became surer. He was wondering how best to handle the situation, and when he thought he walked, just as Enkov had said.

Director Enkov's eyes seemed to glitter and a tiny cruel smile appeared and then disappeared from his dry old lips.

"You asked for the truth, is that not right?" Hawthorne asked.

"Most certainly," whispered Enkov.

"May I ask then why you are here?"

"Because we're losing the war," whispered Enkov.

General Hawthorne nodded, even as he considered Enkov's presence here. Enkov had come with a single bodyguard into his office for a reason. Maybe it was to try to lull him, to put him at greater ease than otherwise. He would have to monitor his words with care. Yet it would be wise to pretend to be at ease, to let Enkov think his subtlety was working.

"During a war of this magnitude we must expect certain setbacks," Hawthorne said. "I explained that during my Directorate interrogations."

"Setbacks, yes," whispered Enkov. "But we've received one defeat after another, and those defeats have come quickly."

General Hawthorne shrugged as he pivoted and paced back the way he'd come. "New Zealand, Tasmania, Australia, Antarctica, we can well afford such losses."

"Not in the swift manner we've lost them."

General Hawthorne didn't respond, even though Director Enkov was right. The Highborn had waged brilliant campaigns. They excelled at space combat. He had hoped land war would have stifled them just a little.

"Volunteers stream into their Free Earth Corps," whispered Enkov.

"True. But it takes time to train good soldiers."

"It takes less time to train garrison troops to hold what they've conquered. That frees the Highborn for further campaigns."

Hawthorne nodded. It was the essential problem.

"Did you expect them to win so quickly?" the director whispered.

"No."

"Then perhaps you're not a traitor after all, merely incompetent."

General Hawthorne stopped short.

"Or will you tell me that you miscalculated?"

"Miscalculated is too strong a word," said Hawthorne. "I misjudged their timing."

A dry chuckle escaped the old director. It made the smoldering tip of the stimstick bob up and down. "Whatever you call it, you were wrong."

Cold fear settled in Hawthorne's chest.

"A general who guesses wrong is useless."

"But—"

Director Enkov lifted a trembling hand. "Swift, Highborn advances have demolished your estimated timeline. Even your little scheme of blowing Greater Sydney with a deep-core burst came to nothing. Worse, our propagandists have been working overtime to defeat the Highborn accusations that we planned such a thing. In all, General Hawthorne, your prosecution of the war leaves much to be desired."

Sweat beaded Hawthorne's upper lip. "I am to be relieved of command?"

"General Hawthorne, I believe you're something of a historian. At least that's what my briefing team told me."

"They are correct, sir."

"Splendid. Do you recall the history of an ancient city called Carthage?"

"Indeed."

"I believe Hannibal marched from there."

"Yes, sir, he did."

"Yes...." Director Enkov shifted to a more comfortable position. "The Carthaginians had an interesting habit concerning generals." The director's features took on a more sinister cast, as he smiled cruelly. "If the Carthaginian general came back defeated or lost too many troops, the city fathers debated among themselves. If the judgment went against this general, they took the loser outside the city. There they stripped him of his rank and his clothes. Soldiers scourged him with whips. They nailed spikes through his wrists and his feet,

145

hammering him onto a cross. That cross they propped upright. They *crucified* him, I believe is the term."

"Yes, sir," said Hawthorne, uneasily. "The Carthaginian's invented the custom that the Romans later copied."

"For the remainder of the war I wish you to consider yourself a Carthaginian general, and all it entails."

Secret Police General James Hawthorne grew pale and found that he couldn't speak. There was a hidden gun in the bottom left drawer of his desk. He wondered what his chances were of reaching it and killing these two.

"...Unless," said Enkov.

"Yes," croaked Hawthorne. He cleared his throat, hating his display of weakness.

"Surely you have a Plan B," whispered Enkov.

"B, sir?"

"Something to implement in case your original theories proved false or misleading."

"Yes, sir."

"Well?"

General Hawthorne thought once more about the hidden gun in his desk. Then he decided that Enkov's briefing team surely knew about it. The bodyguard would undoubtedly kill him before he could open the drawer.

"Sir, there is a Plan B."

"Splendid."

"But it entails great risk."

"I don't like the sound of that, General."

"I don't see any other way out of our impasse, sir."

"Not an impasse, General, but our defeat."

"Yes, sir. Our defeat."

General Hawthorne sat on the edge of his desk. He massaged his forehead and wiped the sheen of sweat from his upper lip. "Sir, to be blunt, the Highborn were a good idea that went bad."

"A good idea?"

"Superior soldiers, sir. Or, to use a metaphor, a better sword than our foes in Outer Planets could wield. Only this sword has turned in our hand."

"I see."

"Actually, one could say it became a magic sword that turned and attacked us."

"Yes, yes, quite colorful, General, but what is your point?"

"Our old swords, sir, break every time we try to defeat the magic sword. My first theory was to throw so many old swords against it that in time the magic sword would become nicked once too often and shatter. That doesn't seem to be happening, or it's not happening fast enough. What we need is a better sword."

"You mean create more Highborn to throw at the first batch?"

"That's not a bad idea, sir."

"It's lunacy. The first batch turned on us. Why not the second?"

"You're probably right, sir."

Enkov scowled. And by that, General Hawthorne believed that his time was limited.

"Sir, what about a new and better sword, even better than the first sword? This new sword we shall be able to control?"

"What are you trying to say?"

"That in deep space a habitat orbits Neptune. Actually, it's in deep-Neptune orbit. It appears to be like any other of the hundreds of habitats orbiting the gas giant. In actuality it's the home to a secret and special project."

"What project?"

"The creation of a new and better sword, sir."

"Men, General?"

"Soldiers, sir, who can outfight Highborn."

"Are you mad? What's to stop them from turning on us like the Highborn have?"

"These are quite different creatures, sir. Their very makeup allows us to implant deep controls."

"Out with it, man! What are they?"

"Cyborgs."

The old withered eyes narrowed. Enkov glanced at his bodyguard. "You mean like him?"

"No, sir. Infinitely more deadly. And if I may say so, sir, most inhuman in their efficiency."

"You've actually made enough of these... these cyborgs to change the war?"

"Not yet, sir."

Director Enkov spat the stub of his stimstick onto the carpet. There it smoldered until the bodyguard crushed it with his foot. "What do you mean 'not yet'?"

"I need the go ahead for phase two, sir."

"What is phase two?"

"If the Director would be so kind as to glance at the holochart on my desk...."

For a second they stared eye to eye. Hawthorne wondered if the old man was going to order the bodyguard to kill him. He began to judge how fast he could jump for the gun in his desk.

Then, with a wheeze, ancient Director Enkov began to work his way to his feet to come and look at the holochart.

2.

Far from the raging civil war—past Jupiter, Saturn and Uranus—orbited blue Neptune. Hundreds of habitats orbited it, and many colonies had sprung up on its various moons. The majority of the space habs had been constructed out of weird ice, making them glittering, colorful motes in the eternal night of space. It insured that the Ice Hauler Cartel was one of the major powers in the Neptune System.

The continuing, growing thirst for weird ice and the constant need for new sources of water had finally led the cartel into experimental ship construction. IH-49 was the third of its kind. It was being readied for a long and hopefully momentous journey. However, within the command module things had already started to go wrong.

"That's impossible."

"What?"

"My game froze."

Osadar Di frowned, not sure that she'd heard correctly. Paranoia came easily to her. Thus, she always checked and rechecked everything that could possibly go wrong. It made her an excellent space pilot.

Osadar shut down her scanning program and pushed VR goggles onto her smooth forehead. She had short dark hair, dark worried eyes and a scratch on her nose. A bit

149

too tall for an ice hauler, she had long shapely legs highlighted by her blue-colored jumpsuit. The suit had a red IHC tab on the left shoulder. The cramped command module held screens, consoles and claustrophobically close bulkheads. The commander sat in the middle of this mess, the pink-faced life support officer to his left and Osadar to his right.

The commander, a tough old man with short silver hair, experimentally tapped his VR monocle.

"What game could you possibly be playing at a time like this?" asked Osadar.

"Antiquity."

"*The* Antiquity Game?"

"Not Earth's. Neptune's."

Because light moved so slowly, three hundred thousand kilometers a second, each planetary grid only linked with computers in its near vicinity. The time lag of say from Earth to Mars—something over five minutes—was too much for players of a complex game like Antiquity to react successfully to each other's moves.

Osadar checked a screen. The commander used ship's AI (Artificial Intelligence) to run his ultra-complex character. A laser lightguide system hooked him into the nearby Neptune III Net.

"What's *wrong* with this thing?" he complained.

"Explain."

"I just ran a diagnostic, and Ajax checks out."

"Who?"

"Ajax!" He scowled. "My character in the Trojan War."

Osadar shook her head.

"The Greeks and Trojans, Achilles and Hector? Didn't they teach you anything in the Jupiter System?"

"Give me the code," Osadar said.

"Eh?"

"I'll see what I can do."

"Oh. Thanks. The code word is Asimov."

Osadar put her goggles back on and manipulated her gloves. "There isn't anything wrong with your character."

"That's what I said!"

"So what's wrong?"

"Ah ha! Found it. The laser-link is down."

Osadar frowned. It was her habitual look. She tried to squeeze off a message to the nearest IHC station. Zero. She ran a diagnostic on communications. Check. So she sent another flash. Another zero. Either the diagnostic lied or IHC had gone off-line, which wasn't possible. For that would mean IHC no longer existed. The Ice Hauler Cartel *owned* communications out here—they even owned her at present. Any space hab orbiting Neptune or one of its moons used their patented lightguide net-web.

The commander cursed in old Angelic. Sometimes he took his historical excesses to extremes.

"Now what?" Osadar asked.

"Ajax crashed! Do you know how much *time* I put into him?"

"Ask the AI why he crashed."

"AI isn't responding."

Osadar's stomach clenched. *She* tried the AI. The ill feeling grew, producing a touch of nausea. Then her eyes, those worried dark orbs, glistened with fear. The AI couldn't answer because its entire ram was being used. What in the devil was going on?

"Ask computing what's wrong with the AI," the commander told the LS officer.

"...Can't, Commander. Something's jamming inter-ship communication."

Fear stabbed Osadar's heart. She tore off her VR goggles and shucked off the gloves. Breathing deeply, she tried to control her panic. Then she unbuckled herself and floated to a portal.

"What are you doing?" asked the commander.

Osadar grabbed a float-rail and pressed her palm on the lock. Nothing happened. She floated to the other portal. It, too, refused to open. She bit back the moan that tried to rush past her teeth. As calmly as possible, she flipped a terminal-head and punched in override. Then she cranked open the portal by hand. On impulse, she set the locks so it couldn't slide shut on her.

"Commander, I'm getting a red reading in computing." The pink-faced LS officer looked up in confusion.

"Osa?" asked the commander.

"I'm going outside to manually override the laser-link. I want Dominie Banbury to hear about this."

"Do you really think that's warranted?"

"Don't you?" she asked.

The commander pondered a moment and nodded. "Wait a minute, though. I'm going with you."

3.

Toll Seven allowed himself a faint smile. Ship's AI had succumbed to his program. The Master Plan went forward with flawless precision.

He shook his bald head—he looked like a robot with plastic flesh, with a shark's dead eyes. He used inner nanonics to dump chemicals into his brain's pleasure centers to dampen his joy. Neither fear nor happiness must mar the smooth working of the plan. Clean concentration was paramount. That blood globules floated past him, under him, over him and behind him meant nothing. The raw stench of gore influenced him not at all. Even more importantly, the adrenaline that had surged through his body when he'd fought ship's security had been carefully drained away by his inner nanonics. The enemy bio-form floated head-down behind him, a trickle of blood still oozing from the torn throat and adding to the floating hemoglobin.

Toll Seven issued the next command through the leads in his fingertips. He'd plugged his first three fingers into computing slots. The converted AI obeyed and locked all inner ship's doors. Toll Seven then slipped a computing cube into the security key. He checked his inner clock. Nine seconds to gassing. Once the IH-49 crew was immobilized, all eighteen of them, he would begin transferring their bodies to his stealth pod. Nothing would be wasted.

"Attention, First Rank," said the AI.

"Yes?"

"Three crew members have exited the ship."

With his broad, seamless face as smooth as ever, Toll Seven slipped a VR monocle over his eye. "Transmit image."

Through virtual reality imaging, he saw the bulky vacc-suits and the twinkling stream of hydrogen spray that propelled them. With a flawless knowledge of the ship's layout, both inner and outer, he realized that they jetted to the laser-link.

His nanonics dumped extra chemicals into his brain and throughout his body. Anger and bewilderment weren't allowed. He considered his options. Gassing would commence in two seconds.

He gave the AI its instructions. Then he pushed off, floated through *Homo sapiens* blood and headed for an airlock. He would have to dispose of these three personally.

4.

Despite the gnawing uneasiness in her gut, the near certainty that Fate had given her this pilot position only to shaft her more deeply, Osadar was awed once again by the sheer gall of her job—no one traveled farther out of the Solar System.

The vast bulk of IH-49 contained fuel for the ion engines. Huge magnetic fields were needed to contain the reaction mass. Thus, fully eighty percent of the ice hauler was fuel tanks and thrusters. It was a long trip into the Oort Cloud to plunder ice comets. The majority of those comets coasted slowly one hundred thousand AU from the Sun. Earth was one AU from the Sun. Neptune was 30.06 AU away. Of course, most of the journey to the Oort Cloud would be made while asleep. Once there and in the name of the IHC, they would crawl over the space debris like a virus, attaching engines, setting up fuel feeders and placing automated missile launchers. It would take many years for the comets to arrive at IHC Pluto Receiving Station. The long history of inter-solar commerce (and piracy) demanded the automated missiles. It was tough work, lonely work, but it would pay well.

The forward part of IH-49 contained the spherical crew hull. To Osadar it seemed as if someone had magnetized the hull and run it over a junkyard. Landers, pods, jacks, missile tubes, coil lines, thruster modules, endless bundles of Wasp 1000 Missiles and a host of engines that would be frozen into the comets had all been attached to the outer hull.

Far to her left winked a green light atop the laser-link. Behind it, dominating space, hung blue Neptune with its few, wispy white cirrus clouds. Triton, the biggest moon, was a black speck against the blue gas giant. The endless space habitats, the majority of them built out of weird ice, weren't visible against Neptune's bulk. Even so, in 2350 A.D. this was humanity's newest frontier, unless one counted the few commercial and scientific outposts on Pluto and Charon.

"Commander!"

"Yes, yes. Spit it out."

Osadar heard both the commander and Technician Geller in her headphone.

"I just lost contact with the LS Officer," Technician Geller said. The LS Officer had remained within the ship.

"What? Impossible." Hysteria edged the commander's gruff voice.

Osadar tried the channel. Zero. She squeezed shut her eyes and forced herself to remain calm. She was gladder than ever she'd taken time to don a zero-G worksuit. Back at the airlock, neither the commander nor Technician Geller had wanted to take the extra effort to get into one. They had donned simple vacc-suits, no doubt figuring a quick look and a wrench could fix what was wrong.

She looked back. Both men dangled in space in their silver vacc-suits. Geller had strapped on a propulsion unit and a tool kit, the commander only a tether. Both men allowed themselves to be dragged by her. Which was simply common sense.

Her worksuit was practically a miniature spaceship. She wore a rigid pressurized cylinder and a transparent helmet dome. The worksuit had an integral thruster pack

156

that contained three hundred seconds of acceleration. Perhaps as importantly, three waldoes—remote-controlled arms—were attached for heavy-duty work. The third waldo mounted an integral laser torch, the other arms had power-locks made to grab onto a ship's hull.

She was beginning to wonder if the worksuit's two weeks of life support wasn't going to be its most important feature.

"Try again," shouted the commander.

Osadar winced, chinning down her speaker's volume. Carefully, she gave a bit of thrust, slightly changing their flight pattern. The two men tethered to her upset the computations. She readjusted and squeezed out a bit more hydrogen. White particles sprayed out of her thrusters. She wasn't rated pilot first class for nothing.

"Is this sabotage?" asked the commander.

"What else could it be?" Osadar asked.

"But how?"

"Or maybe even why?" asked Osadar.

"What?"

"Why bother? All we're doing is getting water for Mars. At least I think that's what Dominie Banbury contracted for."

"Maybe someone wants IHC to renege on its contract," the commander said.

"No," said Technician Geller, "this is inside work. I bet this is part of a takeover."

"Who in the Cartel has the muscle to take on Dominie Banbury?" the commander asked.

"Dominie Yamato—"

"Knows better than to try any of his ninja tricks on Dominie Banbury's projects," the commander growled.

"This does have the feel of something the ninjas would try," Osadar said. During her first weeks of training, they'd pumped her full of Cartel history.

"That's what I'm saying," said Technician Geller.

"Nonsense," said the commander. "The Cartel Dominies aren't fools. To outbid or try a takeover now would be lunacy. There's too much money to be made."

Osadar knew the truth of that. Ever since the Social Unity Government had broken apart in civil war there had been bonanzas of credits to be made supplying both sides. She'd heard the Highborn were winning. Maybe the Highborn didn't want Mars to feed its Atmospheric Converters with trillions of tons of comet-water. For that matter, maybe the Social Unitarians wanted to nix the deal, too. She shrugged. She had no idea what either side really wanted. Thinking about military and political matters only reminded her of all the dead friends she'd lost in the Second Battle of Deep Mars Orbit. And that was something she avoided as much as possible.

What was that buzzing? She checked her headphones, raised gain. The buzzing increased. She lowered gain. Then she raised her eyebrows and turned back toward the commander. He waved frantically and touched his helmet. She waved a waldo arm to show she understood.

Someone jammed communications.

Now what?

Now keep going, she realized, as she stared at the millions of stars around her. In the loneliness of space you don't stop and conjugate, you think and DO before your air runs out. Whomever their enemy was—and this was feeling more and more like creepy ninja work—the enemy knew they were out here. So she had to get to the laser-link and inform IHC what was going on. But if Dominie Yamato was behind this... a cold prickly feeling gnawed her guts. Once she sent the message, well, in her worksuit she would accelerate toward the nearest IHC station and request a pick up from a Dominie Banbury crew. Two weeks of life support would be plenty of time for someone to come and get her. But what about the commander and Technician Geller?

158

Maybe... she licked her lips. Maybe she could convince them to inject themselves with Suspend. Sure, that was a long shot. But they couldn't go back into IH-49 and survive.

Suspend slowed biological functions. It could keep a badly injured person alive longer. If injected into a dying person, it retarded cell death, but only if injected before the heart stopped. That could be critical these days. There was resurrection-after-death with Suspend. Brain thieves used it all the time, supplying black-market chop shops with the needed brain tissue to construct bio-computers.

Osadar tried to calm her jack-hammering heart, but the need for speed compelled her to squeeze more thrust. She held onto the trigger too long. They accelerated away from the hull. She readjusted. Thrust again. They went toward the hull too fast.

"Easy, Osa," she whispered. She concentrated, trying not to listen to the heavy breathing in her ears. Carefully, she squeezed another burst, braking.

She looked back. The commander and Technician Geller gained on her. The tether line was flexible and just because she slowed, didn't mean they did. The commander gathered the extra line, looping it. Good. Smart. He was thinking. But then he was a crusty old space dog. He probably had a plan, would tell her things she should have thought of. Twinkling exhaust sprayed out of Geller's pack. He braked and kept the tether between him and the commander taut.

Osadar shivered. She raised the worksuit temperature. In another few seconds, the commander grabbed her. She had greater bulk in her zero-G worksuit. Still, the shock of the collision jolted her. He clanked his helmet against hers.

"Osadar, can you hear me?"

His voice sounded small and far away, and it was the most glorious sound she'd ever heard. Leave it to the commander to realize they could still talk.

"I can hear you."

He patted her shoulder, then maneuvered so they saw eye to eye. His skin looked pale, and his fear added to hers. She almost asked him if he had any Suspend. Of course, he did, but then he'd have to ask her why she asked. As he attached his vacc-suit to her, she eyed the nearing beacon. Soon they would know the worst. She turned to Technician Geller—

Something caught her eye, something dark and fast, hard to see. Geller must've seen it too. Hydrogen spray billowed out of his tanks. It was too late. He jerked sharply at the waist. Mist blew out of his vacc-suit, and then blood and the gory innards of what had once been Technician Geller. The vacuum of space was ruthless.

Osadar shuddered in terror.

With a jerk, the commander unhooked Geller's line from him. Then he clanked his helmet against hers.

"To the right, by the exhaust port."

Osadar scanned the area. She was going to be sick. Then her eyes narrowed as something moved. She shrieked.

A man with a skintight, almost rubber suit leaped in their direction, even though he had to be over three thousand meters away. He sailed for them, gaining fast.

"Hang on!" she screamed at the commander.

She squeezed thrust in controlled bursts when what she really wanted was to hold the trigger down and blast off. But she was too much a pilot for that; too trained in ways she couldn't change. The man cradled something in his arms that looked like a spear gun. He aimed it at them.

Osadar swung the waldo laser around. It was meant for repair work, but in a fix could double as a close-quarters weapon.

"You think he's a robot?" the commander asked.

"He doesn't look like a bot."

"Not even a Highborn is powerful enough to accelerate that fast in a single bound."

Osadar should have thought of that. The man came on fast nonetheless, his weapon tracking them. The tip of the "spear" was a half-moon blade, as if it was meant to rip open spacesuits and let vacuum do the dirty work.

Osadar understood none of this as she moaned dreadfully. Leaping men with spear guns didn't make any kind of sense in space. He would pass harmlessly underneath them by fifty meters—she'd easily maneuvered out of his flight path. She rotated her zero-G suit to keep the commander away from the gun. Her worksuit couldn't be breached by something as primitive as a spring-driven spear.

The man—if man he was—removed the half-moon crescent blade and attached what looked like an adhesive pad. He aimed and fired, and a filament line trailed the pad. It attached to the foot of her suit. He pressed a stud and reeled himself toward them.

Osadar shrieked again and swung the laser arm. It couldn't reach the spidery line! Her stomach went hollow as she readjusted the laser, aiming it at... what was he?

Through his faceplate, he looked like a robot with shiny flesh, with fake human eyes. He neither smiled nor grinned nor scowled nor frowned. He watched them impassively as he approached, the way a lizard might watch as it sunned itself on a rock.

Osadar clenched her teeth and turned on the laser. It harmlessly beamed past him. For with his arms alone, on the rifle that reeled him in, he swung his body forward, out of the way of the laser, and let go. He propelled himself through space. He wore no security line or any pack other than a slim breathing tank. If he missed them, he'd sail off into space. The risk—no spacer could do that so effortlessly and without a change of expression.

With a pry bar that he'd taken off her suit, the commander jabbed at the man's faceplate. Their enemy latched onto the bar and pulled himself upon the commander. He slid something thin and bright into the commander's suit.

Osadar twisted within her rigid cylinder to see what was happening. The commander's face grew slack. His eyes fluttered.

Grimly, she swung the work-laser.

The man pulled another of his uncanny maneuvers, and sailed upside down over the laser-arm and above her helmet. She craned her neck to look up at him. His fingers were long and spider-like. He reached out. She flinched away from his fingers. Then she grinned tightly. His would be an effort in futility to try to latch onto her bubble helmet. Then, to her horror, small adhesive pads on his fingertips pressed onto her helmet top. With a jerk, it stopped his flight. Gracefully, like a perfect killer, he brought himself parallel with her as if they were lovers. He stared at her. There was no gloating or triumph, no 'Did you see that?' in his eyes. He stared impassively. Anyone but this obvious non-human would have crinkled up the corners of his lips. She'd never see such flawless, uncanny, zero-G maneuvering, and she'd been around plenty of hardened space-hounds.

Although vomit burned the back of her throat, although she knew it wouldn't matter, she brought up a waldo clamp to try to crush him. It wasn't in her to go down without a fight.

He shoved a gleaming steel needle into her elbow. She yelled. Then a great weariness settled over her. *Why*, she wondered. Why go to so much trouble when a simple plasma rifle could've taken care of everything? It didn't make any kind of sense.

5.

Like some obscene, overgrown monkey, Toll Seven rode the zero-G worksuit, braking with particles of hydrogen spray as he brought both captives to his ultra-stealth pod. The vessel was as black as night and spherical, and only a little larger than an old-style garbage Dumpster of the Twentieth Century. The ceramic hull gave the lowest sensor signature of any vessel in human space, and it was crammed with the latest Onoshi Electronic Counter-Measure equipment and decoys.

He floated them into the cargo bay. The Suspend would keep them in the suits, so he simply latched them to a rack and then went back for the others in the ship.

An hour later, he closed the cargo bay. Except for the slain security officer and the technician he'd let vacuum explode, all of IH-49's crew lay like wood in his ship. He entered his command module and set course for home. He timed his burst with the first long burn of IH-49's famed ion engines. The ice hauler would make the trip to the Oort Cloud, but without any crew.

Toll Seven shut off his engine. He would coast for a week. He shut down contemplation mode and instantly entered deep sleep.

6.

Much of Greater Sydney burned out of control. The rest was shambles. Millions wandered the tunnels and ruined levels. Millions more hovered on the brink of dehydration, ready to join the hundreds of thousands of dead. To rebuild Sydney would take months. The Highborn presently fought a cunning campaign to save what they had.

First, they accessed the city's backup computers. Then they declared a general amnesty. Surviving police and SU bureaucrats could keep their old jobs, provided they came to Highborn Mobile HQ in the next two days and declared themselves. Most did, thankfully. It was so much easier to plug trained personnel back into their old jobs than to train someone else who had no idea how to lead. The returning police officers were immediately put in charge of the clean-up crews: which consisted of any able-bodied person healthy enough to work. The former ward, block and hall leaders found themselves given a day's stiff indoctrination, and then set in charge of fabrication and housing. Superintendents and all former SU secretaries ran the new government under Highborn dictates. "Excellence brings rewards," was the first basic slogan, "Life goes on," the second.

The Highborn divided Sydney's populace into three categories. Category one, the highest ranked, was all Free Earth Corps (FEC) volunteers, munitions workers and deep-core personnel. Category two was police, housing, clean up and transport. Category three was everyone else. Rations and chits were given accordingly.

After several days, a semblance of order settled over Greater Sydney. That's when Marten slipped out of the temporary FEC barracks. It happened after the Highborn took Ah Chen. They'd found out she was deep-core. The new rulers only had a few of those and they desperately needed to keep the deep-core mine running.

"You'll be shot," said Stick, after Marten told them he was leaving.

"I've got to find her," Marten said.

"Why?" asked Turbo.

"They didn't ask her if she wanted to go," Marten said angrily. "They just took her."

"So?" asked Turbo. "What can you do about it?"

"That's what I'm going to find out," Marten said.

Omi held out his hand. "Luck."

Marten solemnly shook the ex-gunman's hand. After that, Stick and Turbo shook his hand.

"Stay alive," said Stick.

Marten nodded, and then he turned and walked out of the barracks. It had been as easy as that. The Highborn had posted all the names of the FEC volunteers. They had warned the volunteers that if any of them were caught outside the barracks they would be shot. But Marten had a plan. It was tested two hours later when a police sweep caught him in the middle of a rubble-strewn street, four levels down from the barracks.

"Name?" growled a heavyset, sweating cop. He had a shock rod on his belt, but no stunner or needler. Those had been deposited in Highborn vaults. Two other cops waited behind the older, bald man. They had large plastic shields, batons and wore riot helmets and grim scowls. Dust and sweat slicked their faces. Their uniforms smelled like smoke.

Marten hesitated.

"Give me your name," repeated the heavyset cop as he wiped his sleeve across his forehead. The main air-conditioners worked at ten percent power. From level ten down, the air was stale and much too warm.

"I'm in maintenance," Marten said, and he tried to stroll away.

The two cops with the plastic shields stepped in his path, one of them shoving him back.

The sweating, heavyset cop scowled and took out a rag to mop his face. "Are you a troublemaker?"

Marten shook his head.

"Then give us your name," said the cop who'd pushed him with his shield.

Hoping this worked—it had better—Marten gave then a fictitious name, from one of his mother's forged passports from the Sun-Works Factory. The Highborn had downloaded Sydney's computers and those computers had been linked throughout the Inner Planets.

The older, sweating cop stuffed his rag in his back pocket and unhooked a hand computer, punching the fictitious name into the database. He squinted at Marten as it processed.

Realizing suddenly that this might not work, Marten sidled near the cop who had pushed him. His heart beat faster as he tensed.

The unit beeped and the sweating cop examined it. "This is odd. It says you work in food processing, not maintenance."

Marten went limp. The old names still held.

The other cop said, "You're a liar. They should send you to the slime pits for that."

"Quiet!" snapped the heavy, sweating cop. "That's... that's old-style talk."

The other cop suddenly looked scared.

The heavier cop faced Marten. "Maybe later they'll put you in maintenance. For now head east two blocks until you reach Work Gang Twenty-seven. Tell the foreman Sergeant Jones sent you. And don't skip out, boy. Otherwise it's the firing squad for you."

Marten walked briskly east. But once out of their sight, he turned north. If he were picked up again, he'd have to use a different forged name.

Yet for all his vigilance, another police sweep picked him up two levels down. He used another fake name—he only had two more—and this time couldn't get out of clean up. So for the next few hours he loaded broken concrete and plasteel onto a lifter. It was hard, sweaty work, done under the watchful eye of a former block leader. At the end of the shift, they received a ration of water and a crust of algae bread.

Marten sat with a group of other tired men. They either sprawled on the ground or sat on broken concrete blocks, guzzling the water and chewing the week-old bread.

"Back to work!" said the foreman, clapping his hands to show that he wanted them to move quickly.

Marten rose. Nothing had changed. These men were still ready to bleat to whoever was in charge. The only ones who seemed willing to fight... were the slum dwellers, he realized in surprise. Maybe he would be better off rejoining Turbo, Stick and Omi.

No. He wanted to see Ah Chen again and hunt for Molly. So he worked along the fringe of the group, and then a little farther away yet. The former block leader glared at him, his moist eyes shining. Then the foreman stamped elsewhere. Marten edged a little farther from that spot, checked and saw that no one watched. He strode away briskly.

"Halt!" shouted a cop, who stepped from behind a standing half wall.

Marten broke into a sprint.

"Stop!" roared the cop, and others gave chase.

Marten found it difficult to breathe in the stale, hot air. He was glad the police didn't have any stunners or needlers.

Gasping, he stopped a level later, his throat and chest aching because of the polluted air. How in the world was he going to find Ah Chen or Molly like this?

7.

Marten thought up a strategy thirty minutes later. It happened as he stumbled upon a snoozing cop. Marten had slunk careful through a rubble-strewn street, and ducked behind a building when he heard voices. Then he heard snoring, and to his amazement, he saw an overweight old man sleeping on a cot. It was hot, and the old man had taken off his police shirt, helmet and heavy utility belt. Inspired, Marten took the three items, hurried away and a few blocks later donned the old man's garments.

He tested his plan several blocks later. A squad of three police doing a routine sweep marched toward him. With his helmet on, dark visor lowered, and with his hand on the shock baton swinging at his belt, Marten swaggered toward them. It brought back haunting memories of how his father had once tricked Sun-Works personnel.

"You!" he bellowed. "Report!"

The three men stiffened to attention.

"I said report!" Marten shouted in his best imitation police voice.

"We've rounded up four stragglers, sir," said the sergeant.

"Just four?" Marten asked angrily. "This area crawls with refugees. Find them. Or soon you'll be busting rubble."

They hurried off. With his hands on his hips, Marten watched them go. When they were out of sight, he sighed with pent-up fear and went his own way. Just like in the old days on the Sun-Works Factory circling Mercury, the very audacity of the ploy had protected him. No one would dare impersonate a police inspector; at least no one raised on Social Unity credos.

He reached the Deep-Core Station that he'd entered what seemed a lifetime ago, and he waited until he saw a brown-uniformed deep-core worker strolling home. The man looked young and wore shiny black boots. He smoked the stimstick that seemed habitual with deep-core workers and had an arrogant way of holding his shoulders. Marten trailed him, waiting until no one else was in sight. Then he strode quickly, catching the man unawares.

"You!" Marten said, grabbing him by the shoulder and spinning him around.

The man glowered. "Don't you know who I am? Take your grubby hands off me this instant."

Marten drew the shock rod and touched the man's neck.

With a scream, the deep-core worker fell to the ground, twitching.

Marten felt sorry for him but was certain this was the only way he could gain the needed information. He kicked the deep-core worker in the side, but not too hard.

"You're a straggler!" Marten shouted.

"No!" howled the man.

"Liar," Marten shouted, kicking him again.

The worker covered up. "Please, don't hurt me."

Marten hauled him to his feet, the shock rod poised for a beating.

"I'm a Deep-Core Worker," the man wailed.

"Prove it."

The man dug a wallet from his pants pocket.

"Bah," Marten said, knocking it out of the man's hands. "Fake IDs don't interest me."

The man's eyes boggled. "No one fakes Deep-Core IDs."

"Who is Ah Chen?" Marten barked.

"What?" the man asked, bewildered.

"So you don't know."

"Wait. Yes, yes, I know Ah Chen. S-She's Deep-Core."

Marten barked harsh laughter.

"She's a Third Grade Engineer. They sent her down this morning."

"Down?"

"To the deep station."

Marten's stomach knotted. "For how long is she down?"

"Why do you want to know that?" asked the man, suddenly suspicious.

Marten slapped him across the face instead of using the shock rod again. "You're a straggler."

"She's down permanently, or until they train her replacement. Please, you've got to believe me."

A cold sinking feeling filled Marten. Ah Chen had told him that Major Orlov had slain almost all the deep-core personnel in Sydney. The Highborn would dearly need the deep-core running if Sydney and the outlying areas were to have power. She'd feared the Highborn would take her and send her down-station for a long time, and she'd been right. There was nothing Marten could do for her now.

Marten shoved the man away. "Run."

"What?" asked the bewildered man.

"Run!" roared Marten, raising the baton as if to swing.

The man took off running, slipping and stumbling until he ran out of sight.

Disgusted with his methods and depressed that Ah Chen was gone from him for a very long time, Marten stalked off in the opposite direction. How long could he keep on running and pretending? Maybe long enough to find Molly, he decided.

8.

Transcript #30,512 Highborn Archives: of an exchange of notes between Paenus, Inspector General, Earth, and Cassius, Grand Admiral of Highborn. Dates: February 1 to February 7, 2350.

February 1
To Paenus:
Disaster was barely averted in Sydney. A court of Inquiry thus convenes on the Twenty-fourth concerning it and other anomalies regarding the Australian Campaign. Whether you are in the dock or on the bench remains to be seen.

Luckily, for you, the suicide squadrons were able to breach stubborn city strongholds. Reports indicate that cortex-bomb-laden Earth troops preformed best in this regard. Surprisingly, renegade police personnel showed an avid bloodthirstiness when pitched against Social Unity security forces. Because of these specialist troops, Highborn casualties remained within the accepted limits during the underground city fighting. I am recommending a hundred and fifty percent increase in the number of suicide troops.

That is, however, the only bright spot regarding your premen troops. The Hawk Teams and panzer crews—I wish to remind the Inspector General of staking his reputation upon them if they were given the right training. The Hawk Teams and panzer crews have failed miserably. They lacked adequate zeal and cunning, while the casualties among the Hawk Teams were simply staggering. The panzer crews were worse: timid in the attack and cowardly during exploitation maneuvers. Because of this, Highborn casualties *exceeded* the acceptable limits during the first half of the Australian campaign.

I await your explanations and your plans in order to avoid this in the future, provided you have one, my dear Paenus.

February 3
To Cassius:
Grand Admiral, please forgive my delay in answering. My training personnel are strained to the limit and I am overloaded. We badly need more Highborn drill lieutenants and captains. As it is, I have been forced to take veteran Earth troops off line to use as instructors. Their veteran status is dubious at best, as you indicated in your letter. Earthlings lack fiber and fighting ferocity—I had simply not realized the extent of their non-Highborn qualities. To instill this into them is daunting in the extreme.

One might as well take sheep and teach them to be wolves. The best we can do is to find the rams among them. Unfortunately, we must comb through thousands in order to find one who has the fire. As might be expected, the former policemen have more fire than the rank and file Social Unitarians.

Grand Admiral, despite these grave flaws, I believe the Hawk and panzer teams will improve from campaign to campaign. The very nature of their specialty takes longer to gain mastery than suicide troops. Suicide troops are not so much rigorously trained as highly motivated to make frontal charges. My records indicate that the best suicide troop results came after double doses of Shaker were force-injected. Some suggest we inject Shaker into all our troops. I highly recommend AGAINST this. Hawk and panzer personnel are seldom composed of former policemen, and I believe would become listless and inclined to apathy if faced with forced injections. The Hawk Team and panzer crews wish to live through the conflict and take up civilian occupations afterward.

Rather than point fingers, Grand Admiral, I suggest we thank the Fates that the worst disasters *were* avoided and that we now take extreme measures to ensure they never occur again.

February 3
To Paenus:

Request for extra Highborn denied.

The Inspector General surely realizes that all troops are readying for the next campaign. Social Unity is on the run. We must maintain pressure. Nor do I accept your excuses for listless Hawk and panzer teams. What you've really said is that they are not properly motivated. Motivate them, my dear Paenus, and train them to fight!

February 4
To Cassius:

I will comply as best I can, Grand Admiral. But the number of recruits has swamped my resources. I suggest we make thorough tests for aggressiveness and combat ability, skimming the cream, so to speak, and train the remainder as fire fighters and other emergency personnel.

February 5
To Paenus:

I simply don't understand you sometimes. War on this scale devours vast amounts of troops. Highborn casualties *must* remain within the accepted limits or we will lose. Anything else is superfluous. As it is impossible to advance without sustaining heavy losses, we *must* continue to absorb those losses among our Earth troops. Think of them as fodder, if it will clarify their true function.

If you lack enough training personnel, I suggest you throw the recruits into battle and let the war train them.

Yes, many units will break under the pressure, and yes, they will sustain excessive casualties. So you must rush them through basic training, discover the fighters and make them corporals and sergeants. The units that survive and perform above average will then be pulled out and retrained as Hawk and panzer troops. Use this promise of renewed training as a reward.

Please note the attached New Free Earth Corps unit configuration schedule. High Command has agreed that we must use this influx of volunteers to *push* Social Unity. Train them to fire their weapons, the corporals and sergeants to attack. We must maintain pressure. First grade levies, as they are now officially termed, can sustain one hundred percent casualties as long as they inflict harm upon the enemy.

February 6
To Cassius:
I hear and obey, and may I add, Grand Admiral, that as always your advice is flawless.

I wish to add a note of caution, however. One hundred percent casualties, over time, will undoubtedly cause a decrease in Earth volunteers. I understand the logic of mass wave assaults with expendable troops, behind which our men can maneuver. But surely, Grand Admiral, we must consider what effect this will have later in the War for Earth.

February 7
To Paenus:
Just train your volunteers into fighting troops, Inspector General. That's all I ask.

9.

Marten hit upon the daring idea because he couldn't think of anything else that would give him a reasonable chance of quick success. So the next time he came upon a police sweep, he halted them and snatched the hand computer from the sergeant. Then he punched in Molly Tan's name. A few seconds scan and it gave her occupation as secretary to Highborn Government. Surprised, Marten noted her work place. It was very near the FEC barracks. How had Molly been able to enter government work? She hadn't been a hall, block or ward leader, or…

A troubled feeling spread in Marten's stomach.

"What's wrong?" asked the police sergeant. He was the one Marten had taken the hand monitor from.

"What? Oh." Marten thrust the computer back. "I must report to Highborn HQ."

That shook the three policemen, who had turned suspicious. They hurried from the man that dared go to the bastion of Highborn power.

Marten made his way up the various levels, wondering what he would do if Molly were living with Quirn. That was the only possible explanation for Molly getting a secretary's job in the new Highborn government. As he walked, he thought about all the times they'd enjoyed together, how he'd wanted to marry her. He'd never taken her to bed. In retrospect he wondered if that had been a mistake. He kept telling himself that it was impossible she'd shacked up with Quirn. Blake would have brayed at him, he knew. Good old Blake the disembodied brain. He wondered if Tunnel Crawler Six was still operational. Blake had always told him, "Women follow the power, Marten."

In his daze and without being accosted, Marten made it near the surface levels. The data had said Government House Three. He lowered his helmet's dark visor, drew the shock baton and patrolled in front of the government house. He periodically spoke into his sleeve as if making reports and he watched the arrogant, giant Highborn enter and leave the pseudo-marble building. Tanks were parked in front. Fortunately, the Highborn Military Police ignored him as beneath their notice. They tramped around in their bulky powered armor, immune to everyone.

What kind of future did he have under the Highborn?

Marten shrugged, and prowled. Two hours later, he saw Quirn. The former hall leader still wore a military cap, but he'd shed his block leader cape. He wore a black uniform and limped with his old arrogance. On his arm chatted Molly, just as she used to chat with him as they'd ridden the conveyers. She wore a business suit and a military style cap similar to Quirn's.

Marten stared, transfixed as they strolled near. He heard Molly say, "And then I told him, 'but we must have the pits processing by nine tomorrow.'"

"Maybe they'll send criminals to work the pits," said Quirn.

"Quirn," chided Molly, "that's careless talk."

"Yes, you're right." Quirn gave her a quick kiss on the lips. Then he looked up to see a black-visored policeman staring at him.

179

The former hall leader stopped. Molly did too, also looking up.

"Trouble, officer?" asked Quirn.

Marten simply stared at him, his fingers squeezing his shock rod so hard that his hand hurt. He wanted to beat Quirn to death. Then, minutely, he shifted his gaze to Molly.

"Do I know you?" asked Molly.

Marten had no idea what to say. He slowly shook his head.

"You seem familiar," she said.

"Humph!" said Quirn. "Come, Molly, we don't want to be late for tonight's meeting."

Molly agreed, and they moved on, although Molly looked back once with a worried frown.

Marten wanted to howl, to beat his head against a wall. Molly... despair filled him. How could she? Marten finally swallowed the lump out of his throat. What was left? Nothing in Greater Sydney. He stood there for five minutes, rooted. Then he turned abruptly and headed for the FEC barracks. He was going to slip back among his friends.

10.

In the morning, training began. Marten viewed the training as the descent of man, even though Highborn theories proved antithetical to Social Unity. Marten's awareness of the change of basic assumptions didn't come right away. First, the volunteers from Greater Sydney took a medical examination. Marten endured the probes and pinches, but he hated it.

He donned his clothes afterward and exited through the door the doctor told him. Marten walked down a hall and entered a small room. A huge, uniformed Highborn, an angry-looking giant without any front teeth, scowled down at him. Like all their kind, this man radiated intensity and a heightened vitality. He seemed an auto-trash compacter, eager to crush and destroy. This close to him and in such tight confines, Marten grew tense and worried.

"You believe yourself capable of combat?" the Highborn rapped out angrily.

Marten nodded.

"Speak up, man! Don't cower!"

"Yes," Marten growled.

The Highborn sneered. And he rapid-fired a bewildering set of questions, edging closer the entire time.

After the first few questions, Marten refused to be drawn into a debate. He answered as best he could, and he tried to ignore the superior attitude and the too-close proximity. The giant made it difficult. He was towering, and he was probably three times Marten's weight and was undoubtedly four or five times as strong. His uniform, some type of synthetic leather, crinkled at his movements and showed his lethal muscularity. The snow-white skin seemed much too bright, the face formed of sharp angles and rigid planes. Decidedly inhuman, Marten thought to himself. He didn't like the arrogance. It was more than just the giant's position and power. It reminded him of Major Orlov. The Highborn exuded superiority, as if he, Marten, were simple and cowardly. Despite his best resolve, Marten found himself getting angry at the man's attitude. The Highborn giant loomed closer now and practically yelled down at him.

"No, no!" the Highborn shouted. "Wrong!" And he slapped Marten across the face.

Marten reacted before he could check himself. He lunged at the giant. Then he found himself grabbed by the arm, flipped and slammed onto the floor, hard. It knocked the wind out of him. As Marten struggled to rise, the Highborn picked a marker off the table, held Marten's right hand firmly and stamped the back of his hand. Then the giant picked him up, set him on his feet and propelled him stumbling out of the room and into a new corridor.

The door slammed behind him as Marten's lungs unlocked. He blinked in bewilderment and thought about going back. Then he heard the Highborn holler a question at what sounded like the next recruit. What had just happened? Marten checked the back of his hand. A large number 2 had been stamped there. He touched it.

"Move along," a voice barked through a hidden loudspeaker.

Marten scowled, but he followed the arrows painted on the floor. He came to a holding area, looked for and found Omi, Stick and Turbo. Before they could say much, Highborn herded them toward a parking lot filled with sealed vans. They were hustled onto the vans according to familiarity. Thus, Marten found himself packed with a hundred odd slum dwellers. But not just any slum dwellers, but the gang-members that lived by the fist, blade and gun. Stick and Turbo greeted several old friends. Two drug-running gunmen shook Omi's hand.

Aboard the bus, most of the talk was about the numbers on the back of their right hand. Turbo wore a four. Stick a three. Omi also had a two. They couldn't see anyone with a one. Of fives, sixes and sevens, well, that's what the majority wore.

"What's it mean?" Turbo said, as he rested his head along the side of the van.

The huge vehicle hummed smoothly. The benches on the sides and down the middle were packed with gang members. Each wore the clothes he'd joined with and nothing else, no suitcases, no personal items, nothing.

"Yeah," Stick was saying, "is it better to have a low number or a high one?"

"Marten and I have twos," said Omi.

"So?"

The bullet-headed Korean regarded his hand. At lot of other people were doing the same things. So far, no one had been able to rub out the number, even though many spat on the back of their hand and scrubbed vigorously.

"It's under the skin," growled Marten, who hated the tattoo.

"Seems like most people have higher numbers," Stick said. He'd scanned those around him and across the narrow aisle at those in the middle.

Turbo grunted and rubbed his cheek. "I don't know about the rest of you, but that guy sure clocked me a good one."

"He hit you too?" asked Stick in surprise.

That's when they discovered they'd all been face-slapped.

"Do you think that has anything to do with our number?" Marten asked, wondering if the Highborn's anger hadn't been at him but merely routine. Had it been a test?

Omi arched his eyebrows. "What did you do after he hit you?" he asked Marten.

"Attacked the bastard."

"You're kidding," said Turbo. "He was huge."

Marten shrugged. He was still a bit bemused by what he'd done. "I didn't really think about it. I just found myself lunging at him."

"Not me," said Stick. "I figured he was just waiting for me to do something stupid so he could beat me to death. I figured he was testing for obedience, whether I could take orders I didn't like."

"So what did you do?" Turbo asked.

"Hey, what could I do? The guy towered over me, and he was deciding my future, right? I told him give me my knife to even the odds and let's try that again."

"What did he say to that?" asked Turbo.

"Nothing. He just grabbed my hand and stamped a three on it."

"Huh."

"What did you do?" Marten asked the lanky junkie.

"I told him that was a lousy thing to do. Here they wanted me to fight for them and first thing they did was abuse me. How did he expect me to go all out for them if that's what they were gonna do?"

"And he stamped your hand with a four?"

"Sure did," Turbo said, restudying the big number four on the back of his hand.

"Omi?" asked Stick.

"I tried a chop at this neck." Omi asked Marten, "What did he do when you attacked him?"

"He flipped me onto my back."

The ex-gunman nodded sagely.

"He do the same thing to you?" Turbo asked.

Ignoring the question, Omi regarded his tattoo. He looked up. "It would be interesting to know what a number one did."

"If there is such a number," Marten said.

Stick scanned the crowd. "Might be dangerous to try to find out."

"How come?" Marten asked.

"Couple different gangs in here," said Stick. "Kwon's Crew is over there. And I see Slicks and Ball Busters."

"Yeah," said Turbo, jutting his chin toward the front, "and over there is Kang of the Red Blades."

Marten saw a massive Mongol with black tattoos on his arms. No one sat too close to him. He had flat, evil-looking features, with eyes almost slit shut.

Omi stood and started walking there.

"Idiot!" hissed Stick. "Come back before you start a rumble."

Omi ignored the advice.

"Them gunmen are all alike," Turbo whispered to Marten. "They think they can do whatever they want."

They watched Omi wade past the other gang members, who glowered uneasily. Omi ignored them, moving slowly and deliberately toward Kang of the Red Blades. When he reached the forward area, Omi bowed his head. Massive Kang simply stared at him with his almost closed eyes. His flat, blank-looking face was unreadable. Omi showed him his hand, and then he bowed again and seemed to ask a question. Everyone in the van watched

185

what Kang would do, some in anticipation. Finally, the huge killer showed Omi his hand. Omi bowed his head again and turned. A sigh, a release of tension, drained from everyone. Soon Omi took his place back between Marten and Turbo.

"Well?" whispered Turbo. "What was his number?"

"One."

"What he do when slapped?" asked Stick.

"He said he waited. And when the Highborn reached for his stamp he slapped him across the face."

"You're kidding?" Stick said in awe. "Then what happened?"

"Then Kang said the Highborn set down the stamp he'd picked up and chose another one, the one."

"Did the Highborn flip him?" asked Stick.

"I didn't ask."

"Yeah," Turbo said, "that was probably smart."

Marten thought about the numbers and why they'd been given different ones. He spoke to several other men sitting nearby. They had sixes and sevens. He found they hadn't done much of anything when slapped. What were they going to do to a killer giant anyway? Marten had agreed. A two, was that bad or good? He glanced at the huge, flat-faced Mongol Kang who held court in his part of the van. A two was almost a one. So the Highborn thought he was a lot more like a vicious gang leader than the more harmless sixes and sevens. He wasn't sure he liked the implications.

After several hours, the smooth van came to a halt. The doors swung open and two towering Highborn in powered battle armor gestured for them to hurry out. They did, forming two long lines around a parade ground as more vans disgorged their occupants. All of the recruits were Sydney slum-dwellers.

They were in the desert, several low-built concrete buildings around them. Barracks, no doubt. In all directions stretched a red sand desert. Here and there, gusts of wind stirred up sand. Marten noticed most of the recruits squinted at the harsh overhead sun just as he did. Most of them had probably never been in sunlight before. It was hot—nothing like being underground in carefully selected temperatures. Sweat prickled Marten's underarms.

"This is great," Turbo whispered, who tugged at an already damp collar.

With servos whining, the two Highborn clanked to the center of the parade ground as the convoy of empty vans roared away along the single ribbon of road. Marten figured that maybe six hundred other men stood under the sweltering sun. A squad of beefy Earth soldiers in combat vests and armed with machineguns jogged out of the nearest building onto the edge of the field.

"Regular men," whispered Turbo. All around the field slum-dwellers whispered likewise.

"Silence!"

Everyone fell silent. One of the Highborn had spoken.

Finally, a huge man strode out of barracks. He had to be at least seven feet tall. He was shorter than the Highborn and not quite as muscled. He wore a black cap, uniform and combat boots, with a knife and pistol on a heavy belt. His face was hawkish, with a long, knife-like nose. He didn't really walk, Marten decided, but strutted, knowing that he was putting on a show. There was something odd about his features; something twisted, out of kilter. Maybe it was his eyes, too focused, or the little superior grin that kept twitching into place.

He took his place in front of the squad of armed Earthlings. He clasped his hands behind his back and scanned the slum dwellers. There was some of that strange vitality to him that all Highborn seemed to have. Yet....

"Greetings, premen. I'm Captain Sigmir of Training Camp Ninety-three C. I will drill you into competent

187

combat soldiers within six weeks or I'll see you dead. On the seventh week, you will undoubtedly enter combat of the most ruthless sort. Whether I learn to like you or not is meaningless. You are in an army run by Highborn. I wish therefore to reassure you about nothing. What I will say now is perhaps the most important aspect of Highborn philosophy that you will ever learn," he said, pausing to look at them all. "Remember this: *Excellence brings rewards.*"

Captain Sigmir paused as he inspected the recruits.

Marten noticed that twitching smile again, and the almost hungry way Captain Sigmir watched them. There was something strange going on here.

"Let me say again," said Captain Sigmir: "Excellence brings rewards. In terms of your enlistment, the ability and willingness to kill the enemy is what counts. Little else matters. Neither the...." He seemed to choose his words with care. "Neither the 'end product' Highborn nor I care about your opinions. Think what you like, as long as you kill the enemy. As long as you are proficient at arms, as long as you obey orders on the instant, yes, then you may say or think what you like. Oh, but if you are not excellent, if you are not proficient at arms..."

Captain Sigmir shook his head. Then he removed his cap. He was bald, and an ugly, twisted red scar slashed across his upper forehead. He touched it.

"You notice this, I'm sure. I received it in combat. It killed me." He laughed a little too shrilly as they stared and gaped. "Yes, yes, I assure you I died. Enemy shrapnel tore through my helmet and into my brain. Fortunately, I didn't die on the instant. A fellow officer shot me full of Suspend. I'm sure you've heard how the Highborn are very careful to...." He laughed in that weird way again. "They call it revive, but really it's resurrection from the dead. They fixed my brain as best as possible, restarted my body and—" He leered at them, his grin transfixed.

"Here I am, alive again so I may fight again and possibly die again. My reflexes and thinking aren't quite what they used to be, but who am I to complain? I assure you I'm not that sort of ingrate. Yes, I can still train. Thus, I am proficient at something. Thus, the superiors still give me rank as well as life. You too can gain rank by excellence. Now, an example is in order."

Captain Sigmir put the cap back on and began to strut down the line of recruits. Most averted their gaze. A few dared look into his strange eyes, Marten being one of them. One fellow shivered in dreadful fear. The captain stopped in front of him.

"Show me your hand," the captain said softly.

Trembling, the lad did. He was skinny and shallow-faced, with rounded shoulders.

"A nine," said the captain. He tugged the lad with him into the center of the parade ground. Every eye was riveted upon them. The two armored Highborn clanked to the opposite end of the field as the squad of normal soldiers.

Captain Sigmir let go of the lad's hand and took several steps away from him. "What is your name?"

"Logan," whispered the lad.

"Say it louder!"

"L-Logan."

Captain Sigmir nodded as he scanned the throng around him. The twitchy smile was now firmly in place. "Logan, do you know how to fight?"

The lad looked up at that. He was red-faced and obviously scared. "Yeah, I guess."

"Good. I want you to defend yourself."

"What?"

Captain Sigmir tossed his hat aside and unbuckled his belt, dropping his pistol and knife. "I said defend yourself." He stepped toward the boy, towering over him.

Logan backed up, confused and more scared than ever, although he lifted his fists. Against the huge captain, it was a pitiful gesture.

"In this army, Logan, if you can't fight then you're worth nothing at all."

Logan shook his head.

The captain shouted and kicked. His booted foot swept through Logan's two fists to strike the center of his chest. Logan crashed to the ground. Captain Sigmir calmly walked to him and proceeded to kick young Logan to death. The boy tried to knock the iron-toed boots aside, until several of his teeth went flying. Then small Logan curled up into a fetal ball, whimpering and pleading through bloodied lips. Sweat glistened on Captain Sigmir's face. His scar shone bright red, his strange eyes gleamed and a smile jumped into place every time his boot connected.

During the beating, several men in line grew very tense. One of them finally roared with rage and sprinted at Captain Sigmir, who had his back to the man while he kicked Logan across the side of the head. One of the Earth soldiers smoothly bent to one knee, lifted his carbine and fired a single shot. The enraged man grunted and slammed onto his back, his chest exploding in gore and blood.

Captain Sigmir didn't bother turning around. Instead, he gave Logan a few more kicks until the frail boy relaxed onto his back, dead.

Two soldiers handed their carbines to another in the armed squad. Then they jogged to Captain Sigmir and saluted crisply. The captain nodded as he dabbed his face with a rag. He lifted an eyebrow as he saw the other dead man, but he made no comment. Each soldier grabbed a dead man by the feet and dragged them away.

The recruits, the majority of whom had grown tense, were clearly terrified of huge Captain Sigmir. They whispered their fear, eyeing the two armored Highborn and the watchful soldiers.

"He's insane," Stick hissed to Marten.

"Poor Logan," whispered Turbo.

Marten noticed that Omi and Kang seemed unconcerned, almost as if they understood what had happened. A few others like them, hard-faced recruits, also watched impassively. Marten wondered if they too had once been gunmen like Omi. He shook his head. Here was the primary lesson. Killers ruled among the Highborn. Become excellent killers and they'd pat you on the back. Suddenly he wanted to be far away from here. But that wasn't an option. He was trapped again. He felt that turmoil in his gut again. He could sure use a bottle of synthahol.

Captain Sigmir tucked away his rag. "It may interest you to know that I originated from Lot Six. I was one of the experimental firsts. They called us *beta* Highborn. At the time, it was said that the eugenicists were quite pleased with their efforts. But...." Captain Sigmir glanced at the armored Highborn across the field. "Alas, beta is not superior. Still, a few of us are around; and now they've found a place for us—for us... *misfits*." He peered at the two, nine-foot tall, armored Highborn. Then he shrugged and faced the men. "Perhaps I am not a superior, but here, as long as I produce well-trained recruits, I may indulge myself in life's little pleasures. Providing, of course, I avoid unnecessary wastage.

"Now, let me assure you that poor young Logan would never have made a good soldier. His hand had been stamped a nine, the only nine among you, I might add. It meant that he was extremely passive with little to no cunning." The captain shrugged. "What kind of soldier is passive and without cunning? A soon to be dead soldier. So you see that Logan would have been useless in combat terms. But he still provided use as an example. As such, let us remember Logan. Uselessness brings death. Excellence, well, it provides rank and higher training. Your training here will be hard. Many of you will die, never to rise again. My advice is to make certain you don't become a useless Logan—or don't lose your balance and attack a superior officer. That isn't merely useless, that is rank insubordination. Death is the only reward for that sort of lunacy.

"Also, I wish to address one more issue before you're assigned barracks. Each of you volunteered to the Free Earth Corps. Second thoughts are bad thoughts. The reason why, is that all volunteer lists are sent to the other side. Unfortunately for you, the leaders of Social Unity consider you traitors. The reason that is unfortunate is that should you be captured...." Captain Sigmir grinned. "Don't allow yourself to be captured and don't run to the other side. Torture is what you'll receive. Believe me, I know, for I've seen what they did to my comrades. We overran the enemy holding pens where a few betas had been captured." The captain shook his head.

"Ripped out balls was the least of it. So! Here you are. Here, as Free Earth Corps, you will live or die. Only victory brings rewards. Defeat.... That brings hideous death, if you're not already dead by then. Thus, you must learn to fight. Fight, fight, fight, nothing else matters, men. You must learn to fight."

11.

Marten knew this kind of exhaustion too well. It reminded him of the water tank in the Reform through Labor Auditorium. Pump, pump, pump or you die. But here they switched tasks on you with bewildering rapidity. Knife combat, running, rifle range firing, running, plasma cannon sighting, running, map reading, running, squad tactics to take a hill, running, squad tactics to take a trench line, running, squad tactics to breach a pillbox, running. Day or night, it didn't matter. Stim-shots came constantly. And they ran and ran and ran.

True, he'd never eaten better than here. Muscles on his legs swelled, his already narrow waist became leaner. Run here, run there, it was endless. He sweated almost every minute of the day and drank water like an auto-digger after a long day of drilling. They never let you sleep long enough, either. Bugles blared you to the parade ground. A kick in the side brought you alert on a desert trek stop. More stims, more food, more training, on and on it went. He climbed ropes, rocks and trees and jumped out of buildings, choppers and moving tanks. He dug trenches, used grenades to blast holes into rock, bayoneted dummies and karate kicked three men into the infirmary. What made it worse was that glaring number two tattooed onto the back of his hand. They sweated him harder than most of the other recruits. They demanded he remember tactics, ploys, tricks and how to call down mortar, artillery and orbital fighter strikes. He could set a bone, start a fire with sticks, and poke out a man's eye with a stiffened finger. Run, run, run, crawl under barbed wire, zigzag across a field as shock grenades blew. He didn't dream anymore. The instant his head lay on anything he snored in a coma-like sleep. Catnaps became a way of life.

Some men mutinied. They died. One man foolishly attempted to kill Captain Sigmir. He died, too. A few tried trekking across the desert to anywhere but Training Camp Ninety-three-C. Marten led the unit chasing the deserters. Turbo, Stick, Omi and three other slum dwellers cradled laser rifles as they jogged after Marten. He wore the infrared goggles that saw the fleeing footprints as easily as if they'd been painted in red. Perspiration poured. Their brown uniforms were dark with sweat. Marten especially hated how damp his socks had become.

"Why couldn't they have just cut their own throats," Stick muttered as he wiped his forehead. "I'm dying out here."

"Yeah," Turbo complained, "my feet are blistering."

Marten's gut churned. They were remaking him as a killer. In Sydney, it had been different. They tried to bend you. A brave man could resist. Back at the Sun Works, he'd only used a tangler, although his father had killed. Disobey a combat order here and you died.

The Highborn had lied, he decided. Sure, you could say what you wanted, and that *was* different than it was in Social Unity. But now he was becoming like Ngo Drang the red-suit, the personal butcher of Major Orlov. His gut churned and roiled. The Highborn had him trained like a good little boy. It was more blatant and subtler all at once.

Marten licked his lips, and he veered from the tracks.

"No!" came over the voice-link clipped to his ear. "Follow the track and slay the deserters or you will all be marked as AWOL and immediately eliminated."

Marten glanced back. Omi and the others didn't have the voice-link. But they would be killed just the same. Sure, they had these lasers. They'd all been shown how useless they were against battle armor.

"Warning number two has now been issued," came over the voice-link.

Warning number three would be auto-cannon fire in their backs. Cursing under his breath, Marten veered back onto the track.

"What's wrong with these guys?" asked Stick. "Are they drunk?"

Omi jogged faster until he was even with Marten.

"They earned this," the ex-gunman said. "They knew the rules and they broke them."

"Yeah?" asked Marten.

"Do not throw our lives away," Omi said.

"Don't worry."

"Ah, you're correct," Omi said, as he spotted the fugitives.

Omi barked a command. The ragged hunters, with sweat pouring off them, their chests heaving, halted. One by one, they lifted their laser rifles.

"Do it," Omi hissed at Marten.

Reluctantly Marten lifted his. He saw the four running shapes in his scope. His knuckles tightened. A harsh red beam stabbed across the desert. The others fired, and the beams touched the deserters. The four fell onto the sand, dead.

That's how the days went. But not all of the training was practice. They also taught Marten a little theory. He found out why all the volunteer slum dwellers had been packed into the same camp, why Ball Busters, Kwon's Gang and Red Blades went into platoons of their own kind. Men fought better with their buddies, with other men who knew and cared if they turned coward or not. No one loved the Highborn, but you might stick around and fight when things really got hot if it was your buddies who were on the line. So he, Stick, Omi and Turbo were left together. Nor were his exploits in the deep-core mine overlooked. It was one of the reasons they pumped him full of combat information. And made him an offer.

It happened on the desert target range, during mortar fire training. Captain Sigmir adjusted his scanscope as he looked into the distance.

Marten and his squad waited by their three mortars, two men to each. Marten stood behind them watching, correcting and calling ranges.

In the distance appeared three puffs of smoke, seconds later the sounds of their dull thuds reached them.

"Excellent!" said the captain. "Direct hit, direct hit, eighty-nine percent nearness. The best score so far."

"Pack up," Marten told his squad.

Efficiently, his squad dismantled the mortars, tube to one man, the tripod and base to another. Then they waited for directions. They didn't wait standing at rigid attention, but slouched here or crouched on the ground over there.

Captain Sigmir looked up from his watch. "Marvelous. Marten, walk with me."

Marten fell one step behind as the captain strode into the desert. Training Camp Ninety-three-C lay beyond the horizon in the other direction. Overhead the sun beat down, but Marten no longer noticed the heat—it had been five weeks since induction. He wore rumpled brown combat fatigues and well-worn boots, a helmet, a vibroknife and a simulation pistol. Spit and polish and other parade ground fetishes mattered not at all to the Highborn or to the drill instructors. The only questions that mattered were *could you kill* and *how fast?*

"Walk *with* me, Marten."

196

Marten jogged beside the massive captain, trying to match his long strides. Perhaps the captain was a beta, much smaller than the superior Highborn, but compared to a normal man Captain Sigmir was still a giant.

"Your squads always perform well."

"Yes, sir."

"Yet…. There is a lack in you, Marten."

He said nothing to that.

"There, that's exactly what I mean."

"Sir?"

"You're a brooder."

"Yes, sir."

"More than that, you're a loner."

The five weeks of training had taught Marten one thing, to control his temper, the rage that boiled within him, even as his sense of despair increased. He hated Captain Sigmir, but he felt he masked it so no one knew.

"You use your leadership skills for your own benefit, to think as you wish, to do what you want even if the crowd likes or dislikes it. What I mean is that you aren't using your leadership skills to drive ahead, to make others march to your will."

"Sir?"

"Marten, leadership is a gift. I believe you're squandering yours in isolation. Yes, you are a rock. You stand and do whatever you think is right. Those are all good things, I suppose. But in this war you can rise high if you'll learn to strive to make others obey your will."

"Yes, sir."

They exchanged glances.

Marten didn't allow himself to shiver. Looking into that strange face, so filled with vitality and a strange lust, reminded him that the captain had been dead once. Marten felt it showed.

Captain Sigmir sighed. "I haven't convinced you. But Marten, I'm still going to recommend you as the lieutenant of Second Platoon."

"Sir, I..."

Captain Sigmir held up a powerful hand. "Kang will run First Platoon. Now there's a preman who understands leadership. But you're a much better tactician than Kang. Yes, you're a splendid tactician. Oh, we're quick to note such things. You lack something of Kang's ferocity, or so the superiors believe. I'm not so certain, though. Your rage—" Captain Sigmir laughed. "Oh, yes, Lieutenant, I know very well that an inner rage seethes within you. I can feel it. At times I even think that it's directed at me."

"Sir, I ah—"

"But that's neither here nor there, Lieutenant. Hate me all you wish just as long as you obey me."

"Yes, sir."

"Then you agree to your lieutenancy?"

"Agree, sir?"

"Unless you agree to your new rank you will not receive it. Such is the Highborn dictate regarding rank."

Marten thought about that. Clever on their part, he decided. They wanted him to take some of the blame, to smear on the guilt. What would happen if he refused? Probably Captain Sigmir would post him to Kang's platoon. If that happened, he'd have to kill Kang fast or be the slain one. The ex-Red Blades boss was a sadist almost as bad as the once dead, Lot Six *beta* Highborn strutting beside him. He finally decided it was easier to revolt— when the chance came—if he was one of the guards carrying a gun than if he was one of the prisoners the gun was trained on.

Marten nodded. "I agree."

"Splendid, Lieutenant. I'm overjoyed to hear it."

"One question, sir."

"Hmmm?"

"Who are my sergeants?"

"Your Top Sergeant will be Omi, of course, with Stick and Turbo as the regular Sergeants."

"Very good, sir."

Captain Sigmir stopped, reaching down to put a hand on Marten's shoulder. "One more week of training, Lieutenant, then we will be shipped into battle."

"We, sir?"

"I'm to be the Captain of Tenth Company."

Marten blanched in spite of his best efforts not to.

"Problem, Lieutenant?"

"Begging the Captain's pardon, sir, but I suggest you have a well-trained group of bodyguards."

Captain Sigmir grinned evilly. "Lieutenant, that is well-spoken. Now, back to your squad, my boy, and on the double."

12.

Unknown to the Highborn or to Marten, the civil war entered a new and vastly more dangerous stage when Secret Police General James Hawthorne ordered code A-927Z beamed into deep space via a special laser lightguide flash. As per his orders, and without Director Enkov's knowledge, Beijing HQ started the process by regular e-mail.

On a rather ordinary fish farm orbiting Earth, as yet untouched by Highborn suicide commandos, a communication technician read his e-mail with surprise. As ordered, he pulled up a standard production report and typed in the e-mail's command. To the technician's surprise, a secret computer file embedded in the report scrolled onto his screen. He read it and raised his eyebrows, but he knew better than to question an apparently senseless order when given under such strict conditions. So he aligned the lightguide flash-emitter to the dictated coordinates and typed the *send* sequence on his keyboard. Then he picked up his container of instacaf and took a sip.

On the outside of the space habitat a special laser lightguide tube popped up, adjusted with canny precision and shot a tight beam of light bearing the coded string: A-927Z. The tube then zipped back into its holder and triggered an unfortunate sequence of events, at least regarding the signal officer.

Vents opened in the communication module's ceiling and sprayed a fine mist of combustibles. The officer, with his container halfway to his lips for yet another sip, had time enough to say, "Hey," as his computer files self-deleted. And a pre-timed spark ignited the mist. The explosion shook the entire space hab and demanded the full attention of all fire-fighting personnel and auto-equipment. The signal officer, his computer and various personal effects disappeared in the ball of explosive flame.

Meanwhile, the communication laser flashed through space at the speed of light, three hundred thousand kilometers a second. The lightguide system had a singular benefit over a regular radio message. A tightly beamed communications laser could only be picked up by the receiving station it hit. That, however, demanded precision, and the farther the target, the greater the precision needed. This flash had a long journey in terms of solar system distances, thirty AU or 4,347,400,000 kilometers. Thus, traveling at the speed of light, the message reached the selected target, Neptune habitat, roughly four hours after it had been sent.

The personnel there decoded the flash and read A-927Z. It had an effect similar to a spade overturning an ant colony: boiling activity erupted.

Toll Seven had docked his ultra-stealth pod some time ago, his cargo discharged and stored in deep freeze along with a thousand other carefully stolen people. Workers with hand trolleys entered the locker. Osadar Di, stiff as a log and almost as dead, found herself propped upon one of the first trolleys and rolled to the beginning of a process which would grant her new life but at the cost of her humanity.

Thankfully, for her and her sanity, she had no awareness of the first steps. Set on a conveyer, she traveled to a thawing tank. Immersed in aquamarine liquid, her frozen limbs and torso grew supple. The analyzers attached to her beeped at the right moment and a lifter set her on a new conveyer, where she received a shock of life. Her entire body jerked so hard that she tore several muscles, a minor but not unnoticed matter to the monitoring AI. With an agonizing wheeze, Osadar took her first new breath and her eyelids fluttered. A fine mist rained upon her, killing all bacteria and other biological infestations. In that instant, she awoke to excruciating pain. The torn muscles brought her up sooner than anticipated. Somewhere an alarm rang. At this phase of transformation, her awareness was an unwanted anomaly.

Despite the pain, Osadar felt a great lethargy. Then it came to her that the robotic-looking man who had slain Technician Geller had shoved a needle into her. How long had she been out? She moved her head to the side, and screamed. Staring at her wide-eyed like a deader was the commander of IH-49. Others lay beyond him and they moved on an assembly line. Horror screwed up her face. She bit back a second scream, knowing that her worst fears had all along been right. Life was a rigged crapshoot meant to shaft you in the end no matter what you did.

Osadar tried to move her limbs, but they were so sluggish, and the torn muscles sent mind-rending pain messages to her brain.

Then emergency hypos shot her full of drugs and numbed her nervous system.

"No," she whispered, struggling to rise before she slumped back into unconsciousness. A few moments later she entered the choppers, as the technicians there called them. In actuality, tiny vibroblades sliced the top-most layer of her skin, which was peeled away and discarded into a burner.

The entire process proved grim in the extreme. Director Enkov's bodyguard had in many ways been rebuilt. But compared to what they did to Osadar Di he had merely had his toenails trimmed. They tore her down, removing her heart, lungs and kidneys. Finally, her brain was detached from her spinal column and placed into pink programming gel. The combination entered an accelerated life situation computer. Her brain along with others was electronically force-fed millions of pieces of new data. It was mostly tactical military information and how to use what would soon be her new cyborg body. The program then ran her through thousands of simulated situations:

She dropped Earthward in an attack pod. The pod peeled away and she floated on chutes. Two hundred meters above the ground the lines detached and she plummeted and landed in a crouch. Experiencing events within the simulator as if they were reality, she bounded in hundred meter leaps at the enemy, her thermonuclear slug-thrower chugging in controlled bursts. Within the simulator she target-practiced with dart guns, lasers, regular carbines, knives, spears; hurled grenades at super tanks, manned a laser battery and more. The events played until they became second nature. Within those events command words, obedience conditioning, how to use inner nanonics and other sundry cyborg functions were drilled into her.

At last, the data processing ended. Her brain emerged very different from when it had entered. Something of the old Osadar Di remained, but it lay submerged in the new cyborg personality, or the lack of it.

The reattachment of her brain to a new and improved spinal column was a delicate operation. The scientists and technicians on the secret Neptune habitat had learned to marry genetic human material to machinery like seamless cloth. An armored brainpan was only the beginning of it. She now had power-graphite bones, artificial muscles, millions of micro-nanonics in her bloodstream, an armor-plated body and eyes that could never be mistaken for human. Little was left of the old Osadar Di. And to make sure that that little part could never rebel, obedience chips were liberally sprinkled throughout her nervous system. A tiny powerful governing computer was linked to her brain and embedded within the central mass.

The process from Suspend-dead human to cyborg took two weeks. Training her to use her new body would take another three. Then Cyborg Osadar Di— better known as OD12—would enter the first ultra-stealth pod to make the many-months long journey from Neptune to Earth.

Then maybe Social Unity could finally regain the initiative against the Highborn.

Soldier

1.

13 April 2350

Emergency military conference, Day Two of the Invasion of Japan Sector: 1.19 P.M.

Participants: Enkov, Hawthorne, Kitamura (Field Marshal, Japan Sector) Ulrich (Air Marshal, Strategic Command East), O'Connor (Admiral, Pacific Fleet) Green (Colonel-General, Replacement Army East).

Enkov: You misjudged them again.
Hawthorne: I don't think that's the correct analysis, Director. Strategically this invasion makes no sense. From Australia, they launched the Papua/New Guinea Campaign, which, I might add, has bogged down in the treacherous mountain terrain.
Green: Even Highborn have their limits, it seems.
Hawthorne: Exactly. But to address your question, Director, let me point out that they've captured twenty percent of the small Pacific Islands from Japan to the

Hawaiian Islands to Australia. It seemed clear until two days ago that they planned to build a Pacific Basin Stronghold. Now their supply lines from Australia to Japan stretches past Indonesia, the Philippines and Taiwan.

O'Connor: Over four thousand kilometers.

Hawthorne: Granted they rush supplies and troops in well-armed convoys, but our ability to intercept and destroy them has now—what are those numbers again?

O'Connor: Their transports are thousand-ton Vickers Hovercraft, a rugged prefab design that we believe is already in mass production, with Destroyer Class Hovers serving as escort. Fast V-Boats range as perimeter guards, while VTOL Hover Carriers provide fighters, bombers and their dreaded HK-Leopards. Those search out our submersibles with uncanny accuracy.

Hawthorne: Yes, thank you, Admiral. But what are the improved odds regarding our ability to sink them along this four thousand kilometer route?

O'Connor: A sixty-percent increase.

Enkov: I'm delighted to hear it. As will be the other directors. How much tonnage have you destroyed since the Japanese Invasion?

O'Connor: Ah… none yet, Director. It's still early in the invasion and we have only a few boats along the route. But we believe a pattern has emerged, one that indicates—

Enkov: Here we go again. It's always about holding back to study their pattern, to make sense of these swift moves that seems to paralyze my military men. Yet you just said, General Hawthorne, that attacking Japan lacked strategic sense. What you really mean is that the Highborn have upset your precious pattern concerning their intended behavior.

Hawthorne: They are unpredictable.

Enkov: Or perhaps they are simply more subtle that you, General.

Hawthorne: I take that as a given, Director. Yet I believe they've finally overstepped themselves.

Enkov: Not in terms of sea-borne supply, it seems.

O'Connor: It takes time to reposition our fleets, Director. The bulk of our submarine squadrons lie in Java Strait and the South China Sea, in the southern region off Malaysia. It was anticipated that the Indonesian Islands were their next target. We could have bloodied them well there. The surprises we had in store for them…. Well, it's moot now. Presently, the Highborn supply-line from Australia to Japan brushes near the extreme west of the Philippine Sea but not quite over the Mariana Trench.

Enkov: I fail to see your point.

O'Connor: We must move our submarines carefully, Director. Highborn detection devices are incredibly sensitive. But if we could slip into the Mariana Trench—

Enkov: What difference does that make?

O'Connor: Depth, Director. If we can slip deep enough even their detection devices can't spot our subs, or if they do spot them, short of nuclear depth charges we're safe from attack.

Enkov: Safe, yes, but neither can you attack from the great depths.

Hawthorne: We've developed a new pop-up buoy that will be able to—

Enkov: Correct me if I'm wrong, General Hawthorne, but *developed* means on the planning screen, not yet aboard the submarines.

Hawthorne: Yes, Director. And therein is our chief problem. The former Directorate agreed to the creation of the Highborn because Earth seemed incapable of producing proficient soldiers. This new breed of warrior was supposed to do all of Social Unity's soldiering. Because of it, Earth defenses were allowed to deteriorate. We are the heirs of their errors.

Enkov: More history, General?

207

Hawthorne: Sir, the truth is large military vehicles such as submarines and spacecraft take several years to construct, at least under peacetime conditions. Planes also have a lag time, but not as great. As you know we've accelerated production, but as of now, our space and water-borne fleets are only as large as we had at the beginning of hostilities. Fifty-three percent of our submarines were targeted and destroyed the day Geneva and the old Directorate was destroyed. Since then, Admiral O'Connor has only lost eighteen submarines.

Enkov: And shown little for it.

Hawthorne: I'm not certain I can agree with that analysis, Director. Premature moves only hand the Highborn further chances to complete their original destruction. We must husband our forces until an opportunity of enough worth and one that we can win presents itself. I believe the Invasion of Japan is just such an opportunity. Admiral O'Connor has moved his fleets into position or is in the process of moving them. Yet we must not allow the Highborn the free destruction of our fleets. Rather, I am timing for one sudden swoop upon every aspect of the invasion. Admiral O'Connor will cut their supply lines. Air Marshal Ulrich, who repositions his fighters and bombers along China's coast and slips replacement fighters when he can onto Japan, will sweep the sky of enemy craft. Colonel-General Green has already ordered a mass transshipment of replacement troops from Vietnam to Korea. Once in Korea the bulk of them will be shipped onto Japan and there provide needed ground forces to sweep and destroy the trapped enemy units. It's a bold and audacious plan, Director—Operation Togo.

Kitamura: Named in honor of the Japanese Admiral who destroyed the Russian Baltic Fleet over four centuries ago in a surprise attack in the Tsushima Strait.

Hawthorne: Yes, thank you, Field Marshal. The Highborn have once more struck with surprise. But we're reacting faster than ever and have a plan that has every chance of blooding them much more than *they've* planned for. This, Director, is why we've been husbanding our irreplaceable fleet units.

Enkov: What about the troop build-up in Indonesia?

Hawthorne: We'll leave them there for the moment.

Enkov: A week ago, you said they were our best men.

Hawthorne: Second only to Field Marshal Kitamura's soldiers.

Enkov: Report on that, Field Marshal.

Kitamura: Honored Director, Japan will never fall. Our soldiers have dedicated their lives to Social Unity and promise to hurl back these Supremacist invaders. Three assaults have struck the home islands, at Kobi, at Tokyo and at Sendai in the north. Battle rages hottest in Tokyo—

Enkov: I've received reports they dropped nuclear bombs.

Kitamura: Tactical nuclear explosions of one and two kilotons, yes, Honored One—Precision nuclear strikes that destroyed our "deep-space" laser batteries.

Hawthorne: Beam weapons, Director, capable of hitting spacecraft in near-Earth orbit.

Enkov: Yes, thank you so much, General. I had assumed that's what the "deep space" appellation meant.

Kitamura: Honored One, although they destroyed the laser batteries, they failed to destroy our Merculite missile battery. Six orbital fighters have fallen to our launches.

Enkov: Why didn't they strike that with nuclear fire?

Hawthorne: They did after we scored the kills. But because of our new clamshell shielding—four thousand tons of blast-concrete—the nuclear strikes were shrugged off. Incidentally, several cities have the new Merculite missile bases, Tokyo among them. They were installed six months before the civil war and are among the few innovations the Highborn lack.

Enkov: They've attacked with nuclear weapons. Now we must retaliate likewise.

Hawthorne: I'm not convinced—

Enkov: You've wavered from the first, General. But now I insist we launch nuclear strikes at their main concentrations.

Hawthorne: Dedicated orbital laser stations protect their main troop concentrations, at least if they're true to form. Any missiles or cruise missiles fired at those formations will surely be intercepted. Besides, as long as we refrain from nuclear launches we maintain the moral high ground or at least we'll keep the propaganda value in our court. Most Outer Planets governments have stressed their wish for each of us to refrain from nuclear strikes. If we wish to woo Outer Planets—

Enkov: Meaningless if we're defeated before then. In any case, that's a political decision and well beyond your scope, General.

Hawthorne: Understood, sir.

Enkov: Now a moment ago you said something very interesting, Admiral. You said that the fleets will not be in position for a week. Is that correct?

O'Connor: It could take longer than a week, Director.

Enkov: Then we must strike their convoys with nuclear missiles now. I don't believe they have dedicated orbital stations protecting all four thousand kilometers.

Hawthorne: Perhaps to initiate Operation Togo a few selected targets might be—

Enkov: No, General Hawthorne, before Operation Togo. These nuclear strikes will be made before. I want their supplies and troops stopped now.

Hawthorne: What you suggest is risky, Director.

Enkov: How do you mean risky? They've already struck with nuclear weapons.

Hawthorne: I wish to point out with very limited nuclear strikes. With clean, as far as radiation is concerned, weapons. Large nuclear exchanges between us could easily lead to an irradiated planet.

Enkov: Better that than fall to the Supremacists.

Hawthorne: We are not yet defeated, Director. So I beg you to reconsider this most dangerous process.

Enkov: Field Marshal Kitamura, please continue your report.

Kitamura: Most Honored Director, if you would look at the map. The fiercest fighting takes place here, in Greater Tokyo. Samurai Divisions have hurled the enemy from the nearest underground entrances and advanced a thousand meters. Tokyo volunteers even now stream into battle as Kamikaze squads.

Enkov: Explain that.

Kitamura: Brave men and women and even children are strapped with high explosives. They crawl near or among the enemy and detonate.

Enkov: Incredible! Such dedication must be rewarded. I want lists of all volunteers. Mark them down as Heroes of Earth.

Kitamura: A wise decision, Director.

Enkov: Please, continue with the report, Field Marshal. This is fascinating.

Kitamura: Our casualties are heavy, but our blood flows to oil the path for the rest. Social harmony fills their hearts and others sup at their selfless dedication to the future. In the north, Sendai fell after an hour's battle, but the lines have stiffened here and here. My commanders have assured me that the arrogant invaders will not get past our Fukushima strongholds without massive losses. In the south, Kobi residents have begged my commanders to arm them and let them enter battle. My air fleets have taken sixty-percent losses, but we have destroyed five troop carriers and ten V-Boats. Give me more fighters,

Honored Director, and Japanese pilots will score even more victories. Our deaths do not matter, just that we may save our social unity.

Enkov: Splendid, yes, inspiring. Air Marshal, have you rated success by nationality?

Ulrich: We have, Director. Japanese pilots have scored twenty-eight percent of all known successes. Next are the Germans, at twenty-five percent. American and Israeli pilots each accounted for ten percent. A word of caution is in order, however. While the Field Marshal is correct at the heroics and ability of his former pilots, they were also his best rated. It would be a mistake to ship too many fighters into Japan until the beginning of Operation Togo.

Kitamura: I am sorry, but I cannot agree, Air Marshal.

Enkov: General Hawthorne, has a troop's nationality shown any difference in terms of ground performance?

Hawthorne: Most definitely.

Enkov: Japanese troops do well?

Hawthorne: Very.

Enkov: Then perhaps the Highborn actions become clear.

Hawthorne: You detect a pattern, Director?

Enkov: The Highborn do not hew to your strategies, General, because they do not think like you. Land is not paramount. Men are. Consider. Why strike at Japan? Might it be because the Japanese make better soldiers than the neighboring peoples do?

Hawthorne: Perhaps. Yet a conquered Japan also aims a strategic arrow at Beijing. While I don't see how invading Japan at this time fits into their overall strategy, it is by itself not an unbalanced move.

Enkov: I believe they're more concerned with taking out our best recruiting grounds, then taking those captive peoples and retraining them as Highborn surrogates.

Kitamura: The Japanese will never serve the hated Highborn. We are dedicated Social Unitarians.

Enkov: So did the Australian generals assure the Directorate, as did those holding New Zealand, Tasmania and Antarctica before them. Yet now these nationalities flock to the Highborn standards. You're so fond of history, General Hawthorne. Didn't the Japanese lick the American's boots easily enough after World War Two?

Hawthorne: As the Field Marshal indicated, Director, Social Unity cures many ills.

Enkov: How refreshingly bold of you, General. Are you actually assuring me the Japanese won't join the Highborn?

Hawthorne: I don't intend on letting Japan fall to find out.

Kitamura: We will never fall! On this, I stake my life and reputation.

Enkov: I accept your pledge, Field Marshal.

Kitamura: Thank you, Honored Director. You will see that Japan loves you and honors your socially approved leadership. Even now new armies of volunteers train in the cities' depths. We will boil out and overwhelm them!

Enkov: That, gentlemen, is the kind of zeal we need. Now, General Hawthorne, how soon until this grand assault of yours occurs, this Operation Togo?

Hawthorne: Your timetable, Colonel-General?

Green: Nine weeks at the earliest.

Enkov: Too long, much too long! The Highborn run circles around us because they *move*. By the time we're ready for them, our men are marching into their holding pens or being buried in the field. We have to match their speed, their ability to shift from one spot to the next. You have four weeks, and then you will commence Operation Togo with whatever's ready.

O'Connor: I need those four weeks to slip my submarine squadrons into position. On the fifth week, we might be ready.

Enkov: Fight your way into position!

213

O'Connor: Without surprise—

Enkov: To insure success we will immediately submarine-launch nuclear strikes against their sea-lines.

Hawthorne: Director—

Enkov: My mind is made up on this. I have not struck first with nuclear weapons. But I refuse to sit idly by and allow them to bombard us with impunity.

Hawthorne: Very well, Director. But I cannot guarantee Operation Togo with only a four-week lead-time.

Enkov: Four weeks and I demand that you guarantee it for me, General.

Hawthorne: Perhaps if the Directorate rescinds its policy on the habitats.

Enkov: Negative. They must remain open habitats. Frankly, I find the Highborn agreement to this unbelievable. If they stopped all food shipments earthward, we would face half rations for everyone on the planet.

Hawthorne: They want Earth intact, Director. So unless we change policy I don't believe they will change their open space-farm habitat policy. At least they won't change it as long as they're conquering— As long as they're making advances.

Enkov: Then why ask for Directorate policy to be rescinded?

Hawthorne: Because I'm beginning to wonder if that isn't the place to break them. If we can't break their battle fleet maybe we can destroy one or two Doom Stars.

Enkov: You think that's possible?

Hawthorne: With surprise… maybe. If our new proton beams prove—

Enkov: No! Maybe is not good enough. We will stick to saving Japan. Four weeks, gentlemen, to gather what forces you can and then strike against their invasion. And you must immediately disrupt their four thousand kilometer long supply-line, Admiral. Your submarines are to move now! They are to launch nuclear sea-strikes as close to the enemy as possible. If they own space, we can still use the oceans. I want you especially to target their transports. Until then, Field Marshal Kitamura, you most hold Tokyo. You must defend the Merculite missile battery, no matter what the cost. If that means frontal assaults with your newly trained levies then you must do it.

Kitamura: Agreed, Honored Director. But we will take massive casualties.

Enkov: That doesn't matter. Engage the enemy. Make him bleed until we're ready to drive him off Japan. Then everyone will see that the Highborn are not invincible.

Hawthorne: Shouldn't our objectives be studied in greater detail, Director?

Enkov: You have just been given your objectives, General. Now I want them carried out. If, that is, you can guarantee me success.

Hawthorne: Director, I—

Enkov: Give me victory, General Hawthorne, or we will fall back onto Carthaginian strategies.

Green: Director?

Enkov: Take it up later with General Hawthorne, and consider yourself under the same terms, all of you. Gentleman, the emergency meeting is adjourned. Now, to your tasks!

2.

Convoy A22 left Sydney Harbor at three o'clock in the afternoon Sunday. The first day it sped over the waters at fifty kilometers an hour. Thirty hover transports carried the 20th FEC Division and the 101st Jump-Jet Battalion, which was composed of veteran Hawk Teams. They skimmed over the choppy waves in a diamond formation. Playing shepherd to the transports were four Gladius Class Hovers, small and deadly destroyer sized vessels. They bristled with guns and missiles launchers, and dropped probes as they hunted for enemy submarines. In and out of the diamond formation, they roamed on the prowl. On picket duty twenty to forty kilometers out roved ten V-Boats, hydrofoil ships badly tossed among the waves. Ocean duty left the crews exhausted. A journey all the way to Japan hammered them. In the middle of the transports hovered the VTOL Carrier. Sleek HK-Leopards—reconnaissance planes—and sleek attack choppers lifted from its flat top as they scoured the sea for enemy.

A quarter of the way through the journey, storm warnings forced the convoy off course to the west. The sea grew rougher, until the hovers shut down turbines, settled unto the gray waters and moved like ordinary sea vessels. Overhead, dark clouds threatened rain. On the former cushion of air, the trip had been relatively smooth. Now the men found themselves pitched to-and-fro. Many grew seasick, crawling to the head and spewing or limping into their bunks and trying to endure the endless motion. A few stubbornly continued their crap and card games.

Lieutenant Marten Kluge, his Top Sergeant Omi and Sergeants Stick and Turbo had squeezed themselves around a bolted down table in a little cubby in the rec-room. There they played five-card stud. Each wore the dusty brown uniform of FEC volunteers. Turbo and Stick wore their slouch hats. With a stylus and plex-pad, Omi kept track of the won or lost fortunes. The worn cards rested in a table holder specially made for sea duty. The discards they held with their elbows propped on the table. The room, as did everything aboard the sea-borne hover, pitched back and forth with exaggerated motion.

"Card," said Turbo.

Omi slipped him one.

Turbo frowned as he settled the card into his hand.

"I heard we're gonna be fed into the Tokyo maw," said Stick. "For once Social Unity refuses to be overrun. It's a meat-grinder from what I hear."

Marten shrugged. He hadn't heard anything like that.

"They said High Command wants... some kind of missile battery taken out."

"Merculite missile battery," Turbo said, still mulling over his cards. He'd become the Second Platoon's newsmonger, finding it wherever he found his illegal drugs.

"What's a merculite missile?" asked Stick.

Turbo tugged the peak of his hat lower over his eyes. "It's fast, is what it is. Zooms out in seconds and drops orbital fighters so they plop into the ocean. High Command's gone crazy over it."

"Precious Highborn losses," grumbled Stick.

"Yeah," breathed Turbo. "Twenty credits!"

Omi scratched that onto the pad and quietly set his hand down. "Out," he said.

Stick flicked a gaze over his cards.

Omi's stylus hovered over the plex-pad in anticipation.

"They say it's a blood-bath in Tokyo," said Stick. "The Japanese have lost their minds, is what I hear. They run screaming at you with bombs strapped to their chests, and they blow both you and them to death. Behind them, follow honor-mad Samurai Divisions, one after another in an endless procession. And don't let them capture you alive, either. They got these knives, sharper than my vibroblade. They use them to cut off your balls and—"

"You in or out?" asked Turbo

Stick nodded for a card.

Omi's stylus glided over the pad.

"Two cards," said Marten.

"It's called the Siege of Tokyo," said Turbo matter-of-factly. "And yeah, it's a blood-bath all right, but with FEC Divisions and a scattering of Jump-Jet battalions."

"No panzers?" asked Marten.

"Nope," Turbo said. "They're up north sweeping the home islands, as the Japanese buggers call them."

"What about Highborn?" asked Omi.

Turbo shrugged as he adjusted his hat. He squinted at Marten to make up his mind.

"So we're all killing each other for some worthless missiles?" asked Stick.

"Earth is on the run, don't you know," said Turbo. "But it's gotten too easy for the High Command, so this time they're not using as many Highborn. It's an all-volunteer show."

"The Earth on the run part is right," Stick said. "An old-timer told me the Highborn move all their units like lightning, theirs and the volunteers. He said their staff work is amazing. If they'd ever tried this in the Old Army, said the old-timer, it would have been a balls-up from the get go."

"In and call," said Marten.

With a grin, Turbo spread his cards: three queens, ace high.

Stick threw down his hand with disgust. Marten quietly folded his and handed the cards to Omi. He slid out from the booth and stretched, staggering as the ship rolled. He bumped against the table as the ship swayed in the other direction.

"I'm going topside," said Marten.

Omi grunted and slid out too. "Mind if I join you?"

Marten nodded.

As they left the rec-room Turbo yelled, "We need two more players."

Marten and Omi slid along the corridor and crawled up the stairs. They donned rain gear, slick hats and staggered to the front deck railing, where they hung on. Huge gray waves rose and fell, while darkening clouds loomed threateningly in the sky. Only sailors moved here and there above deck, attaching lines or running to perform some unknown chore. Behind the lead hover followed the other twenty-nine transports. Overhead a chopper thumped somewhere, barely audible over the blistering wind.

Cold salt spray lashed the two men. They wiped their faces constantly.

"I've never been on the ocean before," Marten shouted.

"Just one time for me when my mom and I visited Korea," Omi said.

"You've been out of Sydney before?"

"A year before she was divorced and escorted into the slums. Thanks to my dear old dad."

Marten rubbed salt out of his eyes, glancing at the grim-faced gunman.

Omi's mouth twitched. "A drunk fell overboard that journey."

"Yeah?"

"They stopped the ship and picked him up, but he'd broken his neck, probably from the fall."

"Probably?"

Omi shrugged.

Marten was struck by Omi's moodiness. Normally the man was the Rock, as some of the men had taken to calling him. "What really happened?" Marten asked.

"A thief pinched the drunk's wallet. But the drunk wasn't so drunk and whirled around, starting to holler for help. So the thief, he was a little guy, hardly even a teenager. He used a martial arts move. He snapped the drunk's neck, and was pretty surprised it worked liked it was supposed to."

"So the thief pitched the drunk overboard?"

"Yeah."

Marten thought about that, finally asking, "So what'd he find in the wallet?"

Omi frowned sourly, taking his time answering. "Some plastic, a sheaf of porno pics, nothing much for all the work he'd gone to."

Overhead a bomber zoomed low over the water. It seemed to be in a hurry somewhere. Marten and Omi watched. Thirty seconds later what seemed like small packages tumbled out of the bomber's bottom.

"Depth charges?" asked Marten.

"Seems like."

The packages plopped into the wild sea and disappeared.

They watched the spot. Suddenly, water sprayed upward, twin geysers. They kept watching, but nothing like oil or mangled bodies or anything else surfaced to show that an enemy sub had been hit.

"Turbo tells too many stories," Omi said.

"You mean the ones about convoys that get hit before they ever reach Japan?"

"Yeah."

"You're right. He shouldn't tell those."

"I think they're BS.

"Why is that?"

"The Highborn have the game sewn up," Omi said. "Social Unity is on the run. No way is Social Unity going to train soldiers fast enough to face the Highborn before it's all over."

"Social Unity might get desperate."

"So?"

"Desperate men do dangerous things."

"I suppose…"

3.

One of those desperate men wiped sweat off his face. He was a little over thirty kilometers away, deep under the tossing waves. The captain of the *Riga* stepped behind the tracking officer. The officer tapped a chart, and whispered, "As clear as it's going to get, sir."

The captain closed his eyes. He was queasy. The enemy's hunter/killers were too efficient. Too many fellow captains had already paid the ultimate price for this wild strategy. Yet he nodded. One must obey Enkov.

"Fire one and two," he whispered.

The watch officer stared at him. Everyone else held his breath.

"Fire," repeated the captain. "Tubes one and two."

"Firing one and two, sir," said the firing officer.

The *Riga* shuddered.

In the dark ocean depths, two nuclear-tipped missiles hurtled skyward. Enemy radar and sonar picked them up. Enemy officers roared orders. Planes turned to intercept. Counter missiles left circling bombers. Other bombers and choppers needed less than fifty seconds to rendezvous to the drop zone to let their ultra-powerful depth charges sink. None of them, however, were going to make it in time.

4.

Unaware of their fate, Marten and Omi continued to talk. Then, over twenty kilometers away, an amazingly bright flash lit up the dark clouds. A huge, ominous mushroom cloud arose. It towered higher and higher. Marten and Omi stared at it in shock, their mouths open.

Omi tried to speak, but failed.

Marten's chest tightened with terror. He couldn't believe what he saw. There had been rumors. Turbo had said—His chest unlocked and his numb mind started working from its momentary stoppage. "Get below!" he shouted, shoving Omi toward the nearest hatch.

They turned and ran, staggering and stumbling along the pitching deck. So did other men, babbling sailors who sprinted for the hatches. They jammed the nearest hatchway. Fists started flying, until a boatswain bellowed orders.

The hovers and ships of Convoy A22 acted amazingly fast. Perhaps the ships' captains had been given secret instructions in case a nuclear bomb should explode in their vicinity. Not as smoothly and as in unison as some of their earlier maneuvers had been done, they veered from the nuclear blast. Each ship throttled up, until they fled at full speed. One hover lifted onto its cushion of air, higher and higher as it leapt past the other hovers. Then a glitch hit its engines. The hover's nose sank. A wave rolled and crashed down hard, and the airborne hover flipped onto its back.

That was Marten's last sight of it as the shouting sailors shoved him through the hatchway. He fell down the steps and landed on his hands and knees, and twisted away as others landed on top of him. He crawled, and then unsteadily arose and staggered into the rec-room.

"Nuke!" he bellowed.

Omi shoved in behind.

Shocked, paling faces stared up at him.

At that moment, loudspeakers crackled, and the captain spoke. "All personnel are to grab hold of something solid. A nuclear shockwave will soon hit the ship. Please be prepared. That is all."

In a bedlam of shouts men scrambled for safety. Marten thrust himself at his spot at the card table, clutching the bolted down furniture with all his strength. Seconds later the shockwave hit. The transport shuddered and groaned, and they skipped across the ocean waves like a flung stone. Howling, screaming winds tore over them, and a hot flash caused men to open their mouths. Marten knew they were wailing in terror, but the winds were too loud for their shouts to be heard. Somehow, their hover kept upright. These ships had been built to take a pounding.

Across the table, Turbo stared slack-jawed at Marten. Stick mumbled prayers. Omi squeezed his eyes shut. Finally, no one knew how long, the winds died down and the pitching lessened.

Wide-eyed soldiers sat up. A few of them wept. More than one had broken bones.

"This is war," Omi said grimly, at last opening his eyes.

"I wonder if they targeted a convoy ahead of us?" asked Marten.

"Our baptism of fire," mumbled Stick.

Turbo laughed. "We haven't seen nothing yet, is my guess."

"You're crazy!" Stick shouted in outrage.

"Earth has gotta hold somewhere if they're going to win," said Turbo.

"So?"

"So maybe Tokyo is where they're gonna hold."

"Tokyo is where we're going," Omi said.

"Yeah," said Marten.

"Tell me one thing," whispered Stick.

"What?" asked Turbo.

"How do I go AWOL and survive?"

They each glanced at one another, perhaps all wondering the same thing. Marten knew he couldn't get the image out of his mind of lasering those four poor fools in the desert. Maybe he didn't deserve to live.

5.

Convoy A22 split soon thereafter or at least the eight transports that had survived the shockwave did. It was decided providing a smaller nuclear target was more advantageous than group protection versus submarine torpedo attacks. So a single destroyer patrolled for the four transports of the Slumlord Battalion, minus the HQ Jump Jet and artillery detachments. They had presumably gone down with their ship. None of the V-Boats ever showed up again, and only one other time did they see a chopper. It was far in the distance, undoubtedly looking for a place to land after its carrier had gone down. They also saw a second nuclear blast, a flash that was too far away to send another shockwave rolling over them.

Dispirited and scared, the men gloomily wondered if the dark ocean would become their grave. Luckily, the storm abated the next day and they rode their air cushion as fast as the turbines could whine. Marten led the men in hard calisthenics, exhausting them physically so they didn't have enough mentally to conjure up unneeded terrors. The hovers whisked over the Pacific Ocean all alone. From horizon to horizon stretched the mighty salt sea.

"It almost seems peaceful," said Turbo several mornings later. Rumors said they were a day out of Tokyo.

"It gives me the creeps," Stick muttered. "Everywhere you look is endless sea, water and clouds." Stick shook his head. "It doesn't stop, just goes on and on and on. It makes a guy feel insignificant."

"Aren't we?"

"No," said Marten.

"No?" asked Turbo.

"Breath the air, taste the salt tang. Look at the view and enjoy it, because today you're alive."

"And tomorrow I die," said Turbo.

"Maybe," Marten said, "but today you can affect the world, or if not the world then somebody in it. So that means you're not insignificant."

Turbo shrugged.

"You'd better not feel that way when you're covering my backside in Tokyo," Marten told him.

"Good point," said Stick. "In the old days I told the Blue Jackets the same sort of thing before we strolled the streets for a rumble." He flexed his muscles. The short, stocky youth looked more dangerous than ever in his brown uniform and steel-toed combat boots.

"We're gonna die in Tokyo," Turbo said gloomily.

"We didn't die in Reform," Stick growled.

"Because we were lucky," said Turbo.

"No, because Marten had balls to act," said Stick. "I'll tell you what I think."

"Must you?"

"Life is like a knife-fight. You gotta crouch, glare your man down and grit your teeth. Then you gotta attack before you get a knife stuck in your ribs."

"How can you slip a vibroblade into life?" asked Turbo.

227

"That's not what I mean," Stick said. "It's the attitude."

"Wonderful," Turbo said. "Attitude."

Stick shoved him. "Better keep on my good side, junkie, or it's you who'll get the knife in the ribs."

Turbo squinted down at the shorter, much more thickly built Stick. "I'm combat trained, you ape. You can't push me around anymore."

Stick pushed him again.

"I'm warning you!"

"Knock it off," said Marten. "Here comes the captain."

Captain Sigmir strolled onto the front deck. He'd been jumping between transports, inspecting what was left of Tenth Company. Other than a lone sailor swabbing the middle deck, the captain and they were the only ones topside. Captain Sigmir wore the same black uniform he had the first day. Behind him followed two carbine-toting thugs, his personal bodyguards. Officially, they were his batman and orderly, both corporals and dirty-fighting experts.

"Gentlemen," said the captain.

Marten and Stick saluted. Turbo lowered the brim of his hat.

Captain Sigmir expelled his breath as if someone had slugged him in the gut. His two bodyguards, odd-looking men, grinned at one another as they took up port arms behind the towering captain.

"After shock?" asked the captain softly.

"Sir?" said Turbo, the one addressed.

"Your disrespectful salute, soldier. I want to know what caused it."

"Oh," said Turbo. "It must have been my preoccupation with the joy of being alive, sir."

Captain Sigmir narrowed his strange eyes. Since the end of training camp, he'd been acting even more weird than usual.

"Salute, you idiot," said Stick, prodding Turbo in the ribs.

"Sir!" barked Turbo, snapping off a crisp salute.

"Is your sergeant being insubordinate, Lieutenant?"

"Sir," said Marten, "I don't believe so, sir."

Captain Sigmir clucked his tongue a few times, as he eyed Turbo. "Sergeant," he finally said, "take off that silly looking cap."

Turbo wiped it off his head.

"You seem pale, Sergeant. Sickly."

"I feel fine, sir."

"Indeed?"

"Yes, sir."

"In top physical shape?"

"Sir?"

"I asked you a question, Sergeant."

"Yes, sir. In top physical shape."

"Excellent. I want you to roll up your sleeves and square off against Petor."

The thickest bodyguard, a roly-poly Muscovite with a single hairy eyebrow over his bluest of blue eyes, handed his carbine to the other guard.

Marten tried to explain. "Captain—"

"Please keep quiet, Lieutenant, and watch your sergeant's fighting technique. I'm sure you'll see areas that need improvement. Begin."

Turbo was still rolling up his sleeves as Petor snapped a kick at his left knee. Turbo cried out, flopping onto the deck. Petor attempted another kick. Turbo rolled and clutched the foot, but Petor jumped back, yanking his foot free. Turbo scrambled up. It didn't really matter, though. Despite his comical appearance, Petor truly was an expert at dirty fighting, and twenty seconds later Turbo slumped to the deck, nearly unconscious.

Stick and Marten had grown tense and angry, easing onto the balls of their feet. The second bodyguard, however, had lowered his carbine in an apparently nonchalant manner. Now he aimed it at them. Captain Sigmir appeared not to notice the interplay. He kept licking his lips, chuckling as Turbo grunted or cried out. As the lanky sergeant hit the deck, the captain held up his hand. Petor stepped back, a slight sheen of sweat on his ever so round face.

Squatting beside the fallen Turbo, Captain Sigmir grabbed him by the hair and jerked up his head so they could peer eye-to-eye. "Joy is a wonderful feeling, Sergeant. But where we're going, it's a dangerous emotion. Work on hate, or if that's too difficult for you then fear. Fear of pain or death would be the two most appropriate emotions."

"Yes, sir," whispered Turbo, who was missing one of his front teeth. It lay on the deck in a small, bloody glob.

"I like your attitude now, Sergeant. So run along to the infirmary and see to your mouth." Captain Sigmir let go of Turbo's hair, rose to his imposing height and faced Marten. "I abhor slack discipline, Lieutenant."

"Yes, sir," Marten growled. His stomach had the feeling it once had when Hall Leader Quirn had his hands on Molly, and he had that same helpless feeling as when he'd seen his father slain. He hated that feeling. Today, however, he wasn't that young teenager.

"Oh, it's not as bad as that, Lieutenant. A few scrapes and bruises and hopefully a lesson finally driven home."

Marten nodded sharply.

"Ah, I see a word of advice is in order. Life is precarious, Lieutenant, so you must grab it by the short hairs and force it to accommodate you. Soon we will be in combat. You must therefore learn to enjoy what pleasures you can squeeze out of life, yes?"

"If the Captain says so, sir."

"But you just heard me say so."

"Yes, sir."

Captain Sigmir removed his cap and rubbed the forehead scar. He squinted as he muttered to himself. Then he brightened, set his cap back on and moved a step closer to Marten. "Can it be that you also need more combat training?"

Marten glanced at Petor, who grinned evilly at him.

Captain Sigmir put a single finger on Marten's chin, turning Marten's face so they stared eye-to-eye. "I'm addressing you, preman."

"Sir," said Marten, hating that finger on his chin so much that he could hardly think.

Captain Sigmir searched Marten's eyes.

Marten finally reached up and took hold of the captain's huge wrist, moving it so the finger no longer touched his chin.

Captain Sigmir's pursed his lips. "Lieutenant—"

"Have a care, sir," Marten told him softly.

Captain Sigmir's eyes widened. "Do you have any idea what this means?"

"Do you, sir?"

The astonishment left the captain's face. A weird gleam now appeared in his eyes. "Very well, Lieutenant. Petor!"

"Won't be doing anymore fighting today," Marten said, his hand dropping to his holstered pistol.

"Oh no, Lieutenant, no, no. Perhaps you think I can't disarm you on the instant. So please notice my other bodyguard."

"I am. My Top Sergeant stands behind him."

Captain Sigmir raised his eyebrows, held Marten's gaze a moment longer and glanced back. Omi stood behind the bodyguard. The ex-gunman leaned against the railing. As if resting his hand, Omi had it on the butt of *his* holstered pistol.

Captain Sigmir smiled in a strange way and said, "Very good." Then he turned and without another word marched off, his two bodyguards trailing.

"I don't like this," said Stick, as he helped Turbo.

"No," said Marten, his gut churning. What did that strange smile mean? And why had the captain given up so easily? Marten feared for their future.

6.

The following evening Tokyo hove into view. They saw the fires kilometers before they saw the Japanese landmass. An orange glow sat on the midnight horizon. Even this far out smoke blotted out the stars and the half moon that an hour ago shone serenely upon the sea.

The original port of entry, according to swollen-mouthed Turbo, had been Tokyo Harbor. They would now disembark on the peninsula and in the city of Miura. A seventy kilometer march would bring them near the merculite missile battery, the site of the civil war's most vicious fighting. They feared Captain Sigmir, wondering how he would discipline them. They hoped his Tenth Company operational planning kept him from carrying-out any retribution long enough for him to die in combat.

An hour later, the four transport-hovers docked and the men jogged off in full gear. Instead of marching into the heart of Tokyo, they filed into waiting trucks—ancient, beat-up relics—and they immediately roared off toward the fires in the distance.

A corporal on loan from the 9th FEC Division, a first-wave invading unit, shouted instructions at Marten as the truck bounced along the potted road. Enemy artillery boomed in the distance. Highborn rocket launchers whistled loudly in return. Besides the outer noises, their truck rattled and quavered as its worn engine roared.

"If you see anybody who's not wearing FEC brown, combat body armor or riding the sky on his jetpack, you shoot him!" shouted the corporal, a skinny kid who couldn't have been any older than nineteen. "And don't take off your armor or helmets unless you're underground in a bunker or in the infirmary!"

"What about the Highborn?" Marten shouted back.

"What about them?"

"What do we do if we run into them?"

"Stay out of their way. But if you can't, don't speak unless spoken to. You already know that. Surely your captain has taught you the proper responses."

Stick muttered something unintelligible.

"Now," shouted the corporal. "If somebody waves to you, a civilian I mean, shoot him. If he looks sick or is crying, shoot him even faster. They're all bastards and trying to get close enough so they can blow you and them to heaven. They're all insane in this part of the world."

"What about children?" shouted Turbo.

"They're the worst." The corporal thoughtfully studied the worried soldiers of Second Platoon. "I know it's hard, and you'll feel terrible afterward. But when you see your buddies shredded before your eyes and you're the only one left after several days, it gets easier. So just gun them down and maybe you'll be riding a truck someday telling others how to survive this hellhole."

The men absorbed his words in silence.

"How long you been here?" asked Omi.

"From the beginning. Okay, listen close now. When they tell you it's the big push, they mean you gotta go over the top and storm assault a strongpoint. When they say hold, it means you're surrounded and they can't get any more supplies through until tomorrow. So don't fire everything away in one burst, but start sniping. And if they tell you about how your name will go down in history, well, it's all over for you then. Your only hope at that point is that masonry covers you in an enemy blast but doesn't kill or cripple you—and of course that our side digs you out in several days. If it's the enemy who digs you out." He shrugged. "Save the last bullet for yourself is my advice. Like I said, they're all bastards here. Oh, and don't believe anything they told you about Suspend and revival later. That's all crap. We're all expendable expect for the Highborn."

"How long can this go on?" shouted Turbo.

"I'll tell you how long: Until the Highborn decide."

"What do you mean?" asked Marten.

The corporal shouted, "Couldn't the Highborn take Tokyo if they really wanted? I think so. They've taken everything else. Why not here?"

Marten and his sergeants must have looked unimpressed.

"Hey," said the corporal, "I saw what the power-suited giants could do the first day of the invasion. Nothing could stand against them. If someone could stand, they simply leaped to a different place and attacked from the opposite direction. None of that matters to you. At o-three hundred tonight you're moving into your defensive position. So good luck."

He held out his hand, Marten shook it. "You're not going with us?"

"No, sir. I'm getting off at the next stop to instruct the next batch of fodder."

"Fodder?" asked Turbo.

"Sorry. I wasn't supposed to say that." The corporal grinned, but it lacked sincerity. "Show them what Aussies are made of, mate."

7.

Heavy shelling made the trucks shiver so badly they halted twenty kilometers short of their destination. The men dismounted and entered an inferno. Rubble and ruined, smoldering buildings towered all around them. Smoke billowed into the night sky and flames shot up high in the distance. They felt the heat of it on their faces and the acrid smell seared the inside of their nostrils. Exploding rockets shook the ground and made them duck and start walking in a bent-over crouch. In the near distance mortars crumped. Farther away artillery boomed and occasionally a hellish red laser beamed down from somewhere unseen in the sky. That sound was the worst, a high whine that grated on the nerves and always caused a gut-wrenching explosion.

Hunch-shouldered guides led them through the shattered mess of the city. As they marched, they crunched over broken glass, concrete, spent casings and shredded clothing.

For three hours, they marched, getting sweaty in their steel and ceramic helmets, armor vests and leggings. Sometimes men popped up from trenches or foxholes and gave them a thumbs-up. At other times, hollowed-eyed soldiers simply stared at them. The worst were those who refused to glance over, as if they didn't exist.

"Look at those guys," muttered Turbo. "That's what we're gonna look like soon."

"Quiet in the ranks," said Marten.

They marched to the front, to endless screams, whistles, bangs and thundering guns. And always that red glow showed where Tokyo burned hottest. The stench grew worse and finally they slipped in their nose filters. It was highly uncomfortable, but it made breathing possible again.

A unit of glassy-eyed troops staggered along the other side of the road, away from the front, probably for refit. Their armor-vests stank of smoke and gore, their skin was either chalky or filthy from dirt. None of them could work up a cheer for the 93rd Slumlords.

"See," Marten shouted to Second Platoon, "if we work as a team it's possible to survive."

Ex-Sydney slum dwellers stared at him in disbelief. They looked more than ever like smalltime gang members, drug runners and misfits. Slapping armor onto them and giving them guns wasn't going to turn them into soldiers, not after a mere six weeks of basic training.

Finally, the guides brought the 93rd to a set of underground bunkers. It was five in the morning and Second Platoon, given its own bunker, was exhausted physically and mentally. The men threw down their arms, slipped off their armor and sank onto cots and chairs.

A man popped into the bunker, shouting, "Lieutenant Marten!"

"What?"

"Follow me, sir. Conference, two bunkers over."

Marten hurried after him into another bunker and to a small room filled with the combat officers of the 93rd Battalion/20th FEC Division. Captain Sigmir signaled him to sit beside huge Kang, the Lieutenant of First Platoon/Tenth Company.

Charts came out, a fast pep talk by the Highborn Colonel and some counsel on how to lead their men this first day into combat and then finally their objective. They would hold a 'quiet sector,' a huge hulk of a granary. It seemed the enemy had found underground entry holes into this food storage complex, so they were to watch for crafty, sneak raids. The granary was part of a slow, encircling siege-move on the merculite battery. The massive granary was made out of old-fashioned plasteel. Neither continued enemy shelling, plasma nor wave-assaults had taken it out. Since it anchored tomorrow's planned assaults, the granary had to be held at all costs. Tenth Company would have floor and basement duty, and as it turned out Second Platoon would be the point unit down there. More was said, but after learning his brief, Marten paid the rest slight attention.

"This is it," said the Colonel, another Lot Six Highborn, but saner than Captain Sigmir. "This is what you trained for. Now show us that you premen are worthy of retraining and rank in the New Order."

A half-hour later Stick complained to Marten, "Why us?"

"Why do you think?" asked Omi.

Their part of the basement duty proved to be a maze of fallen rubble, blasted holes in the ceiling that rained a couple bricks every now and then, narrow corridors from one point to the next and a groaning mass above that threatened a cave-in at any moment.

As he'd been trained, Marten put his eighty men into their positions. At the very least, he always left a corporal in charge of a squad. Some of the men grabbed shut-eye—the smart ones, it turned out.

After six hours of waiting, Japanese tunnel rats boiled out of the sewers. They attacked with bellowing yells, vibroknives and shock grenades. From every direction around Second Platoon, or so it seemed, the enemy drove in. The newly trained FEC soldiers screamed in fear, their carbines chattering in the dark. Grenades roared. There was more screaming, and then vibroknives hacked and slashed. The screaming grew higher-pitched. From above, as if timed, the entire granary shook. Static cut out communications. Helmet lamps snapped on, the light washing through chalky dust that floated everywhere. Shock grenades flew at every point of light.

"Turn them off and snap on your infrareds!" Marten yelled. He stood behind a chunk of fallen ceiling. Behind him, two privates fired blindly into the dark. He used his sidearm, firing at anything that moved.

"Omi!" he shouted into his mike. Crackle filled his earphones.

"Banzai!" screamed out of the darkness.

Marten whirled around. A grenade landed at his feet. Marten lunged, scooped and hurled it back, then ducked. It flashed. The blast knocked him against his concrete slab. Three howling enemy soldiers threw themselves at him. One FEC private gurgled as a blade whipped through his throat. Marten rapid fired. Two Japanese flopped against the wall. The last one tried to skewer him in the gut. For a second Marten's armor held as the vibroblade whined against it. He clouted the soldier with the butt end of his pistol. Then he stomped on the man's knife-hand, who grunted in pain. Finally, Marten put the barrel against the helmeted head and pulled the trigger. Gore and blood stained his armor, but Marten was past caring. Six weeks of training and something else deep in him bubbled to the forefront.

"Come on!" he shouted. The remaining private followed him into the darkness.

Picking up men as he went, Marten rallied what was left of his command. Too many, far too many of the former slum dwellers lay sprawled in death or scattered in bloody pieces. The survivors of Second Platoon demanded blood in return. Kicking, biting, firing, stomping and smashing they drove the tunnel rats back into their holes. Then a lull hit as the remaining enemy gasped his last on the floor. Single shots rang out as untrusting FEC soldiers checked the supposed dead.

Second Platoon was learning fast that only fools took chances. Shocked, pale-faced men, their chests heaving, looked to Marten for an explanation. He stared at the darkness out of which the enemy had come. His eyes narrowed. He was a soldier, eh? Then he was gonna do things right! He motioned them to follow him as he retreated, blowing corridors as they went, working their way topside step by step. Ten minutes later a headcount showed him fifty-eight men out of eighty had survived this first encounter with the enemy.

After manning the new positions, Marten called in to report. Captain Sigmir demanded a face-to-face encounter.

"Should I join you?" Omi asked.

Marten eyed the dark stairwell leading down to the basement. He didn't want to face the captain alone, and Omi was his toughest, steadiest man. But that meant the ex-gunman was needed here.

"No," said Marten. "I'll be fine." Besides, what could Omi really do against Captain Sigmir?

"I'm coming then," said Stick.

Marten shook his head and humped alone to Tenth Company's HQ in what had once been the granary's receiving office. There was hot coffee and donuts, of all things. A man typed a report on a computer. The other HQ Company staff, including the two bodyguards, watched and listened.

Captain Sigmir leaned back in his chair. He sat behind a desk. Marten stood at attention before it.

"Lieutenant," asked Sigmir, "how many enemy dead?"

Marten shrugged.

"Lieutenant, you surprise me. You left your basement post, retreated in face of the enemy—"

"Begging your pardon, sir, we first killed them all."

"I fail to understand then why you retreated."

"Because I took heavy casualties, sir."

The captain drummed his huge fingers on the desk.

"Your orders included no such provision as retreat. You must hold your post until relieved or until you're dead."

"That isn't what you told us in training, sir."

The captain raised his eyebrows.

"You said a good commander saves his men through maneuver instead of being bullheaded. I retreated so I wouldn't be outmaneuvered again. They know that basement too well, sir."

"Spurious reasoning, Lieutenant. A barracks lawyer is what you sound like to me."

"I repositioned Second Platoon at the two stairwells that are left, sir. They won't slip up here so easily."

Captain Sigmir slapped a hand onto the polished oak desk. "What? So the enemy is free to dig through the other stairwells!"

"No, sir. I put sensors amid those pile-ups. If they're able to dig through there... sir, we'll know right away."

Captain Sigmir stood. Everyone around them stopped what they were doing, glancing up in fear at the massive, Lot Six, brain-damaged Highborn.

"Lieutenant, you realize that because of this act of cowardice on your part that I could have you dragged behind the office and shot in the back of the head." Sigmir snapped his fingers. "Then you'd be dead and Top Sergeant Omi would take your platoon into the abyss."

Marten stiffened to absolute attention.

"Or perhaps I should march you back to your platoon and throttle you myself, as an example to the others."

"Sir, I—"

"Silence!" roared Captain Sigmir.

Marten's fingers twitched, the only indication that he almost drew his pistol to try to gun down this monster. He was certain that it would be futile, but he didn't want to die without a fight.

Captain Sigmir's eyes gleamed as his weird smile stretched into place. "Step outside with me, Lieutenant." The captain strode ahead and out of the office.

A moment later Marten stepped through, his hand on the butt of his pistol.

Captain Sigmir stood several feet away, his hands on his hips as he peered down at Marten. "So, the preman has balls, does he?"

Marten gulped the lump out of his throat, closing the door behind him.

"You could draw, Lieutenant, and then you'd be dead."

Marten wondered if that was true.

Captain Sigmir showed his teeth in a feral grin. "How little you premen understand us, even me, a damaged beta. Yet I am a Highborn. Do you doubt that?"

Marten slowly shook his head.

"I herd premen into battle, trying to make warriors out of you. It isn't an enviable task, but it is a purpose, and it is one that I will succeed at. Lieutenant, you can't pit your skills against mine. To even think so is sad and hopeless. And so few of you actually have any potential. Yet... I will admit that there is something different about you."

"Sir?"

"Your men look up to you, Lieutenant, and do you know why?"

"No, sir."

"Come now, don't be humble. I dislike such pretense."

Marten licked his lips. Sigmir seemed capable of anything, of any absurdity. He dared say, "I'm not fond of pretense either, sir."

That wolfish grin grew. "Well said, Lieutenant. They look up to you because you've dared to stand up to me. They rightly recognize that as an act of bravery. And now you've taken your platoon out of the tunnels. Yes, it was the correct military move. I knew you were the best of my tacticians."

Marten was bewildered. "I don't understand, sir."

"You've shown initiative, Lieutenant, and you've gained the thanks and respect of your men because of it."

"But.... I've only fifty-eight men left."

"Premen. *Untermensch.*"

"Sir?"

"*Untermensch*, Lieutenant, sub-humans, sheep, fodder, take your pick. So few of them are soldiers, none warriors. The enemy has now shed the useless ones for you."

"Sir?"

"Fifty-eight men out of eighty, Lieutenant, the ones who fought their way out of the horror of hand-to-hand combat in the dark. The fifty-eight: those who might yet make passable soldiers. By posting you where I did, I've done the hard work for you."

Marten stared at Captain Sigmir, at the nakedness of the man's arrogance and madness.

Sigmir clasped his hands behind his back. "Do you know, Lieutenant, that I will gain rank because of the Siege of Tokyo? I will gain a high place in the New Order."

"On our bodies, sir?"

"Exactly! Yes, you do understand. I suspected you might. I have given you the respect of your sheep, Lieutenant. It is my gift to you because of what I will demand. Consider my revelation, and perhaps someday I will allow you to be my aide as I rise in rank." The smile became a trifle sad. "For premen, I'm afraid, true rank is impossible to achieve, no matter what the Colonel told you." The smile became crooked and Sigmir's eyes gleamed. "Do you know, Lieutenant, that in reality Lot Six wasn't a failure?"

Marten spoke carefully. "No, sir, I didn't know that."

"Lot Six was the first of the new men, the *Herrenvolk*, the Master Race."

"Yes, sir."

"Do you truly understand?"

"I think so, sir."

Sigmir nodded. "Yes, perhaps you do. You may go, Lieutenant."

Marten saluted crisply, turned and marched back to his platoon. He realized that as long as Sigmir ran the company that all their lives were in danger. The captain viewed the world through the prism of Highborn concepts of glory.

Marten soon climbed over hunks of concrete and coughed dust out of his throat. Through a hole in the wall, he saw blazing, burning Tokyo. Even though it was day, the black smoke overhead produced a pall of gloom over the doomed city. Tracers flashed and a glob of plasma flew somewhere that thankfully wasn't here. He strode a little farther and shouted the password to a hidden sentry.

Marten soon flopped down within the strongpoint. His men trained their guns at the open stairwell a short distance away. It led into the basement none of them ever wanted to reenter.

"Drink this," said Turbo.

It was hot and jolted Marten's tired brain. At the other strongpoint, Omi commanded the other half of Second Platoon with help from Stick. At least his friends hadn't died in what already was blurring in Marten's mind as a mad, senseless killing frenzy.

He studied his men. Tired, determined soldiers watched that stairwell with grim intensity. Grime streaked their faces, and cuts and bruises. They no longer looked like slum dwellers to Marten.

Turbo had a gash under his eye to add to his puffy lips. He sipped the hot liquid. "This don't make sense," Turbo suddenly whispered, as he leaned near Marten.

"Huh?"

"We can't afford to take losses like this."

Marten thought about Captain Sigmir's words, but he said, "Why do you think the Highborn keep feeding more and more of us into battle?"

"That's just it," Turbo whispered. "That nuke took most of our convoy. How many other convoys have they decimated?"

Marten envisioned the enemy using nukes here. The thought made him sick. "This is Earth's holdout," he said.

"That's what I'm saying. Why don't the Highborn clean it out?"

Marten nodded toward the dark stairwell. "Because these people can *fight*—and don't forget those sea-launched nukes. Maybe the Highborn can't get enough people here to take it."

"I wonder if that's the reason," said Turbo. "Maybe there's a—I don't know, one of their slick, Highborn plans behind all this."

"I don't wonder," said Marten, standing. "Grab some shut-eye. Take a pill if you gotta. I want you fresh in a couple hours when I try to sleep." Then Marten made the rounds to see how his troops were holding up.

8.

Peace reined for nine hours. Then they learned that two more convoys had been nuked and destroyed. There had been no survivors. Each convoy had been earmarked for Tokyo, for the big push to the merculite battery. Soon thereafter, the Colonel of the *Slumlord* Battalion called his captains and lieutenants together in his HQ in the granary's old monitoring station. Most of the surveillance screens in the room had been broken the day they stormed the granary. Bloodstains still marred the walls. They sat in high-backed chairs around a large table. The Lot Six Highborn towered over everyone else.

"There's been a change in emphasis, gentlemen," the Colonel said, standing at the end of the table. He rapped it with a large knuckle. "Advance at any cost is no longer the prime directive. You are now to husband your men, bleed the enemy and wait for reinforcements to get through."

"Sir?" asked Sigmir.

"We've reentered a maneuver stage," the Colonel said. "Verdun tactics—at least until the transports start getting through in numbers—will no longer dictate our actions. Ninety percent of the reinforcements are marked for the panzer drive north and the heavy infantry push to our south. Our goal, gentlemen, is to pin down as many enemy formations as possible."

Marten had learned that the greatest asset of the Highborn was their ability to shift plans. If the situation changed, their goals changed to suit what was possible. It was a daunting power, and he felt uncomfortable in their presence, even if they were only Lot Six, seven-foot tall Highborn. The weird vitality, the intense stares, the *life force* emanating from them made him feel small, weak and inferior. And that made him angry. So he cleared his throat and asked, "What are Verdun tactics?"

The four Highborn glowered: the Colonel and his three captains. The lieutenants, Australian-born all, perked up.

"Mind your place, preman," growled Sigmir.

"Now, now," said the Colonel. "Perhaps an explanation is justified. Verdun was a battle-site in World War One, Lieutenant." The Colonel must have noticed Marten's perplexity. "One side set out to grind down the other through a vast battle of attrition. I think the term 'meat-grinder' has been used among your men. Such a term is rather accurate, as such things go, and Verdun had been planned as a meat-grinder."

"I don't understand," Marten said.

The Colonel glanced sharply at Sigmir.

"I believe he grasps the concept, Colonel," Sigmir said. "What he's trying to—"

"—He'd better grasp it," interrupted the Colonel. "Otherwise he should be instantly demoted to private."

Marten hated their arrogance. Sure, they could outfight and out-think him, but he was putting his life on the chopping block for them. The least they could do was treat him like a man. He asked, "What was the reason for using Verdun tactics?"

"I just explained that," snapped the Colonel.

"I don't mean back then, sir," Marten said, "but for using such tactics here."

"That's quite outside your theater of concern," the Colonel said loftily.

Marten couldn't agree, nor would he let it go. "Sir, do you mean to say that the Slumlords were supposed to grind the enemy by letting ourselves be ground in return?"

"Weren't you listening?" asked the Colonel. "Verdun tactics are suspended until further notice."

"I realize that, sir. My question is why did High Command ever plan to use them in the first place? It seems beneath Highborn military skills."

The Colonel stiffened as the room grew still. The four Highborn gave off a caged tiger feeling, like a mad beast lashing its tail, eager to pounce and kill. The force of it, in a knot of radiating will, hit Marten almost like a physical blow.

The regular men, the FEC lieutenants, grew uneasy and then visibly scared. Kang was a huge man by normal standards but dwarfed by the Highborn. He slid his chair away from Marten until Marten sat alone.

The Colonel worked to control himself. He finally said, "To be frank, Lieutenant, High Command believed that Verdun tactics was all that you hastily-trained premen were capable of."

"But now, sir?" Marten asked.

The Colonel flushed, his snow-white skin turning crimson. "Can't you discipline your men?" he snapped at Sigmir.

Sigmir reached out and cuffed Marten across the back of the head.

Marten jerked around as his hand automatically dropped to his holstered pistol.

"I'd make him point man," the Colonel icily told Sigmir.

Marten released the pistol butt and stared at the table. He'd discovered that the Highborn thrived on premen acts of contrition. It fed their bloated egos and made them feel even more smugly superior.

With the slightest dip of his head, Sigmir acknowledged the Colonel's suggestion. "Yes, perhaps I shall put him on point."

"Fighting spirit is one thing," the Colonel said, "this lack of disciple quite another."

"He will be taught his place," Sigmir assured the Colonel. "Lieutenant, you will remain silent until further notice."

"Yes, sir," Marten said. "I'm sorry, Colonel."

The Colonel sniffed loudly, and then ignored Marten as beneath his notice. "As I was saying—"

An alarm cut him off. Com-lines buzzed and the entire granary trembled—caused by enemy artillery shells hammering against it. Concrete pebbles from the ceiling were dislodged and rattled upon the table. Dust drifted.

"To your posts!" roared the Colonel.

9.

Having slipped onto Japan so that he could lead the fighting from the home islands, Field Marshal Kitamura had given the word for the grand frontal assault. If they could clear Tokyo, then reinforcements could be rushed north and south, and then maybe Japan could be held until Operation Togo. But first tasks first. So quick-trained levies boiled up from the depths. Samurai Divisions gathered their strength and Kamikaze squads strapped on their bombs. What was left of the airforce hurled itself at the largest Highborn concentrations. A massive artillery park endlessly shelled enemy territory.

The FEC 4th Army took the brunt of the first day's attack. It was composed of the broken 9th, the newly arrived 10th and the yet intact 12th, 20th and 22nd FEC Divisions. The remnants of two other divisions, shattered beyond repair, had been taken to the docks and reformed into a garrison brigade. The 23rd and 204th Jump-Jet Battalions provided mobile elites to plug any gaps. Lastly, prowling the back lines, shooting stragglers, regrouping others, in effect stiffening the FEC volunteers by their presence, was the Highborn 91st Drop Assault Battalion. The giants in their heavy combat armor were the terror of both sides. The better-off FEC 7th Army held the city to the south, while the 5th Panzer Corps was to the 4th

Army's north. An offshore battery of artillery-bearing submarines provided the armies with gun tubes, while an orbital laser station was dedicated for Highborn Tokyo use.

Roughly, one hundred thousand FEC soldiers with a smattering of Highborn waged street war against three hundred thousand Japanese. A few of the Japanese formations were the dreaded Samurai Divisions, well-trained soldiers that man for man were more than a match versus the best-trained FEC formations. However, the bulk of the three hundred thousand Japanese were hastily trained civilians, stiffened by police units. They'd had even less training-time than the FEC volunteers. Nor had they the benefit of Highborn instructors. To make matters worse, they were more poorly armed and armored than their FEC counterparts.

The Japanese frontal attack lacked grace. Field Marshal Kitamura knew his soldiers: they were brave but barely trained. Boldly led in attacks their morale might last a week, maybe a few days beyond that. Then newer levies still training in the depths could be brought up and thrown into the cauldron. Of course, complex tactics were beyond them. So he hurled them straight at the enemy, or as he told his commanders, "We'll shove a spear into their guts." To add to the spear's effectiveness, he tied on a bomb as it were onto the tip, in this instance, the Kamikaze squads.

To Marten and his men, the sequence seldom varied.

First enemy artillery pounded their positions. Following almost on its heels screamed the demonic suicide squads. They crawled, ran, limped, dropped down with jetpacks, popped out of sewers, anyway they could they tried to close and detonate. Then waves of hypnotically bolstered soldiers or stim-induced berserks rushed in. They were armed with carbines, sometimes with heavier weapons, always hurling grenades and

251

fighting hand-to-hand with vibroknives and swords if they could. A few times the Samurai Divisions clanked forward in their dreaded bio-tanks.

Almost as bad as the constant attacking, Highborn Intelligence learned that an entirely new batch of recruits, another two hundred thousand, trained deep in the city for the next wave. From intercepted communications, it was clear that Tokyo was to remain a sea of bloodshed, that the city would be held at any cost. Intercepted holo-news reports showed that Social Unity lied to the people of Tokyo trapped below. The holo-shows told of incredible victories, that soon the Supremacists would be hurled back into space.

Above ground, the realities of the situation dictated the strategy for each side and that governed tactics. The underwater nuclear attacks had badly hurt the Highborn ability to re-supply the city. Ninety percent of whatever got through to Japan went north and south. Seldom did anything trickle into Tokyo.

A week after the initial attack, Marten lay hidden behind the twisted heap of a battle tank. The metallic corpse had the dimensions of a dinosaur. He rested his new sniper laser on the twisted tank body, tracking through his scope for signs of enemy. Beside him, Stick gasped, having just run from Company HQ with orders from Captain Sigmir. It was near noon, but that was difficult to tell under these conditions. Like ominous thunderclouds, a vast sea of smoke blotted out the sunlight. From various parts of the city flames and more funneling smoke rose. Here and there behind both lines, artillery tubes spat fire. Marten ignored it all as he tracked across a field of rubble and boulder-strewn chunks of plasteel and concrete. Beyond the rubble stood ruined buildings, their walls immodestly torn away to reveal the various floors.

"Do you believe them?" Stick whispered.

Marten pressed the firing stud. A flash of laser-light stabbed a man crawling toward them—he was forty meters away. The bomb strapped to his chest exploded. Stones flew up and rattled against the dead tank. Marten rolled and slithered through the dust and dirt to a broken sign for Tempko Sake. Stick tagged along. Two Japanese on the third floor of the nearest building stepped forward. Each aimed his electromag grenade launcher at the useless bio-tank—where Marten had just been. Marten lasered them. Then he moved again.

"Well?" asked Stick a little later.

"Well what?" whispered Marten from a foxhole he'd dug earlier. He tracked across the rubble, watching carefully.

"Do you believe the reports?"

"Which ones?"

"That High Command is finally hunting down the last of the nuke-launching subs?"

"Sure, I believe that."

"Do you think *they* know that?"

"Who?"

"The enemy generals!" said Stick.

Marten's eyes widened as the hairs on the back of his neck rose. He jumped out of the foxhole, pulling Stick with him. Hunched over, they sprinted to a trench where several men of their platoon manned a tripod flamer. "Down," hissed Marten.

Everyone flattened himself against the bottom of the trench.

Shells screamed out of the dark sky, hammering against the old tank, the sign and on top of the foxhole. More rubble, stones, dust and miscellaneous items including flesh was flung into the acrid air. The barrage lasted seconds, and then silence ruled again. Marten rose, peering over the lip of the trench as he listened carefully.

He heard the crunch of boots before he saw the gray movement.

"Up," he whispered.

Around him soldiers rose, and now each of them could see the wide-eyed Kamikazes, their lips pulled back in a death grimace as they crawled or bounded from spot to spot toward them. Lasers fired—red lines of agony. Kamikazes curled around them, dying, sobbing and sometimes detonating their grisly packages. From south of their trench came wild shouts of rage. A wave of enemy soldiers high on stims raced at them in a desperate bent-over rush. Carbines barked from enemy hips, bullets whined around Marten and his men. One bullet staggered Marten, striking his heavy chest armor and ricocheting away with an evil *spang*. The flamer crew, veterans now, swiveled their weapon and sighted. A strange belching sound issued from their cannon and an orange glob of plasma burned the enemy squad in a fierce sizzle. Beside Marten, one of his men gurgled with a ripped out throat.

There was no time for niceties. They had to spoil the next probing attempt. Marten pointed to three other men: snipers like him. He led them to the dead tank. In this type of battle sniper work was never done.

"If it's true," Stick whispered in his ear, "the enemy generals must know that."

"What are you talking about?" Marten whispered. He was unaware until then that Stick had followed him out of the trench.

"That the enemy soon won't own any more nuke-firing subs."

"So?"

"So, they've got only so long here then until we're reinforced."

"Yeah, that makes sense."

"So how long until they make a final push with everything they got?"

Marten's stomach grew queasy. Since there wasn't much to say about that, he shrugged and kept tracking the ruins.

Suddenly, one of the enemy dead behind them stirred. He was minus an arm, and only one eye worked. He looked up and stretched his torn lips in a dreadful smile as he reached for his detonation button. That caused his elbow to scrape against concrete. Stick whirled around, saw him, drew and fired.

Marten nodded his thanks. He'd give the enemy this: they fought to the end—the little good it did them. Stick probably had it right. The enemy generals had to realize their situation couldn't last forever. The Highborn ruthlessly hunted the nuke-launching submersibles and pared their numbers. Perhaps worse for the enemy in Tokyo, the orbital laser station religiously hunted down and burnt the artillery if it wasn't quick enough to relocate. But worst of all for the enemy were the Highborn who'd crawled forward and studied their tactics. Just like a few minutes ago, FEC troops fell back at the first sign of attack, so hopefully artillery shells exploded upon empty areas. Often Highborn gun tubes fired then, upon the Japanese assembly areas, uncannily catching them at just the wrong moment. The battle was like a clumsy vid-wrestler fighting a cunning knifeman. The knifeman made deadly little cuts and avoided the wrestler's grapples. But if the wrestler ever got a good hold or if he knocked the knife away…

Relentless day and night shelling and the first-day softening nukes of the original Highborn attack had turned the buildings, streets and the near-surface tunnels of Tokyo into rubble and ruin, and that made wonderful defensive terrain. In a week of fighting tens of thousand of Japanese soldiers had died hideously; burned, shot, gutted and blown to bloody bits. According to the latest reports, more enemy engineer and flamer troops were being

255

rushed up from deep within Tokyo. Sigmir had told them that in ages past flamethrowers had been used for close combat. The flamer was the modern progeny. It discharged a short-range glob of plasma and could kill even heavily armored Highborn. Marten had seen it happen, and he'd seen the rescue teams rushing to the Highborn to take them back to the hospital submarine to resurrect them if they could.

The Highborn who'd studied the enemy had made their reports and recommendations. Now the Highborn colonels and captains intensively trained the FEC soldiers in even smaller unit tactics. Instead of platoons and companies being the units of maneuver and fighting, it had become the individual sniper and the storm group. Storm groups were built around the three-man tripod flamer crew. To support the flamer the others carried sniper lasers, gyroc rocket carbines, machine pistols, and grenades for close-in work. This was no longer street fighting in the usual sense. To stand in the open was too dangerous. Most of the fighting took place inside the ruined buildings or near them.

As he scanned the rubble, Marten uneasily rolled his shoulders. "They're not finished here today," he whispered, feeling the enemy out there.

"Should we fall back?" asked Stick.

Marten considered it, and then shook his head. High Command had at last ordered them to stop retreating. The week of relentless enemy frontal assaults had driven the FEC formations too far out of position for High Command's ulterior plans, or so Sigmir had told him this morning.

Before Omi's team replaced his, Marten fought off two more Japanese probes and one more wave attack. He and his assault group of eight men slew forty-three enemies, losing only the throat-shot private in return. By Highborn standards, it was an excellent morning's work.

Finally he and his team humped back to company HQ, a hundred meters behind the twisted wreck of a Samurai tank. Holes in the ground were the entrances to the various bunkers.

Petor, the single-eyebrowed Muscovite bodyguard, rose from where he squatted and snapped his fingers.

Marten turned and pointed to himself. Petor nodded, his stimstick waggling in his mouth. Then Petor squatted again before the hole-in-the-ground entrance, with his carbine over his knees.

Marten slipped past him and within the cramped command bunker. It was a simple hole with a thick slab of plasteel for a roof. Despite its crudeness, it was impervious to everything but a direct hit from one of the larger shells. A small bulb on a table provided muted light. Sigmir sat in the only chair, while Kang sat impassively on a stool. The Lot Six Highborn poured over a map of Tokyo.

Sigmir noticed Marten, looking up long enough to say, "Lieutenant, good of you to show." Then he went back to studying the map.

There weren't any more chairs or stools, so with his head bent Marten shuffled near and examined the map. A red circle had been drawn around the merculite missile battery that was now far away.

Sigmir peered at the map, as he said, "No more retreats."

"So you told us this morning."

"Correct. Now we have two more days to prefect our techniques."

Marten glanced at Kang. The huge Mongol sat with his eyes nearly closed. He never spoke in Sigmir's presence unless asked a direct question. Only once had Kang spoken about Sigmir to Marten. He'd said, "You'd better watch out. Sigmir will kill you soon."

"Then help me kill him," Marten had said.

257

Since then Kang rarely spoke to him, no doubt distancing himself from a doomed fool.

"Do you understand what the 'no retreat' order means?" asked Sigmir, his weird eyes glittering intently.

Marten nodded.

"But you're merely a preman," chided Sigmir. "How could you possibly know?"

"Captain, sir, if you'll tell me how I've disobeyed your orders I'll—"

Sigmir laughed, cutting Marten off.

Marten glanced at Kang again, who now seemed to study the map with deeper interest.

"You misunderstand me," said Sigmir. "Yes. You follow orders… most of the time. But for the moment that's not my concern."

"Sir?"

"No more retreats," said Sigmir. "Two more days to refine the new tactics. That means only one thing. Can you guess?"

Marten shook his head.

"Why, the order to advance, of course."

"Advance?" Marten asked in disbelief. "That's insane."

Sigmir's smile vanished. He studied Marten. "How is it that you feel qualified to make negative comments regarding High Command's strategies?"

"Through logic, I suppose."

"Logic!" spat Sigmir. "Say rather: a sheep's bleating."

"I take it we're to be reinforced then."

"Don't be ridiculous."

"A second orbital laser platform will be dedicated to us?"

With a thick finger, Sigmir stabbed the location of the merculite missile battery. "I must be the one to storm it."

Marten lifted an eyebrow. "Just you? I'm impressed."

Sigmir grinned madly. "The Slumlords and I. They, and you, will join in my glory."

"I'm sure they'll be thrilled to hear it."

"Does glory mean so little to you, Lieutenant? Then fix your thoughts on gaining higher rank."

"Never mind the glory or the higher rank. I'd just like to survive Japan."

Sigmir sadly shook his head. "What a pale goal you've given yourself, especially when so much is offered you."

"Offered me?" Marten said, perhaps too impudently.

Kang looked up, and then quickly peered at the map again.

Marten understood it as a warning, but he didn't care. The endless fighting reminded him too much of the Sun-Works Factory around Mercury, of his mother and father who had died there. That caused the carelessness that had landed him in the slime pits. "I've *never* been offered a real choice."

"No?" asked Sigmir.

"If I've gotten anywhere it's because I acted in my best interests, never because of the choices offered me."

"Well said! Once the *Slumlord* Battalion realizes that its best interest lies with me they will strive to join me in my glory."

"Aren't you forgetting something?"

Sigmir frowned thoughtfully. "I don't believe so."

"The Slumlords are the Colonel's battalion."

A twitching smile played upon Sigmir's lips. "Yes, today that is true."

"Today? You're not suggesting—"

Sigmir held up an admonitory finger. "Have a care, preman. One word from me and you'll be bound for a penal regiment."

Marten knew of those. They were given the jobs the other side reserved for its Kamikaze squads. Sigmir's threats were never idle. Still…

Marten leaned on the table, studying the plex-screen map. Sigmir had used a stylus to mark the enemy lines and formations in blue. The red-circled merculite site was far behind those enemy sites. He peered at the brain-damaged 'superman' who dreamed of glory and high rank, saying, "The merculite battery is over a kilometer from here."

"Yes."

"The only way you'll get there is by riding on our bloody carcasses."

"Perhaps you'd like to be point man, to show me the way, as it were."

"Is that the prize for telling the truth?"

Sigmir's dark eyes glittered dangerously. "Truth! Here is truth: do as I order, when I order and you may live. But know this, preman, that the day I die and am not resurrected is the day a posthumous letter requests the Colonel to have you shot for insubordination."

Kang's ever-slit gaze widened minutely as he studied the map.

Marten stepped back. He ached to draw and shoot Sigmir, to kill him and have done with it. It galled him that if he tried, if he even dared touch his holster, that Sigmir could probably kill him before the pistol was halfway out.

"Why not have me shot now?" asked Marten.

"Because you can fight, because you have zeal and the killer instinct. I've told you before how rare that is among your kind. For now, I use you. But the day you are no longer of use...." Sigmir smiled. "That's the day the rabid dog dies."

10.

Day and night, the orbital laser platform sought the thickest concentrations of enemy artillery tubes. Then a thick red beam stabbed out of the sky, burning, exploding and destroying the carefully deployed guns. Japanese tanks, headquarter commands, choppers, thick knots of troops humping over the hardscrabble, all tasted the fury of the space-borne laser. At times VTOL fighters screaming over the city simply vanished in the laser's wash. Newly opened tunnels to the deep city melted, air vents exploded and armored personnel carriers became coffins on wheels. Relentlessly, the Highborn eliminated the war-machines and war-fighting capacity of Tokyo's beleaguered armies. More and more it was simply the soldiers themselves who were left and the weapons they could carry. Food trucks were destroyed, radio beacons turned into slag. Rather than a coordinated army throwing itself upon the enemy, the vast horde of Japanese felt isolated, demoralized and bewildered. Still they fought. Grimly, new squadrons of Kamikazes launched themselves at targets of opportunity. The last bio-tanks were dug in and camouflaged.

Two weeks after their grand assault, the Tokyo soldiers lacked almost any artillery, tanks or coordination. Mortar tubes became highly prized weapons, along with captured flamers. The infantry dug-in as they prepared to hold what they'd taken. In the mass of rubble and ruin, they had the perfect defensive terrain. Hungry, thirsty, bitter and terrified, they'd put up as stubborn a defense as anyone had on Earth.

"Time," Field Marshal Kitamura told them. "You're fighting to give Earth time. So you must hang on and fight!"

Only one high-tech weapon was left them: the massive merculite missile battery. Space-borne lasers couldn't harm it, or the orbital fighters dropping from the stratosphere and launching APEX missiles against it. The four-thousand-ton clamshell of ferroconcrete shrugged off every attack. Then, at just the right moment, the clamshell whirled open like a man lifting his visor. Out flew heavy missiles at the retreating orbital fighters as they roared back into the heavens. The missiles had shot down enough of them so that now the orbital fighters flew less over the dying city. Sometimes the heavy missiles were targeted at the submarines off shore. After that, the orbital laser station and hastily deployed anti-missiles were given the mission of stopping the merculite missiles.

Two and half weeks after the initial Japanese counterassault, High Command ordered the 4th and 7th FEC Armies and the 5th Panzer Corps to go back onto the attack and retake Tokyo. They had perhaps three-quarters of their original troops. The Japanese had maybe a little under half of theirs, and that included the two hundred thousand of the second wave assault. The worst casualties for the FEC formations had been in 4th Army, the 10th FEC Division particularly. Units there had been merged and reformed.

Despite their losses, the 93rd *Slumlord* Battalion led the way into the city; Captain Sigmir eternally enthused at the prospect of smashing into the merculite missile station. When his numbers dwindled, as they did with sickening

262

regularity, re-patched soldiers from the infirmaries found themselves sent there instead of returned to their original units. The few reinforcements to get through from Australia also went there. Sigmir refined the tactics. Marten, Omi and Kang best understood and executed them.

The unit of decision had grown very small indeed: the storm group. Each storm group was composed of several assault groups of six to eight men. Marten commanded the most decorated storm group, with Stick and Turbo as his assault group leaders.

Together, leapfrogging each other, slithering through rubble, blindsiding an enemy strongpoint, they broke repeatedly into the selected building. Dirt-covered and terrified, their throats raw from roaring battle-oaths and screaming for help they fired flash/bang grenades through doors and then rushed through right behind, or they slipped in quietly through windows, or they opened holes-in-the-wall with mortars fired directly. Once they were inside, their machine pistols rattled or a gyroc handgun whooshed as it shot a rocket-propelled slug. The heavy rounds were either chemical or high explosive. Grenades, too, by the cluster, took out stubborn defenders.

Then it was close-in work with vibroblades and spades, which in the furious hand-to-hand combat were often wielded like axes. A rigid biphase carbide/ceramic corselet protected their torsos. The rest of their body and limbs was covered by a full bodysuit of articulated metal and ceramic-plate armor. Their helmets had HUD. They were in constant contact with each other, using their built in com-units. Despite so many advantages, they took inevitable losses.

The assault groups didn't go in without support. As soon as the assault group was inside, a reinforcement group followed. Upon taking and clearing a building, the next objective was preventing the enemy from returning.

The reinforcement groups were more heavily armed with tripod flamers, heavy gyroc rifles, mortars, anti-tank missiles, crowbars, picks and explosives. In addition, a reserve group helped the assault groups block off enemy flank attacks. And if it proved necessary, they helped cover the withdrawal of the assault and reinforcement groups.

Refined through daily practice, Marten and the others became experts at this bitter street warfare. Their biggest threat loomed in Captain Sigmir, in his driving lust to be the one who stormed the merculite missile battery. He fed his obsession to the Colonel, who for reasons unknown thrived upon it. Thus in rather short order Sigmir became the tainted soul of the Slumlords.

Three weeks after the initial Japanese frontal assault, Marten slumped exhausted in an underground enemy bunker. Around him on the floor lay the bloody ruins of twelve Japanese soldiers. The last one, the only body-armored enemy, wore the red epaulettes of PHC. Likely, his fanaticism had kept the other eleven at their post. The rest of the room had shot-up furniture and radios and reeked of cordite. The assault had cost Marten's storm group two men. Omi's reinforcement group charged into the bunker and began searching room through room for secret tunnel entrances.

Marten's joints ached and he'd had his fill of battle. Night and day, he killed men, terrified draftees who fought to protect their homes. He had no love for Social Unity, but were the Highborn any better?

Turbo slid down beside him. His thin face had grown skeletal, his eyes sunken and strange looking. For the past several weeks, his supply of drugs had been cut off.

"When's it gonna be our turn to die?" Turbo whispered.

Marten didn't want to think about that. Besides, he'd vowed his father and mother that he'd die free. This wasn't free. It was just free from the clutches of Social Unity.

"Sigmir's mad," Turbo said quietly.

Marten unlatched his canteen, unscrewed the cap and guzzled water. His throat hurt because he always seemed to be screaming orders in the midst of gun-roaring battle. Where a bullet had grazed his armor, his ribs throbbed. He was dirty, scared and half in a daze.

The bunker reeked of sweat, blood and fear. His men moved sluggishly, some eating their rations, some cleaning their weapons, a few staring at the single dim bulb that provided illumination for this main room. Omi's shouts from the corridors proved he'd found a tunnel entrance. He ordered his reinforcement group to bobby-trap it. Less exhausted than the storm troopers, Omi's men bustled to his command, a few moving through the main bunker room.

"Did you hear me?" whispered Turbo.

"Sure Sigmir's mad," said Marten, screwing the cap onto his canteen. "So what?"

"So what! We gotta do something."

Marten rubbed his eyes. His head hurt most of the time and it was so difficult to think.

"*You* gotta do something!" Turbo said.

"Me?"

"You saved Sydney."

"Turbo…." Marten looked away.

"Is this our life then? Slave soldiers for the masters?"

Marten sat a little straighter. He had to survive... and then what? Maybe one of these days he could escape to the Outer Planets. He snorted at the idea. It seemed impossible that he'd survive this abattoir they called the Siege of Tokyo. Surely, within the week he'd be dead while his friends trudged to the next strongpoint.

"It's either kill or be killed," whispered Turbo.

Marten nodded wearily.

265

Turbo glanced at him out of the corner of his eye, as if judging the effect of his words. "You know, personally speaking, I think Sigmir hates you. He uses you, Marten."

"I don't know."

"He's afraid of you."

Marten snorted.

"You're... different," Turbo said.

"I'm just a man."

"Exactly."

Marten faced the thin junkie. "What's that supposed to mean?"

"You're a man, and that scares Sigmir."

"I'm a preman."

"No, we're premen. You're something else, something from an earlier time, I think."

Just then, Sigmir ducked into the bunker. He rattled in his combat armor. It wasn't a battle suit as the nine-foot Highborn wore, but armor much like the storm troopers used. Sigmir held onto a massive pistol, a gyroc gun that fired .75 caliber rocket shells.

"On your feet!" the Lot Six captain shouted.

The tired storm troopers grumbled, stirring as they glanced at Marten.

"What is it, Captain?" Marten asked from his spot on the floor.

In two strides, Sigmir loomed over him. "On your feet, soldier."

Marten slowly climbed up.

"The 9th had penetrated a street ahead of us." Sigmir said in his overloud voice.

"The 9th FEC Division?"

"Gather your men," said Sigmir.

"Look at them," Marten said in a let's-be-reasonable tone. "We just took this bunker. You can't order them into another assault now."

266

"Get them on their feet!" Sigmir roared, "And outside."

"Captain," said Marten, "sir, you can't just hurl us at another strongpoint without letting us rest first."

Sigmir's eyes widened. "Would you deprive me of glory?"

Marten stared into those wild eyes. Around him Omi and the others watched—they'd come to see what the commotion was about. It would be so easy to step back, lift his gun and kill this insane beast. Perhaps Sigmir sensed that, for he aimed that huge pistol at Marten's face.

"Come with me," whispered the Captain.

Omi stepped forward to protest. Sigmir touched the barrel to Marten's forehead.

"Stay back," Marten told Omi. Then he nodded to Sigmir.

The huge Captain pushed him ahead onto the stairs and up out of the captured bunker. It was a steel-shelled dome only a few feet above ground. Behind them and over a slight rise of rubble waited other FEC assault groups in newly dug trenches. In the other direction lay another field of rubble and then a row of skeleton-like buildings. Far in the distance loomed the mighty merculite missile battery.

"Do you see that building?" Sigmir whispered into his ear.

Marten saw a pockmarked building, a vault-like enemy fortress.

"You will storm it immediately," Sigmir said.

"Now?"

"That is what immediately means."

"May I speak, sir?"

"Ah, at last I've found the key to you, eh, preman. You're pleasant enough when a man has a gun to your head. Now listen to me. I've ordered an artillery strike on the building, then—"

Hideous but pitiful screaming interrupted the speech.

Marten and Sigmir jerked to their left. Two Kamikazes popped out of the earth and sprinted toward them, screaming their death cries, their eyes drugged and glistening. Marten threw himself onto the rubble. Sigmir coolly sighted and fired once, twice, the rocket shells barely igniting before slamming into the two doomed men. One of them, however, pressed his detonation button. He exploded and hot shrapnel flew through the air. One small piece sliced through Sigmir's throat. The huge Highborn had taken off his helmet like everyone else, and his gorget guard had been unbuckled. A look of amazement filled his snow-white face. Then blood jetted and the seven-foot Highborn pitched backward.

Horrified, Marten back-pedaled. For a moment, no one did anything. Then Petor ran forward as he shouted into a hand unit. When he reached the corpse, Petor roared, "Help me!"

"Help you do what?" shouted Marten.

Petor pressed a hypo against Sigmir, no doubt shooting Suspend into the Highborn.

"Help me carry him!" Petor shouted.

Marten hesitated. He should have shot Petor before the bodyguard brought out the hypo. Then Sigmir would stay dead. Maybe—

"Fool!" Petor shouted. "Help me or he'll kill you when he returns."

The second bodyguard ran up. Marten doubted he could kill both of them without notice. And Sigmir already had Suspend in him.

So Marten helped the Muscovite bodyguard haul Sigmir to the rear of their area. It was a cleared plaza with a cluster of torn, two-story buildings. As they lay the body down a rescue team of battle-suited Highborn arrived, four of them. Marten watched them bound in one hundred-meter leaps. They landed in the plaza, their servos whining as the half-ton armor crushed bricks.

Two of the nine-foot giants clanked to Sigmir and set him in a black plastic freezepack that they'd brought. The pack had medkits and other strange devices. Needles stabbed the corpse and then the giants zipped the freezepack shut. The other two spoke with Petor, who pointed out Marten.

Marten rose from where a few of his storm group waited. They'd hurried over after hearing the news. Marten walked away from them so he wouldn't implicate his men in case the approaching masters decided he was to blame for Sigmir's death. Marten stood at attention as the two armored giants clanked to him.

They were huge, towering, menacing. Twenty-millimeter cannons aimed at him. Dark visored helmets, like techno-demons, watched him impassively. His weapons would be useless against them in their armor. He wondered why the battalion attached to the 4th FEC Army didn't simply take Tokyo. Mortar tubes and smart missiles were slung on their backs. They seemed invincible.

The one with a sword emblem on his helmet spoke through amplifiers. "You are Lieutenant Marten Kluge, 2nd Patloon/10th Company/93rd Battalion?"

"I am."

"Report."

In short, concise sentences—the way he'd been trained to speak to Highborn—Marten told the two giants what had happened.

After he was finished, the two giants glanced at each other, their dark visors revealing nothing. Marten felt like a naughty child, and that made him angry. But here, in front of these two, he struggled to suppress his anger.

"Why didn't you fire at the enemy?" asked the giant with the sword emblem.

"They surprised us."

"So you threw yourself down?"

"Yes," said Marten.

"An act of cowardice."

"No," said Marten. "It was one of survival."

"You will not raise your voice to us."

Marten hung his head. "I'm sorry."

"Cowardice," repeated the giant.

"Perhaps even retreat in face of the enemy," suggested the other.

"Which is punishable by death," said the first.

Marten looked up. The two armored giants decided his fate. His only weapon was his wits. "May I speak?" he asked.

The dark visors stared at him.

"Speak," said the first, the one with the sword emblem on his helmet.

"Captain Sigmir shot and killed both Kamikazes. It was due to his misfortune of having taken off his helmet and gorget that he died. I reacted instinctively. And I might add that my storm group had just taken an enemy bunker."

"That is immaterial."

"You'll find that my storm group is the most decorated in the 4th FEC Army."

"Meaningless."

"Surely not," Marten argued. "You Highborn are said to honor valor. If my unit is the most valorous, then surely I, as its leader, must be also."

The two giants considered that. Then the first one said, "If what you say is true, your act of... I will not say cowardice. Rather, cunning, is deplorable."

"I don't understand," said Marten.

"You dropped to the ground in the hopes that your Lot Six commander would be killed."

"I've been in battle too long to think that," Marten said, his stomach knotting at their implacable will. "In fact, I've never heard of two Japanese killing a Highborn."

"Say rather: a Lot Six specimen."

"Captain Sigmir isn't a Highborn?" asked Marten.

The two nine foot giants said nothing. Finally, the first one's amplifier crackled. "We are superiors."

"Why explain anything to him?" asked the second.

"So he understands his insolence and why he must die."

"Does my battle record mean so little?" asked Marten, sweat oozing out of his armpits. "Is there no way that I might gain honor among you?"

Again, they were silent, as if he spoke nonsense and they tried to decipher his possible meanings.

"Show us your hand," said the first.

Marten shucked off his gauntlet and showed them the number two tattooed onto the back of his hand.

"He has risen above himself," said the second.

"So it seems," said the first. "Preman—" The giant suddenly tilted his armored head, no doubt listening to an incoming radio message. A few seconds later he said, "Your Lot Six Captain will deal with you upon his return."

As easy as that, they granted him life. Marten's knees almost buckled, but he locked them and refused to kneel before them.

They turned and clanked to the other two Highborn. Together the Highborn bounded away with Sigmir, their twenty-millimeter cannons barking at an unseen enemy as they leaped toward the rear lines.

Omi strode to Marten, who felt limp, drained, surprised to be alive.

The tough Korean studied him closely.

"I didn't understand half of what they were saying," Marten explained. "But I understood they look at me as if I'm subhuman. And you know what?"

The ex-gunman grunted.

"I'm beginning to take that personally."

11.

They learned that one of the new and improved features of Highborn was a gland that squirted Suspend into the brain at the moment of death. Thus, drugs had frozen Sigmir's brain when he died. No damage had been done because of his lack of oxygen. At least so went the theory.

Three nights later, the Slumlords huddled in an underground garage, sitting on chunks of concrete as they cooked their suppers. Suddenly the talking stopped. Man after man looked up, amazed and fearful at what he saw.

Dressed in gleaming new combat armor, Sigmir strode among them. A fresh scar showed where the shrapnel had torn out his throat. He moved with purpose and force. His eyes glittered more darkly than ever and the corner of his mouth twitched as if he considered a joke that only he knew. There seemed to be a new grimness about him, a feeling that a dead man had joined them. Some of the storm troopers shivered as he marched past, a few crossed themselves with a long-forbidden religious gesture.

Captain Sigmir strode to where Marten sat.

Upon seeing the newly resurrected captain, Marten stared for only a moment. Then he jumped to attention and saluted smartly. "Glad to have you back, sir," Marten said, who kept the quaver and more than a bit of hatred out of his voice.

Sigmir peered at him, the odd twitch never leaving the corner of his mouth. Finally, after an uncomfortable length of time, Sigmir whispered hoarsely, "Prepare for a dawn assault, Lieutenant."

"Sir?"

"I *will* be the first into the merculite missile battery."

"...Yes, sir."

Sigmir examined those who stared at him in shock and fear. "Do any here doubt me?"

No one spoke.

"Nothing will stop me," wheezed Sigmir. "Not death, not the enemy, not the lack of guts in my men." Once more, he examined them. Then he turned and strode to where the Colonel conferred with the other Lot Six captains.

"He's a vampire," whispered Turbo.

"I don't know about that," said Stick, who had yet to touch his food. "But he don't die."

"He's going to kill us," Omi said moodily.

"Why do you think that?" asked Marten.

"I've seen that look before. He's mad, stark raving nuts. And if he has to kill us all to get what he wants then he's going to do it."

"We'll see," said Marten.

12.

8 May 2350

The Pre-Operation Togo military conference: 10.26 A.M.

Participants: Enkov, Hawthorne, Shell (Commander, Orbital Sector), Kitamura (Field Marshal, Japan Sector), Ulrich (Air Marshal, Strategic Command East), O'Connor (Admiral, Pacific Fleet), Green (Colonel-General, Replacement Army East).

Enkov: Commander Shell, please report upon the situation.
Shell: Delicate, Lord Director, but theoretically promising. According to our best information, two Doom Stars and other ancillary spacecraft still hold their station in Mars orbit. A Doom Star guards Venus, one has gone to refit at the Mercury construction yard and one is unaccounted for. We suspect but have not yet located the Doom Star in Earth or in the Moon's orbit. Concerning enemy Near-Earth Orbital deployment, three laser stations continue to search and destroy targets of opportunity, as do two of their missile stations. Three Highborn orbital

274

fighter platforms are dedicated to the present Japanese campaign and are in stationary orbit here, here and here.

Hawthorne: Adherence to our space strategy of scattering and therefore maintaining what is left of our deep-space vessels has forced the Highborn to garrison each of their planets with a Doom Star.

Enkov: That is an imprecise statement, General Hawthorne. They control the near orbit of each of the said planets, but not the planets themselves.

Hawthorne: Yes, Lord Director, I stand corrected.

Shell: The Highborn deploy superior electronic countermeasure and detection equipment, Lord Director. But in their wisdom, Space Command long ago placed emergency pods in Earth orbit for just this situation. These pods have been carefully maneuvered into position and are timed to detonate at the commencement of Operation Togo.

Enkov: Which stations in particular have you targeted?

Shell: Two of the three dedicated Highborn orbital fighter platforms and this laser platform.

Enkov: What about the others?

Shell: I have saved the best for last, Lord Director. Breakthrough beam technology and 'total' construction efforts have given us proton beam stations in seven cities. The proton beams are an order of magnitude greater in power and destructiveness, Lord Director. I assure you, the Highborn have never faced anything like these.

Enkov: Our previous beam sites drained the power grid. If these are more powerful, how have you solved the problem?

Shell: The proton beam is charged directly from a deep-core mine, Lord Director. All other city functions are taken offline or run with emergency systems. The proton beams have full and complete use of the deep mine. Therefore, lack of power is no longer a problem. These beams, they will be a terrible surprise for the Highborn.

For the coming operation, these East Asian stations will target the remaining orbital platforms and—

Enkov: You're ready?

Shell: Yes, Lord Director, but I would like to point out that—

Enkov: Thank you, Commander. Orbital Space Command has done their duty. Air Marshal Ulrich, please make your report.

Ulrich: Lord Director, in the Northern Chinese airfields we have reached seventy-nine percent of the projected strength levels. As mandated, the majority of these combat units are medium and long-range bomber formations. Korea holds the bulk of Fighter Command and is at sixty-three percent of projected strength levels. Long range Trotsky Bombers wait in the Siberian airfields at ninety-one percent operational strength. In another week, we could raise all those percentages near maximum.

Enkov: Four weeks was my original timeframe for the counterattack, Air Marshal. In two days, Operation Togo will commence with the units you already have in place.

Ulrich: Understood, Lord Director. But—

Enkov: Thank you, Air Marshal. Field Marshal Kitamura, please make your report.

Kitamura: The love of the Japanese people for their Director spurs them to deeds of unparalleled heroism, Lord Director. Tokyo holds. Kobi fell only yesterday, but after bitter fighting. Unfortunately, in the north the battle-lines have neared the beleaguered capital. Yet we have found the key to victory, Lord Director. While our army units, guard divisions, in particular, hold the gates, the people train underground in the cities. Thus, we launch endless assaults with the Kamikaze squads, maintaining our trained troops for—

Enkov: The Samurai Divisions?

Kitamura: Yes, Lord Director. They are the guard divisions, the heart of Japanese defense. They have been carefully maintained and they will go over onto the assault for Operation Togo.

Enkov: Tokyo has also held because the enemy's supply lines have been relentlessly disrupted.

Kitamura: The people of Japan agree with you, Lord Director. Your precision nuclear strikes have defeated the mongrel forces of darkness.

Enkov: No, no, not defeated, Field Marshal. We must never overstate. But the nuclear strikes have given us the time to marshal our forces for the supreme blow. It seems, General Hawthorne, that you were wrong concerning Highborn reaction to our nuclear retaliation.

Hawthorne: Frankly, Director—excuse me, Lord Director—I'm amazed at the Highborn's restraint.

Enkov: Not restraint, General. Fear. They evidence the fear of those who have overstepped themselves and now see their dilemma.

Hawthorne: But that's just it, Lord Director. If they were afraid, wouldn't they resort to nuclear retaliation on a massive scale?

Enkov: It always amazes me when my generals don't understand the politics of nuclear weapons. The Highborn didn't first use nuclear weapons in Tokyo because they feared, General Hawthorne, but out of arrogance, which is a form of confidence. Misplaced as that confidence has proved to be. Then they were shocked to discover that Social Unity has not lost its confidence—at no thanks to my generals and their timidity. Yet I don't hold that against you, gentleman. As I said, nuclear weapons are political tools, needing political courage to use. Our nuclear strikes against their sea lines have had a devastating effect. Tokyo holds, where every other city has fallen after less than a three-day assault. For over four weeks, Field Marshal Kitamura has held the Highborn at bay, often taking back lost parts of the city, although now they retreat again. Kobi only fell after a prolonged siege and gave the Highborn savage losses. True, in the north their panzer divisions have wreaked havoc. But that's why Operation Togo will begin in two days. Colonel-General Green, is the Replacement Army ready?

Green: The Siberian, Korean and Northern Chinese ports brim with transports and troops, Lord Director. The numbers are eighty percent of anticipated levels, but only fifty-nine percent of hoped for transports.

O'Connor: We've scraped together everything we could, sir.

Green: No disrepute was meant upon the Navy, Admiral. Those damnable orbital laser stations of theirs keep knocking out the transports.

Enkov: Only fifty-nine percent?

O'Connor: River and canal coasters have been reassigned, Lord Director. In another nine days—

Enkov: No, no, two days. Two days!

O'Connor: In two days perhaps seventy percent could be cobbled together to—

Enkov: I'm disappointed to hear you speak like this, Admiral.

O'Connor: The Highborn strike hard from sea and space, Lord Director. I'm not certain—

Enkov: Admiral O'Connor, defeatist talk is not what I anticipated at this conference, not before the beginning of Operation Togo and the start of the end for the Highborn.

O'Connor: I will do my best, Lord Director.

Enkov: Who said anything about best? You will comply with Social Unity's requirements or I will find someone who can. You must employ 'total' effort.

O'Connor: The Navy stands ready to do its duty, Lord Director.

Enkov: Very good, Admiral. See to it that these are simply not false words given under duress.

Hawthorne: Lord Director, I hold to your principles concerning—

Enkov: The principles of Social Unity, you mean.

Hawthorne: Yes, Lord Director. Your serenity during these terrible days has given us strength and vision. But may I be permitted a possible conjecture concerning the Highborn?

Enkov: I called the conference for the interplay of ideas, General. Please, speak freely.

Hawthorne: My reports indicate that very few Highborn have landed in Japan.

Enkov: Three hundred thousand is a few?

Hawthorne: Their ability to raise Earth units and train them to fighting competency is astounding, Lord Director. The bulk of their invasion army is composed of former Social Unity personnel. Surprising, as it is to report, Lord Director, there are only a few Highborn units on Japan.

Enkov: Your report must be mistaken.

Hawthorne: Body counts of enemy dead indicate—

Enkov: Naturally, when Highborn die in battle their High Command has taken every effort to snatch those fallen bodies and hide the fact of their losses from us. The rebel Earth units—nobody loves traitors, not even those who employ them. So of course, the arrogant Highborn does not attempt to save the corpses of those they refer to as premen, not even their own premen. Field Marshal, don't your men make every effort to drag their dead comrades off the battlefield?

Kitamura: Those in the Samurai Divisions especially do so, Lord Director, in order to cremate them and give the ashes of these heroes to their wives and children.

Enkov: There you are, General Hawthorne. I'm sure the Highborn believe we have no Samurai Divisions, at least if they allowed themselves the sort of conclusions you've drawn from their collected dead.

Hawthorne: One wonders if there might not be another conclusion, Lord Director.

Enkov: By all means, General Hawthorne, tell us this possibility.

Hawthorne: Lord Director, the lack of nuclear retaliation and the lack of overpowering Highborn formations within Japan leads me to a frightening conclusion.

Enkov: Fear must be conquered, General. It amazes me the lack of real courage I find in my military men. No, not the men, but in the officers, in the generals, admirals and air marshals. Nine weeks you originally told me— Nine weeks to build up the force to face these ogres we call Highborn. Many of the directors took their cue from you gentlemen. No! Courage, starting with political courage, with will, gentlemen, the will to face the enemy head on by any means necessary. I've given that tool to Social Unity. Those directors who lacked this quality have given way to those of us who don't. Courage to use nuclear weapons. The will to attack faster than they expected us. Operation Togo must and will catch them flatfooted. Then we will hammer them remorselessly. Every plane, every ship, every trained soldier will be thrown at these mongrel ingrates of the scientists and their biological theories run amok.

Hawthorne: Lord Director, what if the Japanese Invasion is simply a gigantic, Highborn trap?

Enkov: Trap? You think that this is a trap? Unbelievable! If my allegiance monitors hadn't kept careful tabs of your incoming and outgoing calls, General—A trap! You'd better explain yourself and this witless attempt at fear mongering.

Hawthorne: Lord Director, fear mongering is not my intention. And I repeat again that we in Strategic Planning agree totally with your theories on will and courage.

Enkov: Not theories, General. Facts!

Hawthorne: I agree, Lord Director. Yet... I hesitate now in, ah...

280

Enkov: No, no, speak your mind.

Hawthorne: Lord Director... fleet and air units are hardest for us to replace, after space units, of course. What if—the Highborn are clever. They must know we will strike back. That at some point we must strike back if we hope to defeat them. So I am compelled to consider this awful possibility. What if they have staged this invasion in order to draw out our last fleet, air and space units? My reports lead me to—

Enkov: General Hawthorne, I will not tolerate this defeatist talk. Not this late in the planning of the greatest attack to ever be launched against the enemy of man. If there truly is a lack of Highborn formations in Japan, it merely shows that our nuclear strikes were even more effective than we thought. They fear to place Highborn where we can hit them. Their losses, I suggest, have been even heavier than you, my generals, have let on in their various campaigns against us. I understand basic military caution. You have all been trained with it. It is the reason a man like me is needed at such a historic moment. But your collective caution has now edged near treason, for it has developed in many of you an unnatural dread of the Highborn. Strike hard, with the most devastating weapon possible, and we will see how quickly the Highborn lose confidence. Operation Togo, fought at the pace of their own attacks, will utterly demoralize them. All the Solar System will see at last that mongrel dogs cannot beat down Social Unity. Now, if I had let your original suggestion stand of taking nine weeks to gather what I've forced you to do in four weeks.... Field Marshal Kitamura, could you hold out for another five weeks?

Kitamura: It would be difficult at best, Lord Director.

Enkov: How will Operation Togo affect Japanese defense?

Kitamura: A successful counterattack will save the home islands.

Enkov: Do you doubt its success?

Kitamura: Please excuse an old soldier, Lord Director. That military disease you just spoke about had infected me. But your leadership, just as the sun drives away shadows, has driven away the doubts I once had. Operation Togo cannot fail!

Enkov: Your honesty does you great credit, Field Marshal. Alas, nothing is perfect, gentlemen. But we must be confident of the outcome, or how can we expect the soldiers under us to fight all out for victory?

Kitamura: You speak the truth!

Enkov: *This* is the Battle for Earth, gentlemen: the successful completion of Operation Togo. It absolutely must not fail. I expect each of you to goad your men to furious action. If there is any slacking in our counterattacks, then I expect each of you to go out and by personal example revive our warriors. If that means you must make the supreme sacrifice—you will be given a hero's funeral, I assure you. The time of planning is over. Our will is set. Now we must act.

13.

Near-Earth orbit swarmed with hundreds of major satellites. Yet more satellites orbited in the 'higher' LaGrange points. Most of these major-sized habitats were the huge farm platforms that supplied the people of Earth with the bulk of their food. They had been declared open, belonging to neither side. So far, each side had in practice left the farm habs open, or at least neither side had overtly used them militarily. Many of the biggest habitats rotated at the L5 and L4 points in higher Earth orbit. These were often industrial plants, using the raw ore of carefully maneuvered asteroids brought from deeper in the Solar System, or blasted off the moon, or purchased from the Comet Barons of Outer Planets. The profusion of habitats made Earth orbit the most cluttered portion of space in the Solar System. In near-Earth orbit, staring down at the planet, were the three laser platforms, the two missile and three orbital fighter stations of the Highborn.

Following their own particular orbits in and out of this profusion of satellites were small ice-coated pods. Year after year, the pods had orbited. Deep in the ice, about the size of a Twentieth century automobile, was a nuclear bomb with rods pointed outward. Those rods were presently trained at the Highborn military platforms.

Message pulses from Earth activated the almost invisible pods.

The explosions threw off massive qualities of x-rays. Those x-rays sped ahead of the rest of the blast. Before they were destroyed in the incandescent fury of the nuclear explosion, the special rods directed those rays in an invisible beam at the orbital fighter stations.

Unbeknown to most of Earth Command, both the Highborn strategists and their Spy Masters had predicted a massive surprise counterattack. Logically, and because of premen emotional makeup, the Highborn strategists believed the counterattack would take place from Earth. The indicators hadn't been difficult to read. And the Grand Admiral's strategy practically mandated such a counterattack. Thus, over the past few weeks the Highborn had slipped their orbital fighters off the platforms. They couldn't afford staggering losses of these craft. Only now had the orbital-fighter construction factory at the Mercury Sun Works shipped its first batch of new and improved space fighters. Thus, only a few of the dreaded orbitals had been left at the platforms. They ran on full automatic. No living beings, especially not superior new men, were on the attacked platforms. The x-ray beams annihilated the few remaining fighters, the robots in the station and maintenance, and one of the laser platforms, which was also devoid of Highborn personnel. The ice-covered bombs destroyed mere shells; Highborn targets set to take the brunt of a blow they suspected had to be coming soon.

Operation Togo had begun with two deceptions, the Highborn's trumping Social Unity's.

14.

Seventy kilometers north of Beijing, in the Joho Mountains, lay a three hundred-year-old complex of coalmines. Deep within those mines was the mind of Operation Togo. This center coordinated the many and various military limbs of the largest amphibious assault in human history.

In the early morning of 10 May, and several minutes after x-rays demolished the Highborn platforms, dim green light flooded the inner command center, and the glowing eyes of a hundred-odd TV screens added to the illumination. The headquarters staff monitoring these screens and providing communication with the outer limbs spoke in quiet whispers and crept about on soft-soled shoes. Air Marshal Ulrich, a thick-shouldered bull of man and a main nerve nexus to the decision node of this brain, glared at the screens showing various northern Chinese airfields.

HB-13 Annihilators were catapulted out of underground runways, lofting the heavy bombers into the dark, morning sky. Behind them followed long-range NF-5 Night Owls and Wobbly Goblins 9000s, the latest in electronic counter measures aircraft. AL-101 Standoff Screamers, which launched near-space missiles, roared up last to do battle with the remaining space stations.

Hundreds of aircraft per hidden base sped into the night sky, heading toward their rendezvous point over the East China Sea.

A colonel muttered quiet words to the air marshal. He checked his chronometer before grunting, "Scramble Korea."

Airforce staff officers leaned toward their mikes, issuing orders. The screens switched to underground Korean airfields, where swarms of F-33 Tigers and A-14 Laser Razors buzzed into the night sky like angry wasps. They headed directly for the Tsushima Strait and Japan beyond. Lastly lofted sleek attack choppers, whomping a few feet above the waves all the way to the islands.

In the circular chamber, left of air control, Admiral O'Connor likewise studied screens. His showed Earth's last carriers, the latest in ship design. The fast, submersible carriers rose out of the deep and whisked toward Japan on a cushion of air. First Fleet and Second Fleet together numbered over twenty of the sub-hover flattops. They launched bombers, fighters, surveillance craft and cunning ECM drones. Third, Fourth and Fifth Fleets contained every other major oceanic unit left to Earth. Serene underwater shots showed an armada of sleek hunter/killer submarines and the much bulkier cruise missile submarines. Yet other screens provided an idea of the incredible number of troop transport and cargo ships at Social Unity's disposal. In the first wave alone fully seven hundred thousand SU soldiers, twenty-five hundred bio-tanks and one thousand cybertanks would land in the beleaguered Japanese Islands to hurl the hated invader off Earth.

Space control, to the left of Navy, waited to order the interceptors into action and to issue the go-word for the merculite missile batteries in Hong Kong, Beijing and Tokyo. Meanwhile, the newly placed and incredibly powerful proton beam stations in Manila, Taipei,

Shanghai and Vladivostok clawed near-Earth orbit, obliterating the remaining space platforms. Already air-launched missiles from the Standoff Screamers roared into near-orbital space to finish off what the beams missed.

General James Hawthorne paced back and forth in the center of command. Against the Lord Director's strictest orders he had kept observers in various farm habitats orbiting Earth. Despite the open habitat order granted by the Highborn, General Hawthorne needed military personnel there to give him far ranging eyes into space. His disobedience was a tremendous gamble in two completely different ways. If the Highborn found out, they might destroy the habs or they might rescind the open order. If they did either, those areas of Earth still under Social Unity's control could face massive starvation. The second danger, a much more personal threat, was that Lord Director Enkov's allegiance monitors—ruthless secret police agents—might uncover his disobedience. They pried everywhere, and were one source of Enkov's unprecedented power. The bionic guards who lined the circular command chamber and watched everyone were the other source.

General Hawthorne briefly mused upon the Lord Director's ways. Enkov believed in blunt power used brutally. The Lord Director had taken captive family members from each of his military officers ranked colonel or higher. These members had become hostages for their good behavior. It was an ancient trick, and so far, it had worked beautifully, at least in terms of maintained loyalty.

General Hawthorne paced as his air armadas gathered like hungry wolves off Japan's shores. He paced as his fleets hurried to disgorge hundreds of highly trained battalions into battle. He clasped his hands behind his back and strode first one direction and then another. He wore no soft-soled shoes, but military gear that clattered on the tiled floor. He paced in the dim green light. He paced, and he smelled danger. Yes, four weeks ago he'd been in favor of Operation Togo. But since then... was this a trap? He couldn't shake the feeling. And if it were a trap... who would shoulder the blame for it? Not the Lord Director.

The minutes ticked by. The general paced, and his staff officers pointedly ignored him as they studied their screens. Tension grew. He radiated it. They felt it. So far, the Highborn hadn't reacted. No lasers stabbed out of space. The stations had been destroyed or damaged beyond use. No orbital fighters screamed down to face his fighters. Again, it was splendid, unbelievable success against negligible Highborn defense. It was unprecedented. No Thor missiles (rocks hurled down from orbit and sped by gravity) bombarded strong points.

The staff officers showed their nervousness in various ways. They wiped their hands on their pant legs or they lit non-narcotic stimsticks or they kept their faces impassive or they checked their chronometers every ten seconds or—only one man paced, his shoes click, click, clicking on the tiles.

None of them, despite the tension, the grimness of not knowing, of waiting, glanced at the bionic security men who even now guarded against treachery. Those carbines, those surgically enhanced muscles had one purpose, one goal: to slaughter anyone who lifted his hand against the State, which was to say against Lord Director Enkov.

General James Hawthorne stopped and blotted his mouth with his wrist.

Air Marshal Ulrich growled, "We have them!"

General Hawthorne thoughtfully pursed his lips.

"We've caught them by surprise," agreed Commander Shell. "We've cleared near-orbital space of them. Japan is ours for the plucking."

General Hawthorne studied the TV screens showing deep space. It was empty, devoid of enemy craft. Subtlety, his bony features shifted from unease, to suspicion and then to a grim certainty. "Scramble the interceptors," he said.

The staff of Space Control turned sharply. Commander Shell took several steps nearer the general before he clicked his heels together. "Sir! Interceptors have limited fuel capacity. They are only to be launched at intervals, thus always keeping a reserve for when the others are forced to land and refuel."

"I know very well what their limits are," said General Hawthorne. "Scramble them all."

"But sir—"

"This instant, Commander."

The interceptors were planet-based space fighters, a turbine-rocket hybrid. The interceptors' magneto-hydro-dynamic turbines used atmospheric oxidizer until they reached the vacuum of space, then they switched to chemical rockets. The use of the MHD power plant in the atmosphere saved the bulky chemical fuel for vacuum use alone, increasing the pitifully short range of the interceptors. Even so, the range limits called for utterly precise use. Those uses had been drilled into every space control officer from the moment he began his training.

"We've gained tremendous successes," argued Commander Shell. He was a small, hawkish man, young for one of such high rank. "Now is the time to hold our cards and wait for whatever moves the enemy can make."

General Hawthorne stared in dread at the screens showing deep space. His gut boiled. Something, a thing he couldn't see but feel, oh yes, he felt it twisting his innards—He refused to acknowledge Commander Shell.

Commander Shell shot an imploring look at Air Marshal Ulrich.

The bull-shouldered Ulrich stepped near Hawthorne. "James," he said. "We have them. But if they have something that can catch us when all the interceptors have landed…"

"No," said Hawthorne, sweat glistening on his face. "If we had really surprised them they'd have thrown something at us by now, some backup, emergency reserve we couldn't have seen before this."

"That's madness!" said Shell. "We took out everything they had in orbit."

"Yes, much too easily."

"Their arrogance was their undoing," said Shell. "The Lord Director was right. We must not let our… *fear* of them unhinge us."

Hawthorne glanced at Shell.

"I implore you, General, stick to procedure."

"This is a trap," Hawthorne dared say.

"What? Nonsense!"

"Highborn don't go down so easily. We all know that."

Commander Shell snorted. "They aren't really supermen after all. We've simply fallen for their propaganda. Our success today proves that."

Hawthorne stubbornly shook his head. "Launch all your interceptors, Commander."

Commander Shell hesitated. "Perhaps a call to the Lord Director is in order, General."

General Hawthorne faced the smaller man. "Anyone disobeying my orders will be immediately shot. Is that understood, Commander?"

Commander Shell thought about that. Finally, he clicked his heels and issued the needed orders.

Air Marshal Ulrich grunted as he stepped beside his friend. He whispered, "You'd better know what you're doing, James."

A soft, cynical laugh fell from General Hawthorne's lips. Then he clasped his hands behind his back and began to pace again.

15.

Not all of the electronic gear on the space habs orbiting Earth was trained starward. Several passive optic sensors of great power watched the planet, the East Asian Landmass to be precise. Its operators squirted a message to a special satellite that sent it on to the Doom Star *Julius Caesar,* presently hidden behind the largest space habitat in the Solar System, the gigantic Tiaping Hab in 'high' L-5 orbit. The vice-commander in charge immediately beamed a message to Grand Admiral Cassius aboard the sister Doom Star *Genghis Khan,* also lurking behind Tiaping Hab.

The Grand Admiral, his eyes alight with the *need* for bloodshed, barked quick commands. The two Doom Stars—each kilometers in diameter—pumped gravity waves and glided forward under emergency acceleration. Although it had occurred much sooner than anticipated, the premen had at last tripped the wire so carefully set for them. Each Doom Star had taken station eight weeks ago in a stealth move and maintained practically zero radiation and radio signature. Now the admiral would pay the premen back for the arrogance of their nuclear strikes and for daring to destroy the space stations. Now they entered phase three of his intricately mapped strategy. Premen were so naively predictable. He just hoped the entire Free

Earth Corps in Japan wouldn't have to be written off. To start training a new Earth Army all over again… he shrugged. As the brilliant preman Napoleon Bonaparte had once so insightfully said, "You can't make an omelet without breaking eggs."

16.

"Commander!" shouted a staff officer, breaking the quiet of the command center.

Commander Shell growled, "Report."

"Doom Stars, sir."

All eyes turned to the staff officer as Commander Shell and General Hawthorne strode to screen S-Fifteen. They hovered behind the staff officer. With unconcealed dread, they studied the growing shapes. The massive Doom Stars gained momentum as they streaked earthward. Spherical as moons and bristling with weaponry, they were launching squadrons of orbital fighters: squat, wicked craft that every person on Earth had learned to hate.

"They've never used Doom Stars this near Earth," said Hawthorne.

"What are they doing here?" muttered a staff officer.

"We've been tricked," said another.

"They're deep space vessels," Commander Shell said. "Caught in Earth's gravity they'll be easy prey for us." He frowned at the screen, at the mass of orbital fighters that were spewed from the two Doom Stars. "How many orbitals do they hold?"

"I thought we destroyed the bulk of them at their stations," an appalled staff officer whispered.

"I want to know which Doom Stars those are," said General Hawthorne crisply.

"The *Genghis Khan*, sir."

"Grand Admiral Cassius's flagship?" asked General Hawthorne.

Commander Shell grew pale.

"Yes, sir. And the *Julius Caesar*, sir."

Somewhere a man retched. The tension in the command center had grown oppressive. The very air seemed to thicken. The Highborn hadn't yet used the Doom Stars like this—they couldn't afford to lose one. Everyone wondered what their potential was when fighting this far down the gravity well of a major planet.

General Hawthorne stared at the two Doom Stars as if he could will them away. The Highborn had out maneuvered them again, and so easily. If he'd known that Doom Stars were so near—disaster loomed.

"Sir," said Commander Shell, "this means—"

"All interceptors at the *Genghis Khan*," whispered General Hawthorne, glad he'd insisted they all be launched. Already a plan formed in his brilliant mind, a risky, all or nothing gamble.

"What?" said Shell. "But that's suicide! The Doom Stars are still too far out. Let them come into closer Earth orbit."

"Don't you think I know they're still too far out?" shouted Hawthorne.

Commander Shell took a step back.

General Hawthorne breathed deeply, once more using his sleeve to dab his features. "Straight at the *Genghis Khan*," he said softly. "We have to buy our boys time and pray for luck. We'll have the added advantage of surprise."

"What?" said Shell. "Surprise?"

"They'll never expect us to throw the interceptors so deep into space."

A visibly agitated Commander Shell collected himself. Once he had been the highest rated interceptor pilot of Earth. His first love still lay there. Everyone knew it.

"General Hawthorne, sir...." Commander Shell straightened his uniform, stepping closer and saluting. "I respectfully beg to report, sir, we cannot afford to throw away the interceptors."

"Thank you, Commander. I understand your feelings."

"Sir! I—"

"I said thank you, Commander." General Hawthorne stared the smaller man down.

At first Shell stiffened, and something in his manner alerted the bionic guards along the walls.

They shifted their attention to him, an ominous, absorbing interest. He glanced at them. A nervous tic twisted the commander's mouth. Now he couldn't seem to bring himself to stare back into General Hawthorne's eyes. Yet he was a stubborn man, and with eyes downcast, he faced the general. "Sir, if we regroup and scramble North and South American squadrons and met the enemy in the stratosphere—"

"No."

Commander Shell swallowed audibly. "Sir," he said, his shoulders hunching and something elemental draining from him. He turned to the screen.

So did General Hawthorne. Already the interceptors popped out of the stratosphere and into space. Their rockets glowed orange as they shot toward the nearer *Genghis Khan*. As far out as the Doom Star was, it would be doubtful that the interceptors would have enough rocket fuel to return to Earth, not after burning their reserves in space-battle maneuvering.

"The orbitals have high ground," whispered Shell.

General Hawthorne knew that in terms of a space battle Earth was a heavy gravity well. That any craft coming *toward* the planet came as if down a steep hill and any craft heading *up* fought gravity, the same for their torpedoes and missiles. As it was, the squat orbital fighters already held every advantage over the interceptors. To give them high ground as well...

Commander Shell, trembling, ashen-faced, turned for the last time toward General Hawthorne. "Sir—"

The general put his hand on the smaller man's shoulder. "We're going to take massive losses today. My only goal now is make them bleed as much as possible. That means some of the amphibious troops have to make it through." In an authoritative voice he said, "Alert the merculite batteries and the proton stations!"

"We can't fire until the interceptors are out of the way," said Shell.

General Hawthorne stared steely-eyed at the screen. "Like you said, Commander, our interceptors don't have a chance. But they can still be of use as decoys."

A staff officer said, "The batteries and stations are online, sir!"

"Tell them to target the *Genghis Khan* and fire everything they have."

Upon hearing those words, a shocked Space Commander Shell slumped into a nearby chair. His eyes seemed to film with tears, but it was difficult to tell.

17.

The bloody remnants of the 93rd Slumlords fell upon a trench line of Samurai defenders. Men fired at pointblank range. Vibroknives whined; the dying screamed and the shock of grenades hurled both attackers and defenders against the trench walls. Then Captain Sigmir jumped down among them. With his gyroc pistol, he blasted Samurais into gory chunks. When his gun clicked empty, he went berserk. Armored elbows, hands and feet, he lashed in every direction, laughing in maniacal glee as he slaughtered those weaker than him.

Then it was over, the trench taken. The survivors crumpled and tore off their helmets, gasping for air. They were shaken and surprised to be alive. Their faces reflected the certain knowledge that they'd been transported to Hell and that no one knew the way back. Slowly, sanity returned to their eyes. They were embarrassed to glance at each other, to know that others had seen them behave like animals so they could endure another hour of life.

Three hundred meters in front of them towered their goal, the end of a savage quest, a cup of blood that they'd paid in pounds of flesh to sip. The mighty merculite missile station was almost in their grasp—it seemed that they would be the first to reach it. After weeks of butchery and dying, the 93rd Slumlords had breached the battery's outer defenses. Few of the original FEC soldiers were left: Marten, Omi, Turbo, Stick, Kang, Petor and a few others. The 10th Company had less than forty soldiers to its name. Those few set up flamer tripods and smart missile sites. The others guzzled synthahol and cleared filth off their weapons.

These past weeks the FEC 4th and 7th Armies had been bled white, lashed to the attack by the Highborn battalions to their rear and the Lot Six commanders among them. The 5th Panzer Corps also prowled the rear lines, adding to the menace for possible deserters. Both FEC infantry armies were like javelins, hurled at the enemy and broken upon them, but not before killing the target. Effective Tokyo defense had ended, except for pockets of fanatical diehards. The toughest enemy clot remained around the merculite missile station. The FEC survivors now stormed those outer lines, pouring their lives away for the dubious honor of being first to breach the high-tech site.

Sigmir reloaded his pistol and ordered weary men to their feet—they had been attacking continuously for thirteen hours. He motioned to Marten, and together they explored the trench system, finally coming to the trench nearest the station that towered five stories tall. Nearly two hundred meters to their left, FEC storm groups clambered out of the trench and ran in a hunched crouch toward the station.

"No!" hissed Sigmir, as he brought up his gyroc, leveling it at FEC troops that belonged to a different Highborn.

As he aimed mines roared out of the ground where the storm groups ran, killing almost all of them in flashes of flames and hot shrapnel.

Relieved, Sigmir lowered his gun.

"Pathetic suicide," Marten said bitterly. He hated Sigmir. The Highborn... he couldn't decide whom he hated more, PHC officers like Major Orlov or Highborn madman like Captain Sigmir.

Sigmir narrowed his intense gaze as he studied the station. His broad, snow-white face was a strange blend of almost sexual relief and twisted, unbearable tension.

"Maybe one of the Samurais we killed has a map of the minefield," Stick suggested.

Omi snorted at the idea.

"We'll have to slither over the top to get there," said Sigmir. "We'll use sonics to detect and then avoid the mines."

"And die to a flamer sweep," said Marten.

Any good humor he might have had drained from the seven-foot Sigmir. His eyes held death, had seen death, lived it and come back again. The tension in him coiled tighter than ever. What made him an invincible warrior, a death-dealing machine, now radiated toward his own men—that might dare thwart him so near his goal. Softly, with infinite menace, he asked, "You have a better idea, Lieutenant?"

"Yes." Marten gestured to the FEC soldiers that had survived the mines and now furiously dug foxholes as protection against gunfire from the fort. "But until we bring those men out there back here we can't use my idea."

"I'll be the judge of that," said Sigmir. "Tell me."

Marten hesitated. The fanatical way Sigmir scratched his throat told him he didn't really have an option—unless he wanted to kill his commander. But with Highborn that was surer suicide than running over the top. "It's simple," Marten said. "Order an artillery barrage onto the mines."

"Perfect." Sigmir rubbed his hands, and he lifted his com-unit.

"Wait," said Marten. "We have to bring them back first."

"Negative," said Sigmir. "There's not enough time for that. Someone else might enter the station before me if we wait."

"You'd murder them?" Turbo asked in outrage.

Sigmir whirled on him.

"He's tired," said Marten hurriedly. "It's been a long thirteen hours."

Stick nudged Turbo and whispered hotly in his ear.

Turbo got that stubborn look, shaking his head. He told Sigmir, "Crawling out there is insane. Worse, it's death."

Sigmir laughed mirthlessly. "What do you know about 'worse than death'?"

Turbo maybe realized his danger. He shut his mouth and shrugged.

"Yes," purred Sigmir. "It's like I thought. You know nothing. So I will teach you." He shoved his pistol against Turbo's face.

"No!" shouted Marten.

Sigmir fired. Turbo's head disintegrated and his torso flopped to the bottom of the trench. Sigmir jumped back, aiming the gyroc at all of them. "Who else questions me?" he asked in a strange, transported sort of way, as if this was the extreme moment of his life.

They were too stunned to react, and the huge muzzle of the .75 gyroc was aimed at them. Perhaps it was the thirteen hours of constant combat. Besides, what was one more death anyway, even if that of their friend? Before they knew it, Sigmir called for an artillery strike.

"Get down," he ordered.

Marten and the others put on helmets and crouched low, their heads between their knees. Soon hellish screams told of incoming fire. The ground shook and buckled as 155mm and 209mm shells impacted with tremendous roars. High explosive shards flew everywhere, shredding whatever was caught in the open.

Marten endured. If he died, then it was over. If he lived... a savage snarl twisted his lips. Turbo!

The barrage stopped, an awful stillness taking its place. All Marten heard was buzzing and an inner roar. He dared lift his head. A bloody haze mingled with the dust and the rubble that had been rearranged. Beyond the worked-over ground stood the mighty merculite station, the same as ever.

He couldn't believe that Turbo was dead, killed, murdered by Sigmir, just as the FEC soldiers out there in the minefield had been butchered.

"Over the top," shouted Sigmir.

At that moment, the four-thousand-ton clamshell of the merculite missile station whirled open. Rockets roared into life, once more making speech impossible. Huge, heavy missiles lifted out of the station, flames belching behind them. Missile after missile rose and accelerated into the heavens.

As they did, Marten and the others climbed out of the trench, sonic locators in their hands as they crawled across no man's land. Most of the mines had been destroyed. But some always remained. A great weariness filled Marten. It made him so tired that he almost didn't care that Sigmir had murdered his friend. Turbo... there would be no revival for a preman, for a subhuman, a nothing to these... these who called themselves superior, Highborn.

As Marten crawled through the plowed-up ground, he glanced at Omi. The ex-gunman had a hard, grim look. A little farther back, Stick clenched his teeth in rage. If they made it across this expanse—Sigmir's day was near at hand.

Marten's sonic locator beeped. A live mine was getting ready to leap.

18.

Over half of Earth's interceptors hurdled toward the *Genghis Khan*. Torpedoes poured out of the interceptors' tubes and their laser cannons spewed at will. The *Genghis Khan's* anti-missiles knocked out ninety-nine percent of the interceptors' torpedoes. Packets of prismatic chaff absorbed the lasers. Then the orbital fighters began a turkey shoot, destroying interceptors as fast as they could target, lock and fire.

Amid the slaughter, the heavy proton beams from Manila, Taipei, Shanghai and Vladivostok shone. Interceptors and orbital fighters—every space vessel caught in the dull-colored beam—vanished. The real target sprayed lead-lined gel, thousand pound layers of it. The gel absorbed protons, dissipating strength. The proton beams didn't flash in pulses like lasers, however, but maintained constant targeting. The gel heated, melted, and then vanished. The *Genghis Khan* sprayed more. Their supply seemed endless. Yet the new and deadly beams kept shining. Closer and closer, the devastating fury of the proton beams neared the Doom Star.

Grand Admiral Cassius roared orders.

Million-ton chunks of rock previously blown off the moon were maneuvered into position. General Hawthorne's assessment teams had considered them mining asteroids brought near Earth for the industrial habs in high L-5 orbit. Their assessment was horribly wrong. Engines attached to the million-ton rocks pumped furiously. Targeting computers guided the rocks toward their impact points on Earth.

Meanwhile, the first merculite missiles streaked out of the gravity well of Earth and toward the *Genghis Khan*. Normally it would have been simplicity itself for the Highborn to knock out the merculites. However, the orbital fighters alone didn't have the ECM power to lock onto them. The *Julius Caesar* tried, but amid the proton beams, the incredible gel mass between it and its target and the orbital fighters, the *Julius Caesar* failed for the first time in its existence. Anti-missiles from the *Genghis Khan* zoomed at the merculites. The heavily armored Earth rockets shrugged off the majority of the anti-missiles. Of course, a few of the merculites were shifted off target by the blasts. A few headed for deep space. Very few of the merculites exploded. But more than one slammed into the Doom Star *Genghis Khan*.

Explosions like volcanoes threw metal, air and flesh into space. Flames roared briefly, mere nanoseconds, before vacuum stole the needed oxygen. The Doom Star was compartmentalized like a beehive, but Grand Admiral Cassius was flabbergasted that the premen had attained this much. The Doom Stars were the Highborn, the essence of their power. If one was destroyed....

More merculites hit the stricken vessel.

Admiral Cassius closed his eyes, trying to contain his rage. He breathed heavily, opened bloodshot eyes and ordered the *Genghis Khan* to break off.

As he spoke, more explosions rocked the massive ship. Damage control reported a full eighth of the ship on fire or destroyed. Another eighth was in immediate danger. The *Genghis Khan* could very well be destroyed if something wasn't done fast to counteract such a tragedy.

Reluctant, enraged, baffled, Grand Admiral Cassius ordered an antimatter strike in near space.

Bombs sped almost instantly from the *Genghis Khan* and detonated just as fast. Killing EMP surges washed over the Doom Stars and down at the merculites racing up. Hundreds of orbital fighters and the remaining interceptors died in the antimatter blasts. Thousands of Highborn aboard the *Genghis Khan* perished or they would die in hours or days from poisoning. Social Unity had never managed to strike such a savage blow before.

The antimatter blasts gave the *Genghis Khan* the time she needed. The *Julius Caesar* finally hove into position. Her anti-missiles and more importantly her heavy beams blew up the next flight of merculites. And now the million-ton rocks entered the stratosphere.

"Scum!" roared Cassius. "Animals! Eat this!"

19.

Cheers filled the command center as the *Genghis Khan* broke off. Men leaped to their feet and hugged one another. The Highborn weren't invincible. They could be beaten after all.

Space Commander Shell rose to his feet and squared his shoulders as he took off his hat and placed it over his heart. Air Marshal Ulrich slapped him on the back. "Brave lads."

"The best," whispered Shell.

General James Hawthorne glared at screen after screen.

"Sir!" shouted a staff officer.

Hawthorne strode to him and gaped at what he saw. It looked like a meteorite. "Where's it targeted?"

"Beijing, sir."

The cheers died as men turned to look at the TV screens.

"Hong Kong!" shouted another man, pointing at his screen and the vast meteorite it showed.

"Taipei!"

"Manila!"

"Shanghai!"

"What do we have that can stop them?" shouted Hawthorne.

Space Commander Shell shook his head. Air Marshal Ulrich was speechless. There was nothing.

"What about nukes, sir," suggested a staff officer.

"Target the Beijing meteorite with nukes!" shouted Hawthorne. "Now!"

A staff officer shouted orders.

On screen, the meteorites streaked toward Earth, the proton beams washing them unable to destroy enough of them to matter.

"Sir! We need Lord Director Enkov's authorization to launch nuclear weapons!"

"Raise him," snapped Hawthorne. "You, order them to launch regardless of authorization, on my authority." Hawthorne found himself spun around to face the captain of the bionic men.

"Belay that order," the bionic man said.

"Look at the screen!" shouted Hawthorne. "Unless I destroy that meteorite Beijing will be obliterated, and so will the other cities. Then Enkov will die. I don't think he's going to thank you for that."

"*Lord Director* Enkov," corrected the bionic man.

"You fool!"

The pressure on Hawthorne's arm increased painfully. In moments, the bone would break. "Listen to me." Then it felt as if his bone creaked in complaint. The bone felt like a piece of lumber under terrific pressure.

"Cancel my order," whispered Hawthorne.

The staff officer said, "But, sir—" A bionic guard put a gun against that man's ribs. "Yes, sir," said the staff officer.

In the rest of the command center, the other bionic security men along the walls trained their carbines on the staff officers. A massacre of debilitating proportions seemed only seconds away.

"I beg you to listen to me," Hawthorne told the bionic captain. "We have—"

"Impact in thirty seconds, sir!"

Hawthorne turned from the shouting staff officer and stared into the bionic man's eyes. It was difficult to think with that bone-crushing grip on his arm. The bionic man didn't seem to be straining at all. Briefly, Hawthorne wondered why they didn't create an army of these bionic men. Then he had to use all his concentration in order to form his words. He said, "Your loyalty and obedience is impeccable, but surely you can see that we must save the Lord Director's life, not to mention our capital."

A sour smile creased the bionic captain's lips. "Disobedience is not allowed. Termination is the result, both yours and mine. I refuse to be terminated."

"Look at the screen."

"Yes, unfortunate."

"Are you willing that the Lord Director should perish?"

"Obedience is mandatory."

"Look," said Hawthorne, trying to turn and look at the screen.

"Negative," said the bionic man, using his infinitely greater strength to keep Hawthorne from turning.

"Ten seconds!"

"I have to order a nuclear strike," General Hawthorne shouted.

"Eight seconds, seven, six, five, four, three, two, one… impact."

From the various screens, bright glares filled the room. The seconds ticked by. Then a rumble, a quake, caused the underground bunker to quiver. Soon the shockwave passed.

"Beijing is gone," whispered a man.

The bionic man released General Hawthorne.

Hawthorne staggered away from the bionic captain. The general gingerly massaged his biceps and wondered if his arm was permanently damaged.

"Manila, gone. Taipei, gone. Vladivostok—"

"Now what, sir?"

General Hawthorne tried to collect himself. It was difficult. The scale of death was… millions, no, maybe a billion dead. He couldn't visualize it. His chest threatened to lock up as his heart hammered.

"The *Julius Caesar* is entering low-Earth orbit, sir, the stratosphere. And the *Genghis Khan* seems to have turned around. It's coming back."

General Hawthorne looked up. The Doom Stars filled the screen, part of the *Genghis Khan* a mass of smoking wreckage.

"We badly hurt one of them," whispered Ulrich.

General Hawthorne squinted. The main brunt of the amphibious assault had yet to be touched by the Highborn. Was it possible to snatch victory from this… this… could one call a billion deaths a mere blow?

"Lord Director Enkov on line seven, sir."

"He's alive?" General Hawthorne asked in amazement.

Before he could say more the bionic captain hustled him to line seven. There he saw the haggard, angry face of Lord Director Enkov. No doubt, the Lord Director was already looking for a scapegoat. General Hawthorne had few illusions about who that would be.

20.

Murderous gun-battles raged in the merculite missile station. The last of the Kamikazes, Samurais, rocket engineers, hastily trained civilians and ex-police officers refused to surrender. They fought with whatever tools were at hand. They were more stubborn at the end than they had been at any other time in the Siege of Tokyo.

Showing no mercy, the FEC soldiers kept coming. After silencing the heavy machinegun ports and blowing the underground locks, the last of the 93rd Slumlords had stormed into the station. Behind the super-thick station walls and below the four-thousand-ton clamshell of ferroconcrete, the merculite station was a vast fortress filled with rows upon rows of heavy merculite rockets.

Perhaps sixty of the huge, armored missiles waited on a conveyer. They looked like bullets on a machinegun belt, and were fed to four blast pans: the launch sites. Between the blast pans raged the gun battles. Bullets and shrapnel bounced off the vast missiles.

Heavy body armor turned the battle in favor of the Slumlords. Remorselessly, they advanced toward the control room. Men in tattered rags crawled along the girders, dropping grenades. They popped out of supply tunnels, guns blazing. Each time, lasers and gyrocs cut them down. Then a last remaining squad of Samurais leapfrogged to the attack. They were outnumbered, outmaneuvered, and blown to bits. Their blood stained three of the rockets that were closest to the blast pans.

Marten led his assault group, their weapons smoking from constant use. Alone or grouped in twos or threes they sprinted, bounded or crawled to new positions. Lasers beamed, machine pistols chattered and gyrocs barked. All around the FEC soldiers, the colossal missiles towered over them. To Marten, they seemed like idols, things that should be worshiped and most of all feared. The merculite missile station was a cathedral to war, to man's madness and killer instinct. It was only right then that men murder men in this place.

"Why don't they surrender?" shouted Stick, slapping a new clip of grenades into his electromag launcher.

"They can't," said Omi, lifting his laser and burning a hole in an engineer that raced at them with a wrench.

"Why not?" said Stick, laying down a pattern of grenade fire that slew another four unfortunates.

"Because they're insane," Omi said, "beyond reason."

Marten marveled at these last Japanese even as he killed them. A squad of political police officers screamed a war cry as they ran at them. They fired stunners, utterly ineffectual against combat-armored soldiers. Some of Marten's men actually stood up, taking the brunt of the stunner fire as they blew apart the pathetic, would-be warriors.

When the last police officer fell, Marten rose. With a wave of his hand, he beckoned his men forward. Sigmir's assault group rose and followed.

Marten paused at the corpse of one of the stunner men. The man must have known his weapon couldn't hurt armored soldiers. So why had.... Marten's chest tightened. He reached down and took a tangler that was attached to the corpse's belt. He hadn't seen one of these since.... His stomach fluttered as he thought about the Sun-Works

Factory circling Mercury. For years there with his parents, all he'd ever used was a tangler, one just like this. It was a policeman's weapon, useless on the battlefield.

A feeling suddenly came over him, an insight into himself. These Japanese were like his parents. They'd never given in, but had died for freedom. Yet what good was dying? He stuffed the tangler in his pack and hurried after his assault group. They knelt behind some missiles, trading fire with....

Marten threw himself onto the concrete floor, an enemy grenade flying over him.

"Look out!" he yelled. He rolled left, behind the nearest missile.

A flash and a scream told of another FEC death. How many had to die before the Siege for Tokyo was over? Then he saw motion, the bomb-thrower sprinting to get nearer them. In a single, liquid move, Marten rose and fired. Riddled with bullets, the bomb-thrower staggered backward, a look of shock on his face.

Marten hated Social Unity, but he felt pity for these poor sods. Then he squinted thoughtfully. He didn't love the Highborn either. He laughed—at last understanding who he was.

"What is it?" shouted Stick, who stood nearby, slapping yet another grenade clip into his launcher.

Marten shook his head. But it had come to him, finally. He belonged to neither side. He was his own side, as his parents had been their own side. *And what side was that?* the cynical part of him asked. *Freedom's side*, he decided.

In that instant, he conceived something new within himself, the germ of a new country, or perhaps one that was very, very old and would be reborn again. In his land—the one he now bore in himself, as a pregnant woman bears a new life—a murderer would pay for stealing another man's life.

"I see it!" shouted Petor.

Marten snapped out of his musing and peered around his missile. He saw it too. It was a door marked CONTROL ROOM.

Sigmir howled, and he dashed toward the entrance. Amazed at the berserk rush, the FEC soldiers of the 93rd Slumlord Battalion watched the huge Lot Six Highborn hurl himself at the door. It burst apart on impact. Sigmir rolled in amidst gunfire. He roared a battle cry as he leaped up and let his gyroc bark.

At the very same instant, the clamshell top whirled open to the nighttime sky. A loud clank sounded as the heavy missiles lurched toward the four blast pans.

"Look at that," shouted Stick. He pointed up into the sky. "What is it?"

Marten peered where Stick pointed. His jaw dropped.

Through a break in the smoke, he saw the full moon. It had a dirty color because of the haze. In front of the moon slid a perfectly circular shape. It too seemed far away. But for something so far away to block out even part of the moon's light, the thing would have to be enormous.

Then it came to Marten, and goosebumps ran up and down his spine.

"What is it?" shouted Stick.

"...Doom Star," whispered Marten.

Stick looked at him as if he were crazy. "Doom Stars don't come close enough to Earth to be seen by the likes of us."

"What else can it be?" asked Omi, who looked up too.

Stick shrugged, and all three of them studied the huge circular shape that slowly slid in front of the moon. Each gasped as the huge shape lit up. Beams, missiles, or that weird gel they'd heard about, something leaving the ship made a play of pretty colors. One of those pretty colors became a beam that slashed through the clouds. Before it could stab within the site, into the merculite missile station, the four-thousand-ton dome whirled shut on its gargantuan hydraulic sleds.

Omi, Stick and Marten exchanged glances. Within the merculite station, the sounds of gunfire, of battle, died down.

"It's finished," said Stick.

Omi raised his eyebrows.

"We've taken the merculite missile battery," the former knifeboy said.

"You mean that Sigmir has," Omi corrected.

"Yeah," said Marten. He knew now that he carried something critical within himself. But if freedom were to be reborn, he had to act the part of a true man today. He nodded sharply to his two friends, asking, "Do you two remember Turbo?"

Their faces hardened.

Stick said, "We remember. But we can't do anything about that now."

"Why not?" asked Marten.

"Because it would mean our deaths," Omi said.

"Given that we'd even be able to kill him," Stick added.

"Do you doubt our abilities?" Marten asked.

Neither of them answered.

"I don't," Marten said. He turned and marched for the control room. A moment later, he heard Stick and Omi behind him.

As Marten entered the bloody room, Stick whispered, "How you gonna make it so we don't die in return?"

Sigmir sat the controls—the panels circled the room. A heap of dead technicians lay on the floor.

The huge Highborn spun in his chair, facing them. "Gentlemen, it is done and I have won."

Marten stopped, with Stick flanking one side of him, Omi the other.

Sigmir glanced at each of them in turn, his dead-seeming eyes searching theirs. With the reactions of an auto-sweep, he fired at Stick. Marten rolled. Omi cursed and beamed Sigmir. The laser light bounced off Sigmir's shiny armor; unknown to them it had been reflected, laser-proofed. Stick grunted. The gyroc shell lodged in the armor joint of his torso and right arm. Then the shell exploded and Stick blew to the floor, dead. Marten fired round after round against Sigmir's armor. The bullets bounced off to little effect, even though Marten was hoping to weaken the armor by repeatedly hitting the same spot.

Sigmir roared with laughter and re-aimed his gyroc. Marten leaped aside. The explosion of the shell threw him hard onto the floor. Both Omi's laser and Marten's machinegun were powerless against Sigmir's superior armor. Realizing that, Marten dropped his gun and drew the tangler from his pack.

"Fool!" bellowed Sigmir.

Marten and he fired at the same instant. The gyroc round was a dud and failed to ignite. It still hit Marten in the chest and threw him backward. The strong sticky strands, meanwhile, tangled the seven-foot berserker.

Sigmir shouted wildly and strained to snap the strands.

Bruised and aching, Marten rose and emptied his tangler onto Sigmir, cocooning him with the wire-thin strands.

"Release me!" roared Sigmir.

Omi shot off the radio attached to the Lot Six Commander's helmet.

Marten dashed to the controls of the merculite station. They were of similar design to those in the Sun-Works Factory. His fingers played over them. Then Marten ran, shouting to Omi, "Come on!"

"Preman!" Sigmir bellowed. "Release me or face my wrath."

Marten didn't pause. He ran out of the control room, shouting orders at everyone to retreat. Above them, the clamshell top whirled open and the missiles lurched toward the blast pans.

"Evacuate the station!" bellowed Marten. "Hurry!"

"Where's Sigmir?" shouted Petor, running toward them.

Marten nodded to Omi. Omi waited until the bodyguard was almost on them. Then he indicated that Petor flip open his visor. He did so. Omi plunged a vibroblade into the bodyguard's face.

***

Panting, running for the nearby trench line, Marten peered up at the night sky. Four missiles launched from the merculite station. Far above, the Doom Star glowed. All around Tokyo and farther a-field terrible laser beams flared.

"Run!" Marten roared.

FEC soldiers ran, knowing that they had only seconds left. They only just made it to the trenches.

Marten landed hard, almost knocking the wind of out himself. The night erupted in a blaze of fire and steel and rocking shockwaves. Marten lay curled into a fetal ball. The pounding was worse than anything he'd faced so far. Heat washed over the trench. Shrapnel that had once been the inside of the merculite missile station flew over in bunches. Bits of dust and concrete rained upon the FEC soldiers, causing each man to tremble violently because he thought it meant the end. They endured the Doom Star beaming of the inner missile site. The intensity of the explosions shook their nerves near the breaking point. Finally, after what seemed an eternity, it stopped.

Marten and Omi uncurled. They avoided looking at each other because each knew from experience that a haunted look would stare back from a zombie's mask. So they breathed gingerly, amazed that they could still be alive.

"Here comes the Colonel," said a man.

Marten dragged himself upright. He wouldn't lie. He'd tell him that Sigmir must have been caught in the merculite station. Everyone knew how insane the Captain was about capturing it. He must not have run away in time, but if the Colonel didn't buy the story…

Marten glanced at Omi.

Omi whispered, "Then we'll have to kill him, too."

Marten smiled grimly in agreement.

21.

General James Hawthorne left the command center in time to forgo watching his carefully assembled armada and army demolished unit after unit by the *Julius Caesar* and *Genghis Khan* Doom Stars. Thousands of bombers, fighters and choppers, wiped out by heavy beams. More than five thousand stratosphere-launched missiles blasted the transports laden with a hundred battalions. Surfacing flattops and cruise missile submarines were finished by a combination of beams, missiles and underwater nukes. And in their place, deeply deployed subs rose and disgorged power-armored Highborn onto Japan.

The careful gathering of hardware and military personnel in the massive build-up... the leaders of Social Unity had made it possible for the Highborn to destroy more units than they had ever been able to find since the start of the war. Perhaps it was true that the Highborn had been bloodied more than ever. The ledger, however, weighed heavily in Highborn favor.

That much General James Hawthorne knew as he rode a fast ground effects vehicle, a GEV, to meet with Lord Director Enkov. The compartment he rode in was sealed from the world. He wore neither chains nor handcuffs, but in the GEV compartment with him sat the bionic captain and five of his most trusted bionic soldiers.

They had hustled General Hawthorne out of the command center. They had marched him past the general's own security men and past the armor units who had secretly pledged personal loyalty to James Hawthorne. Lord Director Enkov had given strict orders concerning the general, and no one had the firepower or the will to take on the bionic guards and thereby thwart the leader of Social Unity.

General Hawthorne contemplated his future. How odd was fate, how twisted and bizarre. He glanced at the bionic captain, and said, "The Lord Director's instincts are impeccable. He had to have fled Beijing only hours before its destruction. His survival skills are unrivaled, wouldn't you say?"

The bionic captain remained impassive. A massively built man, with artificial muscles and stimulant-powered reflexes, he sat ramrod stiff, eyes forward. His five trusted soldiers sat likewise, with the added feature of short, bullpup carbines held in their grimly powerful grips. Armor vests added to their invincibility.

"Enkov does not intend me to survive the meeting with him," Hawthorne mused. He seemed remarkably composed in spite of his statement. "I'm sure he'll ask you to report on my comportment during the operation."

The bionic captain minutely changed position, so he stared impassively at the general.

"I tried to do my duty as I saw fit," said Hawthorne. "I of course will tell him that you were simply trying to do yours."

"I obeyed my orders."

"Of course," said Hawthorne. "And like the Lord Director I too believe that obedience is the highest military virtue. Of course, not all virtue belongs to the soldier. Some must belong to the commander. Chief among the virtues he should possess is loyalty—Loyalty to one's subordinates and to one's own orders. Otherwise

318

a commander is merely whimsical and therefore not worthy of obedience."

The bionic captain allowed himself the tiniest of frowns, and a faint downward twitch of the smallest portion of the left side of his mouth. "Lord Director Enkov does not plan your death to be a pleasant one."

"Such is my own belief."

"Yet you are calm."

General Hawthorne shrugged. Then he sat still, a tall gaunt general with wispy blond hair, bony features composed and a row of medals on his chest. The bionic captain had allowed him time to don his dress uniform, a considerate gesture.

Soon the GEV stopped, settling onto the ground. The door opened and the bionic captain and his five soldiers escorted the general step into an underground bunker. The ultra-clean garage of the bunker held many tanks and GEVs and a company of black uniformed allegiance monitors aiming pistols at him. They wore black helmets with dark shaded visors. All of them were tense, ready for anything. .

The bionic captain marched his five men and General Hawthorne past the allegiance monitors and into a sterile white corridor. More bionic men stood at attention along the corridors. No one said a word as General James Hawthorne's heels drummed upon the tiles. Impassively, they watched. How carefully and zealously Enkov had built up this special Corps of new men, Hawthorne thought. Surely now the Lord Director had to rule with a greater severity than before. A purge would be in order, a cleaning out of the traitors in the military who had allowed such an unprecedented disaster. At least Hawthorne was certain this was how Enkov would be thinking. Today, Hawthorne himself would be the first scapegoat.

They finally reached a steel door—the end of the corridor, end of the line. The door slid open, and the captain and his five most trusted men marched the general into a small room, interrogation sized. Lord Director Enkov sat behind a rather small desk. Flanking him stood his original bionic bodyguard.

A plain wooden chair sat before the desk.

"Sit," wheezed the old, wrinkled man who held supreme power.

General Hawthorne sat.

With a trembling, palsied hand, Enkov stuck a stimstick between his withered lips. His eyes seemed to glitter with promised death for everyone who had failed him. As the stimstick glowed into life, the Lord Director pointed an accusatory finger at the general.

"You failed."

"May I speak?" asked Hawthorne.

The bionic captain shifted uncomfortably.

Enkov noticed. His eyes narrowed suspiciously. He leaned back in his chair and eyed the captain of his guards at the military command center of all Earth. It had been a post of high rank, surely one of the Lord Director's most trusted positions. The evidence of the captain's five-man security team, still armed in his presence, showed the truth of this.

Enkov asked, "Do you have something to report, Captain?"

"He did his duty," General Hawthorne said.

The Lord Director lifted his bushy white eyebrows. Red smoke drifted out of his nostrils. "I don't recall asking you a question, General."

"No," agreed Hawthorne. "But it's time we told the truth, you and I. And heard the truth, too," he said to the bionic captain.

Enkov glanced from the bionic captain to the general. A mixture of caution, suspicion and—was that fear?—

mingled in the old man's features. He noticed the port arms of the five trusted bionic soldiers. The Lord Director leaned toward his intercom.

The bionic captain, the one who had stopped General Hawthorne from using nuclear weapons to stop the million-ton meteorites, gave his men a subtle finger-signal. They raised their carbines and riddled the Lord Director's bodyguard with bullets.

The Lord Director jerked back in his chair, surprised and bewildered at this sudden turn of events.

"You are relieved of duty, sir," General Hawthorne told Enkov.

The stimstick dropped out of Enkov's mouth. Then he snapped forward as his old, palsied hand reached for the intercom button. The hand never made it. The carbines spoke again. And the ancient, Lord Director fell to the clean floor, dead.

***

A half-hour later, the bionic guards ushered the General into Director Blanche-Aster's office. She sat in a wheelchair, a red plaid blanket over her useless legs and a bulky medical unit hooked into her and keeping her alive. Her face was drawn and old and she wore a turban because it was rumored that all her hair had fallen out. Her eyes yet shone with dangerous life.

"General Hawthorne," she said in a surprisingly strong voice.

"Director."

"By killing the Lord Director, you have committed a horrible deed."

"I stand by it," he said, determined to die with dignity.

"Do you? Do you indeed?"

"The Lord Director's arrogance cost Earth too dearly," General Hawthorne said. "He had a debt to pay and I merely helped him pay it."

"That's claptrap, General. Your neck was on the block and you did what you had to in order to save it. Or do you think me so dull that I'd actually believe that you're committed to saving Earth?"

General Hawthorne clicked his heels together. "Director, I think of nothing else."

She studied him with those dangerously bright eyes, with those deeply knowledgeable eyes. "A single word from me, a nod even, and you'll be dragged out and shot like a murderous junkie."

"Yes, Director."

"Don't interrupt me, General."

He tilted his head in acknowledgement.

"I could first have you tortured, lingeringly tortured, the scene saved on video for the world to watch."

His stomach knotted, but he kept the bitter emotions off his face.

"Yet I need someone to run the war, General. I need someone who can hurt the Highborn. You've hurt them. Tell me, if you fought this war under my direction, could you win it?"

He peered straight into her eyes. "I could."

"Director," she admonished.

"Director," he said.

"I'm reinstating you as the Supreme Commander of Social Unity. And I insist that you defeat the Highborn."

"I will do my duty, Director, to the very best of my ability."

"Hmm. Yes, I really do hope so." A hard, wintry smile twisted her face. "So hadn't you be off then, my General?"

General James Hawthorne saluted smartly, turned on his heel and marched out of her office. He had a war to win.

22.

Transcript #42,124 Highborn Archives: an exchange of notes between Paenus, Inspector General, Earth, and Cassius, Grand Admiral of Highborn. Dates: May 13 to May 17, 2350

May 13
To Cassius:
Hail the Grand Admiral! Glorious! Victorious! The very Earth trembles at your audacious blow struck amidst treacherous sneak attacks and a startling new enemy beam weapon heretofore unknown. I salute you, Grand Admiral. Your strategic brilliance awes us in Training Army, Earth.

I am pleased to inform you that ahead of schedule Australian levies E, F and G have been trained to competency and await FEC Army assignments. Alas, not all is perfect. We still await the Antarctica transshipments of the new Praetor Mark III panzers. Three battalions of veteran panzer crews have been assigned them, but until we receive the transshipment, training will continue to be delayed. Otherwise, Grand Admiral, excellence reigns in Training Army, Earth.

May 14
To Paenus:

The Japanese furnace all but devoured our FEC Divisions. Despite overwhelming losses, however, they held. You are to be congratulated on your training procedures, my dear Paenus. The panzer crews proved disciplined, although yet lacking in true exploitation zeal. Still, under the circumstances of narrow, built up fronts and mountainous terrain, I am not displeased with their performance.

Paenus, our glorious victory of 10 May moves the Campaign for the Solar System into its next phase. I must ask that you scour the FEC Divisions recently thrown into the Japanese cauldron and designate several "hero" units. At once, contact Commander Brutus of Ninth FEC Army so he may award honors to the deserving premen. The numbers need not be large, but only "heroic" formations must be chosen. Said troops will be transferred to Training Commandos, Space. I regret your loss of these trained soldiers, but we are stretched everywhere. Your quick compliance is appreciated.

May 15
To Cassius:
Long live the Grand Admiral! To hear is to obey. My inspection officers fly to the Japanese Islands even as I write this missive. They will scour the FEC formations and present you with heroes or with premen with enough savagery, skill and battle luck so they will not sully the reputation of the Commandos.

May 16
To Paenus:
Your choices, I know, will be excellent. And ensure, too, proper pomp and circumstances during the honor ceremonies in order to heighten FEC morale. As you know, the premen are a touchy species, given to dramatic emotional displays. But then you know this better than I,

my dear Paenus. Are you not the architect of our valorous FEC formations?

Salutations and Congratulations on a duty well preformed.

23.

The 93rd Slumlord Battalion, all seventeen survivors, wore dress uniforms as they waited on parade to be pinned with medals by the Inspector General of Training FEC Army, Earth. Highborn Superiors were here along with some of the older Lot Six specimens. Mostly FEC soldiers stood at attention, panzers roaring past and orbital fighters zooming in a thunderclap across the sky.

"They honor us," said Kang.

"Are you so easily impressed?" Marten asked.

The big Mongol scowled. "Look at the orbital fighters, the panzers, the battle-suited drop troops."

"So what. A little razzle to dazzle us into obedience. I'm unimpressed."

"Then you're a fool," said Kang. "Paenus himself honors us. And we're to be transferred to Training Commandos, Space."

Marten glanced at Omi, who stood on the other side of him. The ex-gunman kept his face impassive. Marten turned back to Kang. "We're leaving Earth, that's all I care about."

"What's that supposed to mean?" growled Kang.

Marten merely grinned. He stood at attention, waiting for Paenus to come and pin him with a bit of tin. The decoration was meaningless. Turbo and Stick were dead.

Almost everyone he'd trained with in Australia was dead. He wondered how Molly and how Ah Chen fared. He'd probably never know. But one thing he did know: He would be free, somehow, whatever it took. And now the Highborn were sending him off-planet. Well, he'd only come to Earth in order to escape the Sun-Works Factory. From orbit around Earth it would surely be easier to escape to the Outer Planets and be free than from deep within this gravity well.

"Here he comes," growled Kang.

Marten stiffened to ramrod attention. He hoped Social Unity and the Highborn killed each other off. Then maybe men would be able to live as they'd been meant to live. He knew that once he escaped from the Commandos that he'd make his dream into reality. But first, he must survive this bit of frippery. He pasted a look of awe on his face, trying to think how a dog would feel being petted by its master. Let them think what they wanted, for now. Soon enough they'd find out the truth, and then let both sides beware.

24.

Meanwhile, in deep space between the orbital paths of Neptune and Uranus, the first, ultra-stealth cyborg pods continued their journey to Earth.

The End

24177374R00187

Made in the USA
Middletown, DE
20 September 2015